The Firm's Deception

LT Richards

Published by Silver Fox in the U.S.A.

Print ISBN: ISBN: 978-1-7348861-7-7

eBook ISBN: 978-1-7348861-8-4

ACKNOWLEDGMENT

I WOULD LIKE to thank all of our friends who have been instrumental in developing this book. They have been inspirational and supportive. I would like to thank a few people who were key in reviewing *The Firm's Deception* and provided constructive feedback in its development.

Thank you:

Katherine G.

Vickey O.

Reginia D.

Sarah H.

Brett

"It's barely five o'clock and we're already drunk, I said, my voice slurred, as I draped my arm over Jimmy's shoulder. Our feet stumbled over the cracked pavement, hands clasped onto half-empty shot glasses, like a pair of drunken sailors haphazardly returning from shore leave.

Senior skip was a memory I'd never forget. The annual tradition of escaping from high school for a week, usually spent doing something mundane like bowling or camping, had finally come to an end. My buddies and I were eighteen, and we decided to go all out with a trip to Mexico. Our first day didn't disappoint with a deep-sea fishing trip that involved a lot of beer and a few sizable fish. Luckily, the first mate did all the work. He cleaned the ten fish we caught and asked us what we wanted to do with them. We looked at each other, laughed and said, "We don't know, we don't have anything to put them in." I guess we didn't think that far.

"We can donate these to the homeless kitchen if you'd like, señor," the captain declared from his deck as he arranged his mooring line in a meticulous pattern.

"Absolutely, let's do it," I said, raising my can of beer. We had plenty of evidence from our photos of our catch, and helping those in need seemed like a worthwhile thing to do.

Our second day involved just as much alcohol as the first. After several shots of tequila, we stopped by a tattoo parlor to check out the artwork on the walls. Prices were affordable. Jimmy slurred, "Let's get ..."

At that moment, I noticed an image that resembled the tattoo my father had, and before I could think, I shouted, "How much for that eagle design, and can they make it smaller and put it on the inside of my arm?"

The artist nodded. "Yes, sir, the tattoo would look great. It will cost you about twenty US dollars."

"Will I get free tequila if I get it?"

"No, sir, you shouldn't drink while getting a tattoo. It's not good for you," he said. I thought for a second before I made up my mind.

"I'll take that chance then. Will I get free tequila if I still go through with the tattoo?"

He shook his head and shrugged once more. "Yes, sir, but it will be an extra ten dollars."

"That isn't free," I stated.

His response was a shrug of resignation: What can you do?

How many times can someone shrug their shoulders?

"All right! Let's do it," I answered, settling the matter. I sat down in the chair.

The guys laughed just as the artist began to make his first scratch with the ink needle in my arm. Jimmy said, "Dude, I was kidding about the tattoo. We're going to get another bottle of tequila and come back to get ya."

The radiating heat from my arm was a little worse than a sunburn, but it was the most memorable thing about my father I could think of getting. The detail of this small eagle was identical to the one he'd gotten in the army. I watched the artist take care to scratch the ink into my skin with his small machine. The dull humming of his tool continued while his assistant kept my glass full of some of the best-tasting tequila I'd ever had, but at eighteen, I'd only tasted the cheap stuff we could get our hands on illegally back home.

As the eagle came to life, my mind was flooded with memories of my father. He had been a good man, kind and loving toward my mother, Elaine, and me. But even with all his admirable qualities, I couldn't shake the feeling that he wasn't there for us as much as he could have been. As an army engineer, he was frequently deployed to undisclosed locations, and we were left to fend for ourselves in his absence. His nuggets of advice were helpful, but they couldn't replace the void left by his physical absence.

It was strange how a soldier, a weapon of war who had been trained to kill without hesitation, could be so nurturing and patient. He always used discipline as a way to raise us up instead of tearing us down; something I now found unique in this world.

His love for eagles was intriguing as well. It had started when he was first assigned to the 326th Engineer Battalion in the 101st Airborne, which had an eagle logo. From then on, pictures and small statues of eagles filled our home. We even watched eagle documentaries together when I was little. But as much as I wanted to love eagles like he did, it only reminded me of how distant he was with us at times.

My heart ached as I remembered him telling me how majestic eagles were, how strong and patient they were. They only took what they needed and observed everything before making a decision. If only he had observed our family before deciding to leave us behind so often.

I still remember that fateful day when the knock on the door came. My mother began crying almost immediately—she knew what it meant, as she had seen this before with other spouses whose husbands never returned. The story they told us of three hundred soldiers trapped on a ridge with heavy enemy fire was etched into my memory. There was my father and the other engineers working as hard as they could on a bridge to rescue those trapped soldiers under fire; there were the three hundred men and women he saved that day, all filing past my father's casket during his funeral; telling me thanks for my giving up my father to save them.

The buzzing noise stopped. "All done, señor."

I wiped a tear from my cheek. The work was impressive and more detailed than I could have imagined for a tattoo. It was a bald eagle, and I could even see its eye looking at me. Although that could have been the effect of the tequila I'd been drinking all day.

"You like?" the artist asked.

I nodded, unable to take my eyes off the artwork. I walked up to a mirror to get a better look. It was brilliant work.

"That will be fifty US dollars."

"Wait, you said thirty with the tequila!" I groused, thinking I'd been had.

"I said around twenty, señor. I put a lot of detail in this art. It was my best work, and quality costs more."

I looked at him and shook my head as I handed him the fifty dollars. I would have paid the same in the States, and the artwork was better than I could have imagined. Now hopefully I wouldn't fall ill from a dirty needle.

"We're back, bro, and you're two shots behind," Darian said, pouring tequila into a small shot glass and handing it to me. I wiped a tear from my eye with my shirt sleeve and lifted the glass to my friends. With another glance at my eagle … or to my father, I tipped the glass to my lips. Down the hatch.

"Don't drink too much, or you might get sick, señor," the tattoo artist warned.

"Why juu say that now when you gave me all that 'free' tequila earlier?" I scowled at him, recognizing my drunken slur again.

He just waved at me and walked away.

The others were getting a bottle of some amazing agave delight in the adjacent store, or so they were told. They looked at my arm. The red glow around the artwork was quite prevalent from the irritated skin, but the picture was perfect. They gave the standard glance—"Cool"—and poured more tequila.

"At least Brett isn't a virgin when it comes to tattoos, right guys?" one friend joked. The room erupted in laughter. It may be true that I was probably amongst the few seniors in school who hadn't lost his virginity yet, though this wasn't something I was particularly bothered about.

*　*　*

Our last night in Cancun, we went to a club recommended by the hotel's bellhop. Everyone knew that bellhops had all the insider information.

The ladies were gorgeous—their young Latin bodies alone were nothing short of stunning with flawlessly toned figures and mesmerizing eyes. I had one of the most beautiful dancers on my lap, and Jimmy said, "Come on, Brett, why don't you take her into the back room? It won't cost much."

I glanced at Karla's barely-covered assets and shook my head. Although she was attractive, and I fought to keep my eyes from her revealing cleavage, I wanted something more meaningful than a random hookup for money.

Karla asked, "Don't you want to come into the backroom?" Her plea reminded me of when my sister wanted something from me—usually she got it—however, not this time around.

"No thanks," I said. "You're lovely, but I'm heading back to my room instead."

I stood up and helped her off my lap. The sight of my friends passionately making out with their girls sent a chill down my spine. Karla looked like a bellhop who delivered luggage to your room with her hand out for a tip.

"Can I have a tip for my time?" Her personality turned from wanton whore to businesswoman-like the flip of a switch.

I pulled twenty bucks from my wallet and handed it to her. "I'll be in my room, guys. Have fun. I'll see you in the morning to check out at eight, right?"

Jimmy didn't even look up at me, too busy groping his girl's ass as she ground herself into his crotch. "Might be a late night, but yeah—eight in the lobby."

As I left, I walked past the small stage near the entrance. The girl dancing was barely eighteen and smiled right at me. I could almost hear her siren song luring me closer, but I'd already decided I didn't want my first time to be something cheap like this.

When I walked by the tattoo shop, the same artist was putting a tattoo on a woman's breast. Her tits were in full view of anyone who should walk by the storefront. She saw me looking at her, hoisted her drink up, and winked. I laughed and continued my walk, remembering the artist's warning about alcohol and tattoos.

Why do hotels have to be uphill when you've been drinking? It was after eleven, and all the vices were on the street. Every genre of prostitute was lined up along a building, asking me for a good time, as were generous dealers offering me a free sample of their inventory. I was half a block away when I saw one of the most beautiful women I'd ever seen standing at the corner of our hotel. Her skintight, red minidress showed every beautiful curve. Her smile was just as captivating as that dancer's at the strip club. She didn't have a chest, but the rest of her body and her face was incredible.

"Hey, señor, perhaps you like some back door, or maybe some yum yum?" Her voice was deep. I stopped to try and comprehend her words.

"What did you say?" The salsa music in the background may have distorted what I heard, and I leaned in so I could hear her better.

"You like back door, or blow job?" she said, and then when I looked down, I saw the middle of her dress bulge out.

"You're a man?" I exclaimed, quickly stepping back, trying to figure it out.

"I'm all woman, señor, only I pack a little extra meat." She laughed and walked away.

I was amazed at how great she looked, but with a cock.

Nearing the hotel entrance, I stopped for a moment to look around and take in the smells—an exciting blend of car exhaust and pot. Although this trip was an experience I'd remember forever, I didn't think it would be on my repeat list.

I was glad I could convince my friends to get a quality hotel. After walking by some of the cheaper hotels with the vast amount of *marketing* in front of them, the extra cost for a higher-end hotel was well worth it.

A chandelier hung from the ceiling with ornate, scary-looking vines and flowers. The edges of the leaves were trimmed in gold which gave the light a soft green tint. Tiny pieces of cut glass were sprinkled throughout the foliage like stars on black velvet.

The tropical plants along the walls, reaching toward the sunlight cascading through the windows, made the lobby feel alive. Just before I got to the elevator, I saw a bartender wiping out glasses with a towel.

"The bar is open until midnight, señor. You still have time to get a drink."

I turned to see the man behind the bellhop counter. *What the hell? I could use another drink before I crash.* I smiled at him and turned to the bar.

The hotel was quiet and calm with soft Latin music floating through the air. Just what I needed to relax and get ready for bed.

The small man was in his early fifties, with gray strands among his shoulder-length, black hair. His shirt strained against his belly, and his red bowtie was off center. He looked up at me when I approached and smiled as he set down his towel to pull out a clean glass for me.

"What would you like, señor?" His painted smile was flawless, but his eyes told me he was ready to go home for the night.

"Tequila on ice, please."

"Good tequila doesn't need ice, señor. Would you like to try some?"

"Sure!"

He took a beautifully painted blue and white bottle off the shelf, poured a generous sample into a shot glass, and slid it my way.

Smooth was an understatement. I thought the stuff at the tattoo parlor was good, but this had a silky texture on my tongue and no real burn in my throat. It was by far the best I'd had on the trip.

"Wow, very good. Yes, I'll have this. How much?"

"Five dollars, double for eight."

"I'll take a double." I gulped down the last of what was in the shot glass as he slid a tumbler my way, just like in an old Western movie—stopping at my hand. I'd sleep soundly tonight.

"I'll have what he's having."

My moment of solitude had been abruptly interrupted.

A beautiful brunette who could easily have been my mother's age walked up to take the adjacent seat. Her diamond jewelry and form-fitting burgundy dress suggested she had just come from an event.

"Juan, I assume you managed to convince this handsome young man to try your homemade agave juice?"

"Señora Vicky, it is the finest tequila in all of Mexico … even if I did make it myself." The bartender cast his gaze at me and raised his eyebrows expectantly.

I took another sip; the knowledge that it was homemade did not change its flavor, in my opinion. It was still smooth and delicious, but now I understood why it was so cheap.

As Juan splashed a generous portion into a glass, the woman said, "Even though I usually give Juan shit about his homebrew tequila, I must say it is the best I've ever tasted."

Juan beamed as he pushed the cork back into the bottle and placed it on one of the middle shelves among alcohol selections.

"So, are you going to join me for a drink or just stare at my tits?"

Shit! Was I that obvious?

"Um, I'm sorry I wasn't …"

"It's all right, I'm proud of them. Come on, join me. What's your name?" Her confidence was intimidating, but I figured I'd entertain her for a little while, at least until I finished my drink.

"I'm Brett." *Now what should I look at?* I didn't want to be caught looking at her abundant cleavage again. I nervously looked around and then at Juan, who just shrugged as he wiped out a glass. *Why does everyone shrug around here?* I just wanted to wind down before I went to bed.

She was in her forties, and I was stunned to see the most brilliant cobalt blue eyes as I moved closer. They were almost too mesmerizing to look away.

"If you're going to seduce me with your eyes, at least let me do the same," she exclaimed.

Heat flooded my face. I didn't know how to respond. *Is she coming on to me?*

She placed her hand on my leg. "Relax, I'm just giving you some shit. I had a dreadful night and am just trying to let loose a bit. How about you? What brings you in here so late and all by yourself?"

She looked me over like she was trying to buy a young horse. All that was left was for her to check out my teeth.

"My friends are at the strip joint down the road. It's our last night here. We came down for senior skip for a few days."

Her Cheshire grin was intriguing, almost as though she had found a secret or some prize.

"So, while your friends are getting laid by pretty girls, you decided to come here and drink alone? Are you into girls? It's all right if you're not. I'm just curious."

I snapped my head toward her, trying to keep my gaze above her neck, but her breasts were nearly falling out of her dress, and I couldn't help but glance at them. The skintight dress molded around them, just covering her nipples. How she wasn't falling out was beyond me. I looked up into her eyes.

"I am into girls, but I just didn't want to pay for something meaningless like that." Catching myself looking down at her cleavage again, I turned to look toward Juan. He smiled at me and nodded as though he knew something.

When I brought my attention back to Vicky, she sipped her drink and continued smiling as she blatantly evaluated me. It was a little uncomfortable but also exciting. That tequila was beginning to work. She leaned toward me slightly, and alarms of arousal went off in my body as her perfume surrounded me. It was like a drug coursing through my veins, and my reaction was immediate. I tried to think of some way to adjust myself without disclosing how hard she made me.

"Perhaps you'd like to spend your last evening with a meaningless experience which you wouldn't have to pay for?"

I wanted to reply, but I couldn't find any words. She placed her hand on my leg again, this time caressing it and sliding it up my thigh.

"That is if you want a real woman to show you an amazing time on your last night in Cancun. Besides, I know you're dying to get your hands on these tits. Aren't you?"

She placed my hand on her breast, sliding it along her protruding nipple.

I nodded, and then she placed her finger under my chin, pushing my mouth closed. I was embarrassed at my immaturity, but it didn't seem to faze her.

She threw back the rest of her drink, took my hand, and said, "Juan, add it to my room."

"Yes, Miss Vicky."

"Where's your room?" she asked.

My heart was pounding so loud I thought the entire world could hear it as I led her up the stairs to the second floor. We reached the hallway, and a shiver of anticipation ran down my spine. Then we stopped at room 215, and my gaze stayed locked on the door number as I gasped for air while coming to terms with what I was about to do. I felt my body trembling with anticipation until she turned me to face her, our lips desperately searching for one another in an electric kiss.

She tugged me closer to her and ravaged my lips in a passionate kiss until I could feel a heat burning through me in waves. Suddenly she placed my hand on her breast where I felt her nipple pulsing against my palm. Vicky then grabbed my wrist and guided it under her dress. The heated sensation of her nipple caressing across the skin of my hand sent a jolt of desire to my core that made me tremble with pleasure. Her fingers moved along my zipper, and the pressure against it amplified my lust until I could barely contain myself. I couldn't help but devour her with passionate kisses. My mind was no longer in control of my body.

"Let's continue this in your room," she whispered.

I caught my breath for a moment, opened my eyes to see her intoxicating smile, those piercing blue eyes, and saw my hand caressing her breast as though it had a mind of its own. She looked down at my hand and then back up to my eyes and smiled.

"You're such a sexy man. I want to see what a young stud like you can do."

It took me a few seconds to realize this was happening. I hastily dug out my room keycard and opened the door, and she walked in behind me. No sooner had I set my keycard down on the dresser had she grabbed my arm and spun me around.

She pushed me down in a chair next to the bed and made quick work of my belt. In one fluid motion, she had my shorts off, allowing my virgin cock to pop up like a catapult.

She gripped it with one hand and moaned, "Mmm, very good first impression."

Her soft hands were a welcome change to my own hand, and then when I didn't think I could be further aroused, her warm tongue methodically circled around my head.

Her eyes were closed as she moved my head to her cheeks, almost savoring the touch against her face. My heart was like a bass drum with no music sheets to play off. I was no longer in control of my breathing nor my body.

I'd never wanted anyone or anything so desperately in my entire life. Every fiber of my being was lured to follow her wherever she took me. It was like a subconscious instinct that was now in control, and I wanted more. I *needed* more.

"Mmmm, precum. I love it." She stroked my cock, squeezing out a few drops of dew from the tip, then looked into my eyes and slowly licked it away.

An internal earthquake of muscle spasms rocked through me in reaction to her touch.

"You have a fantastic cock. It's, like, the perfect size."

I'd never compared myself to other guys and doubted I'd ever find myself comparing while hard either, but a hint of pride danced in the back of my mind to know I was well equipped.

She took my cock in her mouth, all the way to the back of her throat. After a slight pause, she pushed farther down. My body reacted involuntarily with a jerk. I gripped her hair, and with an animalistic instinct, I thrust my cock farther down her throat. The sensation of her throat tightly squeezing my cock while her lips reached my base caused my stomach to spasm.

My arms shook as I felt her head trying to come up. She gagged and pulled off. Tears in her eyes had me alarmed, but she laughed.

"Yes, perfect size. I like a confident man who uses a little force, but you gotta let me come up for air at some point." She laughed again and continued sucking, licking, and gliding the head of my cock along her face. It almost seemed like she was worshipping me, or at least my cock.

Although I was a virgin, I wasn't new to jerking off. I knew what it felt like to get off, and somehow, she knew when I was about to come and would stop and kiss my thigh or grip the tip, to go slower and then back at it. She spent what seemed like an hour enjoying my cock with her mouth and hands. She would caress my legs and occasionally look up at the aching expression on my face to monitor how close I was to coming. Each time the pressure built up more and more, and each time, I internally begged her not to stop. I wanted to shoot my load like a volcano.

"Something tells me you're not going to last much longer," she said while licking the tip.

She stood and took off what little dress she had on and then slid off her black, lace thong. Her bare mound and huge breasts were mesmerizing. This time I caught my mouth open and closed it. She leaned in closer, guiding her firm, pink nipple to my mouth. I wrapped my lips around it and instinctively began sucking as I lifted my hand to grip her other breast. After a moment, I switched. I didn't really know what I was doing, but it seemed to come naturally to me. I felt as though I was floating through a dream.

"Now, let's see how well that young tongue of yours works." She pulled me up from the chair.

I took off my shirt, and she lay down on the bed, parting her legs wide to expose herself. I stared at her gorgeous, naked body until she motioned for me to come to her with her finger.

I couldn't believe I was about to do this; it felt so surreal. My heart raced with anxious excitement as I made my way between her legs onto the bed and kissed the soft skin of her knee. I inched my lips slowly up her thigh, stopping at a small tattoo right below the crease of her leg adorned in just the letters SD with some colorful flowers around it. I sealed my lips over the ink and traveled farther toward the heat radiating from her core.

The unfamiliar yet irresistible aroma swirled around me, stirring an insatiable hunger within me that led me straight down to her center without warning. I lapped eagerly against her labia before flicking my tongue up to her clitoris. This was my first taste of a woman, and it hit like crack cocaine on a cold winter's night—I couldn't get enough!

My primordial instincts kicked in full force, and my movements became more rapid and heated as I feverishly tongued her pussy, tasting every sweet drop of pleasure she had to offer.

She grasped tightly at my hair. "Woah there, tiger," she breathed between moans. "Take it easy, we have all night."

I greedily devoured her with my lips and tongue, letting my fingers wander inside her wetness. I explored every inch of her as if it was pure gold. My body shuddered with anticipation as I imagined what it would be like to thrust within her depths. I licked and nibbled at her clit, pushing myself harder against her until she grabbed a fistful of my hair and pulled me tightly into her core.

"Do it harder," she whispered, so I complied, pressing my finger in deeper before swirling around her entrance so expertly that she could do nothing but groan in pleasure. Her body quivered beneath me, and her hands pulled me in closer as I sucked on her clit more forcefully, sending waves of exquisite delight through her veins. Suddenly, a hot stream of liquid flooded over my face and neck as she came undone beneath me—an unexpected surprise! The sensation was overwhelming. The sweet taste of her arousal filled my mouth along with confusion. *Did she just piss on me?*

I backed away and looked at my soaked bed as she was catching her breath. She had to have seen my expression of shock and confusion.

"Haven't you ever seen a woman squirt before?" she asked.

I didn't want to show my ignorance, but there it was as my head jerked to the side, indicating my lack of experience.

"It's not pee. It's just an inner liquid that comes from a woman when she has an incredible orgasm, and what you gave me was incredible."

Not sure what to believe, I just stared.

Tilting her head, she asked, "Do you smell pee?"

I smiled then, realizing there was no pee smell. And it tasted almost sweet. It was just strange having experienced it for the first time.

"Now," she parted her legs wide, and I saw her entrance glistening with pleasure, "why don't you slip that gorgeous cock of yours inside of me and really make me come."

Shit. I didn't have a condom. I stood still for a moment in panic.

"What's the matter?" she asked.

"I don't have a condom," I admitted. It felt like I'd won the lottery and showed up to collect without my winning ticket.

"I'm clean, and I can't get pregnant, so if you're clean, then let's get to the fucking," she stated without care.

Her inviting entrance and my cock were like a force that screamed, *get in there and fuck her.*

Urged on by the intensity of the moment, I lunged between her legs. My length slipped effortlessly into her waiting heat. A sensation like never before coursed through me as her wet walls clung to my cock like a second skin. I had only dreamt of such pleasure, yet even then it was far beyond what I could have imagined. She clawed at my backside and yanked me with each thrust until my balls pressed against her tight derriere.

"Oh god yes, fuck me! Harder! Give it to me now!"

I gasped in response, slamming into her with all the force and passion that filled me. Her body shuddered beneath mine as she coiled in pleasure, bloodcurdling cries escaping her lips. An ocean of ecstasy escaped from her inner sanctum and soaked our bodies. In that moment, nothing else mattered other than plunging relentlessly into her until our passion reached its breaking point.

"Yes, fuck me until you come," she ordered. "Don't stop until you finish inside of me."

I lifted myself to gaze at her breasts, swaying to the rhythm of my thrusts, and looked down to watch my glistening cock slide out and slam back into her. It was much more erotic to see than any porn I'd watched. The slapping of skin on skin was nearly deafening as I continued to fuck her. It was the most exhilarating experience I'd ever had.

She cried out, "Yes, keep fucking me. I'm coming again!"

The raw power of her voice burned through my veins like molten lava, and with those words she set me into motion. I lunged forward, driving myself harder and deeper into her than ever before until I felt every inch of her around me. Our bodies collided with each other as I let out a guttural scream, thrusting faster and faster until finally I reached my peak and unleashed a surge of pleasure that rocked my entire being. I opened my eyes to find her glowing, blue gaze locked onto mine, both of us spent and exhausted from the intensity.

"That was some of the best sex I've had in years. Thank you."

I wouldn't dare tell her that was my first time, but I was beaming from the compliment.

"I need to get going. I'm leaving in the morning. I just want you to know I desperately needed this."

She got her dress on, held her shoes and panties, then leaned down to kiss me. It dawned on me that it was the only time we'd kissed all night other than in the hallway.

"Thank you, and I hope all goes well for you," she said as she walked to the door.

She left the room, leaving me wholly exhilarated in a soaked bed. *Was I just used?* Part of me was pissed, but the majority of me was elated.

It was two a.m., and I had a few hours before meeting the guys to catch our ride to the airport. I couldn't sleep on the wet bedding and mattress, so I flipped it over and slept on the uncovered bed.

When I met the guys downstairs, they were boasting about their hot women at the club. The smell of booze was overbearing.

Jimmy said, "A shame, Brett. You could have gotten your bean snapped last night. Those girls were hot as hell!"

I put my hand on his shoulder in complete glee and replied, "Maybe I did."

Then I saw her heading toward the hotel exit with another man and luggage. Her jogging clothes covered much more than her dress last night, and she had her hair in a ponytail, but her gorgeous figure still made my cock twitch, especially since I knew what was under those clothes. She looked back at me as she walked out the door to a taxi and winked before stepping into the car.

"No fucking way! You fucked that MILF last night?" Jimmy asked, his eyes bulging out as he stared after her. The taxi door closed.

"I don't fuck and tell," I boasted.

"You dog! She is hot as hell. Well, good, our mission is complete," he said, turning in his key to the front desk.

"What mission is that?"

"For you to lose your virginity. And it seems like you pick them better than I could."

* * *

As soon as I stepped through the door, Mom noticed my new tattoo. She gave me a disparaging yet accepting smile and said, "I was hoping you wouldn't do anything like this, but it looks exactly like your father's."

She pulled me in for an embrace and continued, "Still, I hope that getting the tattoo is all you did while down there. There's plenty of tempting opportunities for a young man like you."

My illicit rendezvous filled my memory once again, but instead I told her, "No worries, Mom. I didn't do anything Dad wouldn't have done."

Her eyes lit up with worry before she laughed and responded, "That doesn't make me feel any better!"

Oh damn! She does know …

Mom's face softened with warmth as she smiled and declared, "It's nice that you still love your dad after all these years. He was—and still is—a great man. I can see him in you."

I had to become the man of the house when I was ten years old. My mom and four-year-old sister were all we had left in our family. My sister and I were best friends, and I tried to be there for her. I knew my father would want me to take care of them the best I could. For now, I did that by working a part-time job after school and on weekends to help my mom pay the bills.

Tears welled up in my eyes, and I took my bags up to my room, plopped myself on the bed, and stared at my tattoo, trying to remember my dad. I looked at my nightstand to see an assortment of college letters. No doubt Mom had set them there while I was gone.

I was late to apply for colleges, and many of the smart kids already got early selection. I procrastinated until my mom forced me to apply.

My grades were great, and I figured my 3.85 GPA would get me into any college I wanted. Mom walked in to find me looking at the collection of colorful school emblems spread across my bed.

"Oh, you got your letters. What do they say?"

"They all accepted me."

Tears filled her eyes, and she smiled behind her hand. I could tell she was proud of me, but I laughed a little as something else occurred to me.

"I wish one had denied me so I wouldn't have to decide which one to pick."

"There are bigger decisions in life than that," Mom replied with her usual calm composure. "Look further into each school and work out which will offer you the best education for what you want to do with your life."

What did I want to do with my life? It was clear that engineering was my path, but beyond that ... I had no idea.

"Mom, I don't know what I want in life."

She sat next to me on the bed and placed her hand on my leg. Her warm smile always brought comfort. "Your father was uncertain about his future as well, but he was talented in his field of work. He embraced life with open arms and had a great time while it lasted," she said reassuringly. "Life is too short for you not to enjoy it fully. You'll make the right decisions."

She started to walk out and then stopped to look at me again. "Also, I know you haven't dated much in high school, and I realize I put a lot of responsibility on you, but there will be a lot of opportunities to date when you're off to college."

"Mom! I don't need the talk." I glanced up at her and then realized I couldn't look at her and think about sex.

"You've become a very handsome man. You're fit, confident, and respectful. The girls will be lining up to ..."

I could feel my face burning. I needed her to stop. "Okay, Mom, thanks."

Her straight-lipped smile told me she wanted to say more. Thankfully, she didn't.

She walked out as I stared at the acceptance letters on the bed. "Just make sure you use protection!" she yelled from the hallway. I could hear a laugh in her voice.

I stared at the doorway, shaking my head. Then I realized … this is really happening.

Brett

I settled on a major that combined robotics engineering and computer science, and Virginia Tech had the perfect program. I had just enough to pay for tuition; some of it was from scholarships, some from what my father had left me, and the rest from my savings.

It was a very stimulating major, and I gave it my all. Working out at the gym was something I looked forward to each morning; an hour-long session always cleared my head and made me ready to seize the day. I cycled through powerlifting, repetition lifting, and aerobic activities to keep my body in shape and perhaps bulked up to a proud definition.

Occasionally, I indulged with the guys and attended a few parties. I was amazed at how much more confidence I gained from pulling off a 4.0 grade point average and getting laid. Somehow, I lucked out. At my first frat party, I had sex with a gorgeous brunette sorority girl. They must have some sort of intel report with each other, because after that, a new one was selected to hook up with me at every party. My friends would get frustrated at the girls nearly throwing themselves at me. One fraternity offered me full membership if I just taught them how I do it. I would have hated to tell them that some forty-year-old MILF taught me a lot my first time, but on second thought, they just might praise me.

A new girl would flirt with me at each party while the others would watch. I finally reached a point where I'd just ask her to a bedroom after a brief introduction and she would follow me. It became almost mechanical over time as she would suck on my cock, I'd perform oral on her, slip on a condom, we'd fuck, and then go back to the party. It was still hot, but I wasn't sure what else to do, and I never received any complaints.

* * *

Time passed quickly, and I found myself in my senior year of college, making the rounds at industry day. It was chaotic. About a hundred companies were looking to hire engineers, but roughly a thousand engineering students were looking for jobs. After interviewing with five of the six companies I was interested in, I was exhausted. I didn't know much about the last company on my list, but I forced myself to walk over. As I approached the last company, I saw an exciting sign that looked like gears within a watercolor image of a horse and the name Parnum Fectum at the bottom. The graphics were brilliant and intriguing, with a look of some advanced robotics technology. Perhaps I'd misjudged.

I walked up to the booth. A beautiful woman was standing at the table. She had dark hair, almost black, that looked like silk resting on her shoulders. Her eyes were a cobalt blue, an eye color I'd seen only once before. But that was a long time ago. She smiled as I approached, and I was so captivated I couldn't walk away if I'd wanted to. Her black skirt suit with a white blouse complemented her figure nicely. My exhaustion vanished, and newfound energy raced through my veins.

"Hi, I'm Grace," she said, holding her hand out to receive mine. Her soft, warm grip against mine only amplified her allure. She was probably the most beautiful older woman I'd ever met, and again I was reminded of that woman in Cancun. Vicky. She had the same incredible blue eyes.

Grace

Taylor stepped away to the restroom, leaving me solo to manage our recruitment booth. I didn't usually attend these, but Taylor's assistant, Trish, was on vacation, and I had a previous meeting with the dean of the college engineering earlier in the day.

This university had been a treasure trove of bright minds and modest expectations for salary over the years. Taylor created an attractive recruiting display that was doing its job of sparking curiosity and promoting my company at the same time. I firmly believed bringing in creative minds with strong personalities was key to our success. So far this year, prospects had been slim. We only had one more scheduled interview at our recruiting booth, and no one had impressed me yet.

A tall, well-built young man approached our table in a nice suit, no tie, and a blue, button-down shirt. His short, dirty-blond hair, well-defined jawline, and hazel eyes were appealing. He looked familiar. As he got closer, I saw his eyes were more of an emerald green with bursts of gold. He passed the initial presentation test. I smiled at him and watched his eyes check me out, from my Louis Vuittons to my hair. *How cute they are not knowing how to check a woman out subtly. At least he's attractive.*

Holy shit! Cancun! This was the boy I hooked up with in Cancun.

I was surprised he didn't recognize me. Usually, everyone remembered my eyes, but then again, my hair was longer, blonder, I'd lost about thirty pounds, and I used a fake name when he saw me last. Plus, I was more professionally dressed.

"Hi, I'm Grace." I reached out to shake his hand. He appeared calmer and more confident than most candidates we met for the first time at this age. Many had nervous smiles as though they were vacillating between fear and optimism. He squinted slightly as though he was trying to figure out if he recognized me.

I found myself not so subtle either in scanning him over. He'd filled out a little more. He had broader shoulders than I remembered, and I hadn't noticed his masculine jawline last time.

"Hi, I'm Brett."

"Oh, yes, you're the last one on our list to interview. Are you graduating this summer, Brett?"

"Yes, ma'am. A double major in mechanical engineering and computer science with an emphasis in robotics. I spent as much time in robotics as the school provided, hoping to land a career in some cool programs."

Hmmm, quite respectful with good manners. He kept his eyes on mine as we talked, and the confidence he projected was stimulating. I noted only an occasional glance down at my blouse—but he was still young, and I wasn't one to complain about being gazed upon. In fact, I enjoyed it. But was he looking at me as just some stranger with big breasts, or was he trying to remember where he'd met me before?

"Brett, we're looking for some mechanical engineers with those skills, and we have some great robotics programs for the Department of Defense."

"Is this Brett?" Taylor walked up with a glowing expression of optimism, but she had no clue I'd already fucked him. How would she? After five years, I'd almost forgotten about it myself.

"This is my director of human resources, Taylor Williams. Ms. Williams, this is Brett."

I watched his demeanor as he shook her hand. He appeared confident as he focused on her eyes, but again, he couldn't help the occasional glance at Taylor's blouse.

"Do you have a special focus area, Brett?" Taylor asked while picking up her notepad, already prepared with Brett's education information.

"I've enjoyed robotics and would like to do more with that. I didn't know your company did research in that area, and Grace indicated you have some DoD contracts."

"We do indeed," I said, "and gaining more recognition for our creative approaches to micro-robotics."

"Cool, I would love to work on those projects." Brett beamed as he looked up at our banner behind the table, illustrating pictures of our robotics work.

I gave a subtle nod to Taylor, and she smiled back, understanding what I had in mind.

As Taylor boasted about our company to Brett, I thought about how he might fit into our alternative endeavors.

Taylor and I had been together since the beginning of the company. She was my second hire after my engineering partner developed a micro battery that could hold a hundred times more energy than any other battery to date. That gave us our first large contract, for which I hired Taylor to help recruit further.

Taylor and I couldn't be a better match. It was even more serendipitous when we discovered our shared interests for darker entertainment. We were both attractive, single women who enjoyed men who wanted to submit to us. I was married until three years ago, when my husband became jealous of my success. As I became more dominant in and out of the home, he became weaker. The more docile he'd become, the more demanding and dominant I became. I wanted to dominate him in the bedroom too. At first, he complied with my sexual demands, but then believed he was too humiliated to continue. I gave him a million dollars and told him good luck with his next life.

I didn't have time for weakness. While I enjoy gripping a man's balls until he begged for me to stop, the thought of a man who could stand up to me had a certain appeal too. Not the type of alpha man who boasts about his cock or stamina the way my sales reps did, but one who demonstrated confidence in a more subtle way. One who could take a woman and know what to do with her.

A few years ago, Taylor and I created a secret club called Secretum Dominationem, or SD for short. A concept I had thought about for many years. We found that prominent women wanted to live out their femdom fantasies in a private setting. Everyone who entered had to wear a mask and follow our explicit rules. Consent was key, of course. We provided the space for women to step into the role of Domina with any man who volunteered to role play as her slave, or servus. It was surprisingly easy to find men of all ages who liked to be dominated by a woman. We had them sign nondisclosure agreements, and anyone could leave if they no longer wanted to continue.

"Brett, are you available this evening?" I asked. "I'd like Taylor to take you to dinner and explain more about what our company offers. And perhaps you can provide more insight to us on what your five-year plan might look like."

Taylor was beautiful, confident, and intelligent; she could almost command attention in a room by merely walking into it. She projected an alluring presence, which made her a great partner in captivating the attention of clients, employees, and servi alike.

Taylor nodded in concurrence and asked, "Would seven p.m. work? I'll stop by to pick you up. Where are you staying?"

Brett seemed surprised by the sudden dinner offer, but Taylor's ability to close the deal had always been impressive. She seemed to have an almost magical touch to get people, especially men, to comply with her interests. Brett gave Taylor his address, which she wrote down on his profile page.

We shook hands, and I said, "Brett, I want you to know that there's no pressure in any decision you make. We're a growing firm and offer many opportunities to those who want to be successful."

He smiled and then shook Taylor's hand too.

As he walked away, I breathed a sigh of relief that he didn't recognize me from Cancun.

I turned to Taylor. "I think he'll fit in nicely. In fact, I know he will." Memories of that night five years ago flashed through my mind, and I couldn't keep the smile from my face. My instincts told me he was just what I was looking for.

Taylor tilted her head, raising an eyebrow. "The one for the engineering position or the one for …?"

I smiled at her, nodding. "Both."

Taylor

Before heading out, I put together my best outfit—a Versace formfitting, blue, sleeveless dress, thigh highs, and black, strappy heels. It wasn't exactly the usual attire for college interviews, but this evening might require me to pull out all the stops.

I examined myself in the mirror from different angles, running my hands over my hips, stomach, and breasts. *There's no way he'll deny this tonight.*

I topped off the look with some more lipstick then headed downstairs where the driver waited for me with the door open. After giving him the address, we were on our way.

When the driver pulled up to his apartment, he was waiting outside wearing the same clothes he wore during the interview. He was still a student and probably didn't have many choices. He walked up and opened the door.

"Punctuality is an excellent quality." I smiled at him from the back seat behind the driver.

He climbed into the car beside me, his eyes studying my contours from head to toe. He seemed hungrily drawn to my demeanor and the shape of my dress. As soon as his gaze lingered on the fringes of my dress, I knew he was mine.

I understood that Grace wanted me to tantalize him, both to employ him at our company and to see if he was appropriate for our private club. We had been offering a place for powerful women in high-profile positions to fulfill their lusty desires on men in exchange for tremendous fees and confidentiality. The males would come forward and volunteer themselves as our submissives.

However, we were receiving more and more requests for a Dominus to whom these same women could submit. A man who could tunnel into a woman's mind with confidence and determination. Who could hypothetically make a woman orgasm before he even removed her clothes just by his words and touch. A man whose whispers and warm breath on a woman's neck could make her core ache with need.

We searched BDSM groups and other fetish organizations. All we found was the same type of alpha power-trip male who wanted a woman kneeling at his side as he pet her and demanded she do certain acts to show her unwavering submission to him.

The man we were looking for would be young and handsome and could learn how to read a woman's desires. One who wasn't so knowledgeable that he couldn't be taught. Someone who could practically hypnotize a woman's mind, control her with passion, and build up lust rather than intimidation. Grace believed Brett was the man we could groom for that role. I'd find out just what type of potential he had tonight.

As we approached the restaurant, I saw him fidgeting with his hands clasped and adjusting his jacket. He stared anywhere but at me, until I asked him a question. Then he would glance at my eyes, my cleavage, and look away. "It's okay. You can relax. It isn't a date, just dinner." I placed my hand on his leg. His slacks were pulled tight over his thighs and groin, and I was already impressed with what I saw. It took all my restraint to keep me from ravishing him right there in the seat.

"I know, but I've never been with a woman on a date like this. I mean, not a date; dinner is what I meant."

"Like what, Brett? As I said, it's simply a dinner to discuss your working for us." I slid my hand along his leg.

"You're very beautiful, and well, everything seems to be happening so fast, and …"

I continued sliding my hand up his thigh, then reversed it back toward his knee. He stared at my hand instead of making eye contact. The bulge in his pants had grown more impressive.

"Relax, Brett, we're just having dinner." I gently slapped his leg with a laugh.

He nodded as the car pulled up to the restaurant. Une Touche De Virginie or A Touch of Virginia. It was an exquisite restaurant that mainly used Virginia products on its menu.

The valet opened the door for both of us. As we approached the entrance, I purposely stumbled. Brett was quick to put his hand around me to prevent my faux fall.

"Thank you." I gave him my best demure smile and placed my hand on his chest. He looked into my eyes and then deviated to my cleavage. I let him gaze for a moment, letting the tension build, waiting for his eyes to come back to mine. I placed my hand over his, and the thought of his large hand grasping my throat flashed through my mind, sending a little thrill through me. When he finally looked back into my eyes, he blushed. *So innocent.*

Brett opened the door. *A gentleman. Good start.*

A host in a tuxedo escorted us to a beautiful table with white linen, wine glasses, and a lit candle in the middle.

"A bottle of your best Cab," I requested.

* * *

While we sipped our wine, I explained more about the firm, how Grace guided it to where it was today, the benefits, the engineering group he would be working with, and all the things I knew would entice him from a professional point of view. He was eager to learn more specifics about the robotics labs, but I had to tell him that most of the details couldn't be discussed until he became an employee.

I couldn't help but look into his eyes. How the gold blended in with the emerald green was something I'd never seen before. He wasn't only beautiful, he was enthralling. He was the kind of guy who made a woman want to rip his shirt off and throw it to the floor, along with her inhibitions.

Now I needed to work on the extracurricular interests.

"Where do you see yourself in five years, Brett?" I smiled and added a bit of an eyelash flutter. My eyes never left his as I sipped my wine, attentive to his every word. Even his deep, masculine voice reached my aching core.

He laughed. "Hell, I haven't had a chance to think about five years from now. I'm still trying to see myself walking across the stage to get my diploma."

I laughed as he gulped more of his wine. Refined he was not, but still … I picked up the bottle and gave him another generous pour, hopefully loosening him up a little more.

"Do you have a girlfriend?" I asked inquisitively.

"No, I don't have a girlfriend." He blushed and looked away.

Could he really be as innocent as he appeared?

"A handsome man like yourself, I can't believe it. I'm sure you've had many girlfriends over the years?"

He looked up at me and smiled. "I've had my fair share of fun in college, but I've never been in a relationship with anyone in particular. My father passed away when I was young, and we were on our own. I grew up helping my mother raise my sister, and then in college, I focused on my studies and worked to help pay for my schooling. The life insurance the army paid out helped pay off our house and some of my tuition."

"That must have been tough, all that focus on family and studies. But it sounds like you were sowing your seeds quite well in college then?"

He nearly choked on his wine, and his face turned bright red. Perhaps he had some experience after all.

"I don't think I'd call myself a Johnny Appleseed, but I had a good time." Now I nearly spit out my sip of wine. Impressively witty, but he was adjusting in his chair and nervously looking at the table. I needed him to calm down. I filled his wine glass again.

He quickly drank through his third glass. "So, you're not married?" he asked.

I smiled and tilted my head, a little surprised at him taking the lead on a personal question. "I'm not married. I like to keep my options open, and I haven't found a man who can keep up with me. Besides, I seem to find that I enjoy life by seizing the moment when it comes by." I knew my glimmering smile and comment would exacerbate his nervousness, but I also wanted to put some provocative thoughts in his head. Judging by his rosy cheeks, I'd succeeded. He wanted to get laid.

Our food arrived, the standard small portions you get at upscale restaurants. While we ate, I continued savoring my first glass of wine and emptied the remainder of the bottle into Brett's glass. I surely didn't need to be intoxicated to fuck. In the event this was the only time I'd have him, I wanted to remember every moment.

"What type of women are you attracted to?" I asked as I signaled for the check.

He looked into his wine glass, purposefully avoiding eye contact with me. "I like confident women, cute, and attractive, obviously. I like women who are witty and have a certain smile that melts me." He glanced up at me again and then looked down. I could tell he was smiling, and his reddish cheeks were giving him away. My bait was working.

"Is something wrong?" I reached out, placing my hand on his.

"It's just that you have that smile I was talking about."

He's hooked.

I placed my arm into his on the way to the car, and I was impressed that he naturally bent his arm to accept me. He opened the door for me, and I let my dress ride up a little, exposing my panties as I got settled. "Oh, I'm sorry about that," I said. His open mouth and gaze on me told me all I needed to know.

Most of the drive was quiet. After two bottles of wine, consumed mainly by him, I thought he would be more talkative. I placed my hand on his leg, my fingers just inside the curve of his thigh. "I really enjoyed the evening with you."

This time he looked into my eyes, then to my lips. I knew he was fighting to keep from taking me right here in the car.

We arrived at my hotel. "This isn't my apartment," Brett said, sounding confused as he looked out the window.

"Oh, the driver is used to driving me back here. I didn't think to tell him to take you home." In reality, I'd told the driver to take us to my hotel. I didn't think the little white lie would hurt. "He can take you home … or …" I placed my hand on his leg. "You can come up with me for some more wine."

His smile and wide eyes answered for him. "Sure, I could go for some more wine."

We walked into my suite, and I had a bottle of chardonnay in the wine chiller behind the bar, which I'd indulged in earlier while getting ready for dinner. I opened it as he walked around the room to look at the historical wall hangings of the local area.

"Wow, this is a beautiful hotel room." He looked out the window at our view from the fifth floor. It was dark, but the moon's glow over the Appalachians was always an incredible sight.

I strolled up to Brett and handed him a glass of wine. "A toast. To your new future. May you be successful in everything you do." We clanked glasses and took a sip. He appeared a little more relaxed but didn't confirm his future would be with us.

I placed my hand on his arm. "Would you mind if I got dressed into something a little more comfortable?"

He inhaled sharply. "Uh, sure," he said and quickly drank some more wine.

After a spritz of Versace on my neck and another on my stomach, I touched up my lips and modeled in the mirror. *Damn, I look good.*

I walked out wearing only my cream-colored, silk robe, holding my glass of wine. Brett was replenishing his. I wanted him more relaxed with the wine, but I didn't want him with a drunk dick tonight.

I placed my hand on his arm. "Brett, do you think I'm attractive?"

He gazed at my nipples protruding through the silk fabric. His hand moved, and his face turned red. Something was holding him back.

I slid my fingers over the fine silk, along my breast, then slowly over my nipple. "Would you like to …?"

He grabbed the back of my neck and pressed his lips to mine, wasting no time penetrating my mouth with his tongue. I stretched my arm to set my glass of wine on the table, leaning just a little to find it.

I ran my fingers ran through his thick hair. I wasn't drunk, but his scent and the short bristles of his evening shadow against my cheek were intoxicating enough.

My mound lightly brushed against his leg, and I felt a thrill shoot through my core.

"You can if you like," I whispered.

His eyes locked on mine. "Can what?"

"You want to touch them, don't you?" I continued a light caress over my nipple. "You can touch me if you like."

He set his glass down and stood back to gaze at me as though I was some statue at the Louvre.

He gripped my breast and circled his palm over my nipple, then gently circled the palm of his hands ever so softly. Goosebumps rose like an electric current through me, bringing my body alive with want and anticipation.

His hand glided to the back of my neck, and I closed my eyes at his sensual touch for a moment before he gripped the back of my hair and my eyes jolted open. He tilted my head to the side, pressed his teeth into my neck, and then dragged them along my skin to my shoulder. My entire body shuddered. The subs back home never did this to me.

The cool air rushed over my body as he opened my robe. He stood back and gazed in amazement at my body. I could actually see his chest heave with each breath as he contemplated what to do next.

Brett

Was this really happening? Taylor was gorgeous, much more attractive than any woman I'd met while at college, and her breasts were mouthwatering. One lady in school had shown me the way she liked for her hair to be pulled, but I hadn't done it since.

Taylor had me so worked up that my primal instincts kicked in as I grabbed hold of her tresses from the roots and drew her near.

Her hand softly slid up my neck and into my hair. My skin erupted with goosebumps as her breath lightly grazed my neck.

"Would you like to learn what women truly desire from a man?" she quietly asked. Her piercing blue eyes were captivating, and even though I had some experience, I always enjoyed learning something new, especially from a beautiful and more experienced woman like Taylor.

Her lips gently touched the hairs on my neck. At the same time, she continued to whisper, "A woman wants a man who will control her but not be arrogant about it, a man who will seduce her mind and make her want him, make her desperate for more. She wants her mind so seduced that her body offers itself to him." She moved to the other side of my neck. "There's an art to it. For starters, whisper into my ear what you want to do with me. And be true. Never think of dirty words as you once did, think of them as erotic, enticing words that seduce your partner, making her want more and more of you."

It was like she was some kind of witch or enchantress. My mind was overwhelmed, and I could feel all my energy flowing to my core. I didn't understand what she was doing to me, but I desperately needed more.

She tugged my shirt out of my pants and ran her fingers through my hair. Our lips came together, just barely touching as she whispered in a sultry tone, "A woman likes a confident man, one who knows how to take what he desires. Tease her, touch her lightly so she yearns for more."

I complied, placing my hand on the back of her neck and softly caressing her skin.

"Yes, that's it," she sighed.

My fingertips moved to her face, stroking her cheek and along her neck. Abruptly, she grabbed my thumb with her teeth, and I froze. She then placed my index finger in her mouth and sucked slowly with closed eyes, clearly wanting more. My body throbbed with pleasure as I became aroused. All this from her sucking on my finger? Women truly amazed me! I wanted so badly to be released from my clothing.

"What do you want to do with me? Tell me what you want ... and don't be embarrassed."

I wanted to tell her how much I wanted to fuck her, but I blushed and couldn't do it. At a college party, I would just ask a girl if she wanted to go fuck and she would say yes. We went upstairs, had sex, and came back down to the party. This was different, so much more. Taylor was more as well.

"Do you want me to suck your cock?" she managed to ask while circling her tongue around my thumb.

I nodded again like I was in a trance.

"Then tell me. Grip the back of my hair, tilt my head to the side, and whisper into my neck to suck on your cock." She took my hand and placed it behind her head. "Make sure you get a good grip so you can force my head to move."

I closed my fingers around a fistful of hair, and she gasped.

"That's it. Now tell me to kneel and suck your cock while you gently guide me to my knees."

I was in some kind of hypnotic state; my lips barely touched the hairs on her neck, and I whispered, "I want you to suck my cock."

She smiled. "Now I want you to guide me down with your hand. Be firm but gentle so that I can understand what you desire while still respecting my boundaries."

I placed a strong grip on her hair and guided her onto her knees. "I want to see your lips around my cock." The idea of giving orders felt strange, however, she grinned as she kneeled.

She unbuttoned my belt and trousers before letting them fall to the ground. I was slightly taken aback at seeing myself standing in front of her like this. She kissed the tip over the fabric, then moved around the sides of my boxers. I could feel an eruption stirring inside me and wasn't sure how much longer I'd be able to hold it back.

She reached up and caressed my scrotum through the fabric. I glanced downward, attempting to control my racing heart. It seemed like she was hoping for further instruction from me.

"Take it out," I demanded.

"What should I take out?" She smirked as she continued to move her lips along the outline of my member.

"Pull my cock out?" *Oh my God … I said it.*

"Mmmm," she uttered under her breath as she tugged at my waistband, eventually lowering my boxers to the ground. My shoes were removed, and my pants pushed away from my ankles. I looked on in anticipation as my cock swayed back and forth like a branch in the wind.

Her hands made their way up and down, feeling my length. She then leant forward and kissed around my balls before making her way up to the head. Her lips formed an O as she enveloped me with her mouth. One hand stayed caressing my testes while the other moved up and down my shaft. I could not take my eyes off her; it was something I'd never seen before: a woman so consumed with desire for me that she would kiss, lick, and massage me all over.

"Slow is what a woman wants—the ability to experience every moment without rushing it," she murmured while still playing with my testicles and slowly moving her fingers along the tip of me. I watched in admiration as my penis peeked deeper into her throat, only stopping when it seemed as though she might gag. She pulled back and did it again, this time more confidently.

She gazed up to me. "What do you want now?"

"I want you to take my dick down your throat," I uttered in astonishment. Without any hesitation, she took me inside her mouth, allowing my entirety into her gullet. There was a brief pause, but then she pushed herself farther with purposeful movements. As she reached the base of my penis, she moved her lips back and forth as if she were fucking my cock with her throat.

I'd never experienced anything like it and was about to lose control when she pulled away. "Is that what you wanted?" she asked softly. I simply nodded as I was too overwhelmed and stunned to respond. All I desired at this point was to slide myself inside of her.

She stood up, clasped my hand, and placed it on her bare mound. She whispered into my ear while caressing my neck, "Gently slide your finger through my slit and explore."

Her wet warmth was smooth and exhilarating. I grazed my fingers along her folds. I wasn't new to exploring a woman's pussy, but Taylor was different, and I wanted to prove myself to her for some reason.

I stopped at her clit and circled my fingers around that spot while slowly applying pressure. When her breathing heightened, I pressed into her entrance. She gasped and kissed my lips, nodding, assuring me it was good.

"Kiss my neck under my ear," she whispered.

I kissed her and slipped my finger inside. She was so soft and wet. I reached my finger up inside and searched for that little spot, waiting for her reaction to tell me I was there.

She gasped. "Yes, that's it, good, good. Now, what would you like to do to me? Tell me."

I wanted to slide myself into her, but I wasn't sure how to answer her. I attempted to guide her to the bed, but she stopped me.

"Not until you tell me what you want to do to me."

"I ... I ... I want to slide myself into you."

"Do you want to fuck me?" she asked.

I nodded urgently, but she said, "Tell me you want to fuck me, and tell me you want to fuck me hard. I want to hear confidence and determination in your voice."

Why did I need to say it now? I'd never had to say it in college. Okay, sometimes I did—but it was always expected. I wasn't sure I had the nerve to say it, but she was practically begging me to tell her—and I wanted to fuck her so desperately.

I slid my hand up to her neck, caressing it, then across her throat to her chest when she gasped. I slid my hand back to her throat, and she gasped again, tilting her head up. She smiled with her eyes closed.

"Yes, grip my throat harder," she said in a tone somewhere between demanding and desperate.

"I want to fuck you mercilessly," I whispered.

She gasped again and nodded. She lay back on the bed and held her legs open. She slid her hands down her milky thighs on either side of her mound pulling herself open to expose her inner pink flesh. I placed my cock at her entrance and was about to push myself into her when she said, "Tease me. Slide your head through my slit, rub my clit with it, and then surprise me. It is all up to you, but a woman doesn't like a simple fuck. She wants you to change it up, titillate her."

I watched my head slip into her entrance, sliding it barely inside and then out, gliding it up to her clit, and then I slipped it back in, but primal instincts took over, and I forced myself into her. She arched her back as I began thrusting in and out of her. My body began to shudder as I gripped her hips. I groaned like a wolf who'd conquered his prey as I came. My legs shook, and my ass cheeks clenched as I shot wave after wave into her. I couldn't let go and was magnetized to push in as deep as possible.

Once my body relaxed, I looked into her eyes.

She smiled. "Mmmmm, that was fantastic."

I pulled out of her, watching myself slowly slide out, mesmerized at how beautiful she looked. She patted the bed next to her, motioning to join her.

"That was amazing!" I said, my breathing still heavy. Typically, I lasted longer than that, but none of the girls in college turned me on as much as Taylor.

She smiled while twisting my chest hairs into little spirals. "Just keep in mind that not all women like what I like. The true challenge and reward is to find what each woman likes by exploring her body." She kissed my nipple. "Exploring their mind." She moved up and nibbled on my ear, sending shivers through my body. "And exploring their soul. Then you can give her the best satisfaction she could ever want. And in return, you'll have some of the best sexual experiences of your life."

I gazed at her body, wanting to memorize every detail. I'd only been with one other older woman, but something about them was an incredible turn-on. Perhaps their confidence in what they wanted.

She kissed my neck again and whispered, "So what do you think? When do you want to move out West?"

Grace

Brett walked across the stage to get his diploma. Soon he'd be the newest hire in my expanding company. I had a feeling he would work out just fine.

While I visited a few universities on the east coast to provide a substantial donation, I made the trip to Brett's graduation to lock in the deal with him in person. I was reasonably confident my offer wouldn't be easy to refuse.

According to the rundown Taylor gave me on her extended interview with Brett, he was a bit less experienced, which made sense, given his age. It might be a risk for what we wanted, but he was also intelligent, attractive, and learned quickly. It was a worthwhile risk.

The ability and desire to learn were what interested me. I prided myself on my ability to find some of the most brilliant people outside of the likely sources, like MIT. Then I taught them to be the greatest. Other than my sales and business development staff, most of my male employees were engineers or IT experts comparable to any in the nation. I paid them well to keep them, too.

The dean congratulated the class, and the auditorium erupted in cheers. I walked outside, expecting to catch Brett taking pictures with his family.

Moments later, I saw him and two women exiting the auditorium. They walked into a line where others were waiting to take their picture in front of the engineering school sign.

"Congratulations, Brett." I reached out to shake his hand and then shake the hand of the woman I presumed was his mother. "Hi, I'm Grace Skyler. You must be Brett's family."

"Yes, I'm Elaine, Brett's mother. This is Kelly, my daughter."

Elaine looked to Brett, motioning him for an introduction, but he appeared a bit shocked to see me. "She's the owner of the Parnum Fectum firm in California that I interviewed with." He blushed, probably recalling the *depths* of his interview with my incredible HR director.

Elaine smiled and looked back at me. "Oh, that's great. I'm sure you didn't come all the way out here for Brett's graduation."

"I had to go to DC and some other places on the east coast for a meeting, but I decided to take a detour and see my new superstar cross the stage. That is, if he accepts our offer to come work for us."

I could see that Brett was uncomfortable. He smiled at me as though he was undecided. Maybe Taylor didn't charm him as well as she usually did if his commitment was in limbo. It was a good thing I decided to come.

"Well, I don't want to take up all of your time, but I'm interested in you, Brett. Give it some thought, search around and find out what salaries you might start at, and I assure you, my offer will convince you that we are the company for you. I have many great things planned, Brett, and I'd like you to be part of them." *More than you know.*

"Thank you, Ms. Skyler. I'll let you know next week. I appreciate you coming out to see me graduate."

I pulled a graduation card from my bag. "You're very welcome, and here's a little something I wanted you to have for graduation. Taylor told me you are worth every bit and more. No matter what you decide, I appreciate the opportunity to meet you again and your lovely family."

I shook Elaine's hand. "It was a pleasure meeting you, Elaine. You have an incredible and brilliant son, and I hope he decides to come work with us."

Elaine put her arm around him and smiled. "I'm sure he'll make the best decision for him. Thank you for coming out of your way to visit."

I smiled at Brett and walked back toward my car, realizing much of his strength and confidence appeared to have come from his mother.

I glanced back and saw him opening the envelope. He looked up with shocked eyes, and I was certain that little gift worked.

I hoped so, anyway.

Brett

I was scared shitless to see Ms. Skyler walk up to us, especially after my evening with her HR director. She had to know what we did. I played it cool while she introduced herself. I didn't know what to expect after that evening with Taylor. I couldn't imagine sex with coworkers would be acceptable, much less with the HR director.

The envelope she left me was blue, and my name was written on it in a small, bold script, similar to a formal invitation I saw in a renaissance movie. I looked at it while we waited in line for pictures by the engineering school sign.

"Are you going to open it?" My mom nudged me with encouragement.

I didn't know what to expect in this envelope. *What if it's blackmail pictures of Taylor and me, and my mom sees it?* Now I was making myself even more nervous. Wait, I was still new to the world—being blackmailed would be silly.

"Go ahead and open it while we stand here waiting. She obviously wants you to work for her. I guess you made a great first impression." Mom placed her hand on my shoulder with more anticipation than I had. *If she only knew.*

I looked at the line in front of me and thought pictures weren't that important, but Mom was proud, and it would be too awkward to just walk away. I slowly opened the envelope and saw a card. I pulled the card out and peeked inside to see a slip of paper. *Whew, no pictures.*

The card was a typical congratulations card. I looked up to see my mom eagerly awaiting. Kelly was staring at some of the other college boys walking by. Opening the card, I saw that the piece of paper was a check for ten thousand dollars.

My mom gasped. "Oh my! Your interview must have been exceptionally detailed."

I didn't look up at her, but she was spot on. I could feel my eyes widen. I had never held a check for that much money before. I've never had that much money at one time before. With the check gripped in one hand, I read the inside of the card.

Congratulations, Brett!

My HR director informed me that you have a great desire to learn. I was impressed with you as well in our short discussion. I believe Parnum Fectum would benefit greatly from your employment and want to show you my interest in hiring you. This check is a graduation gift to you whether you join our firm or not. I want you to know that we will always be interested in you and hope someday you decide to work for us. Your starting salary would be $80,000/year with full benefits. Please compare to other offers and let me know your decision. I wish you and your family the best future possible.

Sincerely,

Grace Skyler
CEO
Parnum Fectum

"Wow, that's a lot of money! You must have made a great first impression with your interview."

The image of Taylor's body popped into my mind. I couldn't look my mother in the eyes and answer, so I just stared at the card and the check and mumbled, "It was an excellent interview."

I looked up to see Ms. Skyler standing in the parking lot by a car, smiling at me. I smiled back, and she got in her car and left. I didn't know she was the CEO, and she made me an offer like this? What could I possibly have that others didn't?

When we got home, Mom had a little celebration cake for the three of us.

"Are you moving to California?" Kelly asked.

All eyes were on me. I'd helped Mom raise Kelly since she was little, but now she was fifteen. I owed my mom a lot, and it would be difficult to leave them now.

Mom walked up and hugged me. "You have done more than we could have asked of you, Brett. You would have made your father proud, but you need to seek your destiny. We will be fine here, and with that much of a salary, you can travel home to visit anytime you want."

"Or fly us out to you!" Kelly yelled out. We laughed.

"Thanks, Mom. I think I'll take the offer."

Taylor

I took Brett's acceptance letter to Grace's office to tell her the good news. "You offered him eighty K? We've never offered any new engineer that much."

Grace leaned back in her chair, twirling a pen in her fingers. "Didn't you say he was just what we were looking for?"

"Yes, for the SD role. But if the other engineers find out what his salary is, we could be facing some serious backlash." I chuckled nervously.

"Have him sign a nondisclosure agreement," she replied without hesitation. "I want him on board."

Her eyes narrowed as she spoke, with an expression of determination I had become accustomed to seeing. I knew there was no changing her mind. With a heavy sigh, I asked, "What date do you want him to start?"

A smirk crossed her lips, and she tilted side to side in her seat. "As soon as possible," she answered with a devilish grin.

Realizing she was thinking with her SD hat on versus her company hat, I grinned back. She was a fantastic visionary, and while I was sure Brett would work out great, there were some complexities this time.

For the past few years, some of the engineers we hired were also secretly indoctrinated into SD as submissives for our Dominae to enjoy. I would focus primarily on the single men. They had no idea Grace and I were the ring leaders of that secret group, and we wanted to keep it that way. Not all engineers were lustful geeks, but we'd found enough of them to invite via a personal, untraceable email address with a tempting monetary bonus if they pleased their Domina for the evening. Since each Domina paid us ten thousand dollars, the least we could do was pay these volunteers a few hundred to ensure discretion and enthusiasm. Making them sign a firm non-disclosure agreement also helped keep a high level of discretion.

They would have an orientation with a Domina and see what excitement they could be offered. Almost every one of them accepted the invitation. Dominae were typically high-profile elites from various corporations or political affiliations who paid a substantial fee to take out their stresses on the servi. Everyone wore a mask, so it was difficult to see who anyone was at the monthly events.

I made all the necessary arrangements for Brett to fly out next week to start his new career and his new adventures. I had to admit, I was interested in seeing his growth in SD as well. *Hell, as gorgeous as he is, I'd like to see a lot more of him too.*

Brett

Saying goodbye to my family was difficult. I hugged my sister and then thanked my mom for everything. Then I took my carry-on and went through security. Taylor said the rest of my belongings would be picked up and shipped to me when I was ready for them.

My only other flying experience was to Cancun, which was like being in a sardine can, so flying first-class to San Francisco would probably spoil me for future travel, but I enjoyed every free drink and my luxurious space while I could.

When I arrived, I went down an escalator and saw a man in a black suit holding a sign that read: *Brett Jenkins.* I walked up and said, "I'm Brett."

"A pleasure meeting you, Brett. I'm Raymond, your driver." He pointed to my carry-on bag I had next to me. "Is this all of your luggage?"

"Yes, this is it."

He reached for it. "Allow me to carry it to the car."

I followed him as he asked, "I trust you had a good flight?"

We had some small talk about the flight and what life was like in Virginia. He had a friend who went to the University of Virginia, which wasn't far from where I attended, and told me he always wanted to travel out there someday.

About an hour later, we pulled up to the Ritz Carlton near Silicon Valley. It was the most impressive hotel I'd ever seen. Raymond walked me inside to the desk clerk and introduced me.

"Good evening, Mr. Jenkins. Your room is ready, and we have your payment on file from the Parnum Fectum Engineering Firm. Here's your key."

She handed me a credit-card-like key. Raymond asked, "Will there be anything else, Mr. Jenkins?"

I stood there in awe. My treatment was nothing short of feeling like royalty. "I don't think so."

"Excellent. I will be here at eight tomorrow morning to pick you up and take you to the office. I hope you get a good night's sleep."

I walked into my room and stared in amazement. It seemed larger than my mom's house. It was incredible with a sofa, large screen TV, fireplace, a small kitchen, a bar stocked with alcohol, and a bedroom and bathroom that looked like a king would stay here. I set my bag on a small, floral-printed, cloth bench near the bed and placed my suit in the closet. It was the suit my mom had gotten for me when I graduated college. I didn't know if I needed a suit, but I thought I'd wear one on my first day.

Taking advantage of the stocked bar, I grabbed a beer and searched through the TV for a hockey game. It was eleven p.m. in Virginia, but only eight p.m. in California, so I struggled to keep my eyes open.

I woke up in the chair to see some chef making buffalo cauliflower nuggets. I cringed at the TV, contemplating if cooking was now considered a sport, and couldn't you just buy buffalo sauce and put it on the nuggets?

Damn, it was two a.m. *I need to get to bed.*

I stumbled into the bedroom, set my alarm for seven, and went back to sleep.

My eyes opened to no sound. I looked over to see that the clock read five a.m. *Ugh! Jet lag sucks.*

I was sluggish standing up, and my eyes were still heavy. Maybe a shower would bring me to life again.

The glass and marble in the bathroom reminded me of some posh scene in a movie. There was a dial behind some towels near the shower. I turned the knob, causing heat to emanate from the area, and I realized it was a towel warmer.

The shower controls were outside the stall, and I could set the temperature by pushing on an arrow like the thermostat on a wall. If only I knew what temperature to set.

I laughed. All I'd ever known was to put the handle between red and blue. I guessed at about one hundred degrees on the shower and stepped inside when the water was warm. It was like rain falling from the ceiling. A warm, gentle rain that I didn't want to leave. I washed up, turned off the water with the little stop button outside the door, and reached for my towel. The warm, white towel against my skin was softer than anything I'd ever felt, making me wonder why this company would be this interested in pampering me. I was just a young engineer.

The echoing knock at the door was a bit alarming. The clock on the nightstand read seven a.m. "Room service," a voice called through the door.

Horror movies started flashing through my mind. I looked through the peephole and saw a man in a black vest and white shirt at the door. "Mr. Jenkins, I have a breakfast buffet for you."

When I opened the door, he pushed in a cart full of covered dishes and removed the lids: eggs, bacon, sausage, fruits, smoked salmon, coffee, and orange juice.

"This is amazing." I pulled out my wallet.

"No, sir. Your company has paid for it. Enjoy."

He walked out, and I dug in. Everything was amazing. I'd never tasted orange juice this delicious before.

Once I got my suit on, I envisioned my mom proudly standing next to me in the mirror reflection as she did at my graduation. I took a deep breath and smiled at the start of my new life.

*   *   *

Raymond opened the door to the car, and I stepped out to see a brick and glass three-story building that would make Frank Loyd Wright proud. It almost had a castle look with stone blocks, yet modern lines and window features. It was awe-inspiring.

I followed Raymond to the front door and saw Taylor standing there with another woman. Images flashed through my mind of that evening—our so-called interview. I couldn't help the warmth on my face, and my cock stirred to life as my mind reminisced about what I did with her body.

She wore a black skirt to her knees and a cream-colored blouse. I had every contour of her under those clothes memorized.

"Welcome, Brett! I hope your accommodations are suitable," Taylor said as she held her hand out to shake mine.

I shook her hand and then reached to shake the other woman's hand standing next to her.

"Hi, my name is Trish. I work for Ms. Williams, and I'll handle your in-processing paperwork."

Taylor escorted us upstairs to the HR office. I couldn't help but glance at her ass, remembering that night—a night that I'd probably—*hopefully*—never forget. We stopped at a table. "Trish will take care of all your in-processing paperwork, and then we'll show you around the firm. Grace wants to have lunch with you, so we scheduled that at noon. Do you have any questions?"

"Um, no. Thank you for everything." Her gorgeous smile warmed my cheeks again. I couldn't take my eyes off her, unable to shake away the images of her lying naked in bed, and those gorgeous lips wrapped around my cock.

"I'll leave you in Trish's competent hands." I watched her walk down a hallway. Her sway was almost hypnotizing. I'd love to …

"Mr. Jenkins, would you like to have a seat?"

I subtly shook my head and focused on the folder that Trish had set on the conference table.

The in-processing was time consuming. I'd heard of a 401K, but I never knew the details. Trish thoroughly explained my benefits, the processes for logging my time, and the code of conduct for the company. I'd probably pay more attention to her if she wasn't so beautiful. The light reflected brilliantly in her glossy, black hair. I tried to discretely determine if her long eyelashes were real. Regardless, they accentuated her beautiful blue eyes like a model from *Vogue*. Fortunately for me, she was dressed conservatively in a plain dress suit; otherwise, I'd probably forget everything she said.

"All right, we're all done. Welcome to Parnum Fectum," Trish said brightly.

I reached out to shake the hand she'd extended and replied, "Thank you."

She paused a moment, almost as though she was assessing me. I'd tried to be subtle in checking her out, but based on her smile, I'd failed. She let go of my hand and said, "Now, let's take a tour of the company. Your lunch with Ms. Skyler is at noon."

The test lab on the first floor was incredible, and there were many different sectioned activities going on. "What's in there?" I pointed to a room that said CLASSIFIED.

"Oh, that's where we work on our government programs that are highly classified. We do a lot of different types of engineering here. Once we get your security clearance completed, you'll get to learn more about some of those programs."

The elevator ride to the third floor was quiet. Trish may have been a couple of years older than I was, and I couldn't help but check out her hourglass figure in the elevator door's reflection. I hoped to learn more about her, but it was best to get settled into my job for now.

Trish introduced me to the sales and marketing teams. Many were well dressed in suits. Everyone looked upbeat and positive, introducing themselves to me with an attitude like they wanted to sell me a used car. I couldn't help but smile at the positive energy on that floor, but I'd rather be building something in a lab.

We went to the second floor. "This is the engineering division," Trish said as the elevator stopped.

We walked out to a sea of cubicles and rooms of near silence—a stark difference from the third floor. I followed Trish across an open area with a large conference table and algorithm-filled whiteboards on every wall. We walked down an aisle of cubicles to an office. "This will be your manager, Steve Briggs. Steve, here is your new engineer we just hired. Brett Jenkins."

A shorter man with a shaggy beard stood up from behind a desk with piles of varying-colored folders. He had a small table with a couple of chairs, and all the walls were dry erase boards with calculus equations written all over them.

Steve reached out, and we shook hands to greet one another.

"I'll leave him with you for an hour, and then he has lunch with Ms. Skyler. I'll stop by to take him to her office," Trish said and turned away. "I'll see you shortly, Brett."

"Come on, my boy," he said.

Boy? He was maybe ten years older than me.

"I'll take you on a little tour and introduce you to the team."

He introduced me to several others, then brought me to a cubicle with two desks angled slightly in a V shape. "Todd, I'd like to introduce you to our new engineer, Brett."

A man approximately five years older than me stood up. He had dark, curly hair and thick, dark-rimmed glasses and was wearing the typical engineer attire of a plaid shirt and khakis.

"Hi, Brett. Welcome aboard," he said. "I guess you'll be sitting there." He pointed to the desk next to him, empty except for a computer keyboard, mouse, and monitor in the middle.

"Great. I'm looking forward to learning the ropes," I said, which caused Todd to snicker in a way you'd see in a *Revenge of the Nerds* movie.

"What's so funny?" I asked.

"Oh … nothing." He pushed his glasses back up his nose and stopped snickering.

I didn't think much of it.

Steve said, "I'm going to show him around on some of our projects. He's got lunch with Ms. Skyler today."

"Oh, wow, I never had lunch with the big boss. You must be someone special," Todd said sarcastically with another snicker.

Steve took me around to look at some of the company's projects, and I was excited to see the robotics work.

"I love robotics," I said. "It's what initially turned me on to this company when Ms. Skyler told me about it."

"Good, we need help in that area. I'll have that be your primary focus."

I was pretty excited to work on something I enjoyed in college. We walked back to his office where Trish was waiting. "I hope I'm not late," Steve said, looking at his watch.

"Nope, right on time. Thanks, Steve. Come with me, Mr. Jenkins."

Grace

Beaming didn't come close to how I felt as I hung up the phone. I'd just landed another large deal—for twenty million dollars. Now having over a half billion in contracts, I felt unstoppable.

The fact that I was a successful CEO and a secret domination sex club owner wasn't something I felt guilty about at all. I liked to think of it as discreet networking. I provided the clients an avenue to explore a part of themselves they could never do elsewhere. These powerful, prominent women paid well for a high-class and discreet location to act out their dark desires. I was all too willing to provide that setting for them and potentially land a profitable deal or two along the way.

The twenty—or now twenty-one—deals I'd gotten from SD Dominae had probably brought in over half of our contracts to Parnum Fectum. Taylor was the only other person who knew of that connection.

The door opened; Trish came walking in. "Mr. Jenkins is here for your lunch appointment, and the caterer is here also."

"Send him in. We'll eat in my office."

Brett walked in behind Trish.

"Brett! I'm so glad to see you again." I walked up to him and shook his hand. "Have a seat while they set up our lunch." I motioned toward a couple of chairs by a coffee table. "How are your accommodations?"

He looked apprehensive. "My accommodations are incredible, but ..." He looked around and then glanced at me. He seemed to have trouble making eye contact. *Damn, he remembers me, doesn't he?* "I'm wondering why me?"

I sighed in relief—internally. "Look at me, Brett."

His eyes instantly locked onto mine, almost like a child does when his mother demands the same.

I smiled. "You are a talented man, and from what Taylor informed me of, you have a lot of potential. I pride myself on finding potential that can help take my company to new levels."

As soon as I mentioned Taylor, his face flushed, and he looked away. Hopefully we'd be able to cure him of that uncomfortable reaction at the mention of Taylor's name.

"I want you to know that I know about your evening with Taylor, and everything is okay. You're both adults, and you shouldn't be ashamed. We won't terminate anyone here for workplace relationships providing it doesn't interfere with the job. Okay?"

His face turned crimson while he nodded and looked down at the table.

"Look at me, Brett … okay?"

Brett looked into my eyes and formed his lips into a smile, but he remained flushed.

"Lunch is served," the restaurant waiter announced.

I looked into his eyes and softly said, "It's all fine. Just relax and enjoy your new career."

During lunch, I asked Brett about his background. He shared how he helped his mother raise his sister after his dad passed away and how he had to work extra hard to do well in school and take care of a household. Taylor was right about him. He had the potential to be exactly what we were looking for, but he'd need to have a lot more confidence, not to mention an understanding of a woman's body, if we were to succeed in our newest addition to SD.

"Did you see the robotics we're working on, Brett?"

He nodded. "Yes, it looks fantastic. Steve said he'll have me working on one of the projects."

"That's great. Once you get your security clearance, you can see some really cool things we're working on in the classified vault." His enthusiasm had me excited. "What are your plans for living arrangements?"

He pondered a moment. "Well, really, I haven't given it much thought. Everything has happened so fast and all I brought with me was one carry-on bag."

I remembered Trish lived alone. She wasn't part of SD, but she might appreciate a small bonus for taking him in for a little while.

"Let me look into something for you. Perhaps I can set you up somewhere for a little while until you find a place for yourself."

We were both finished with lunch. The waiter warmed my coffee and filled Brett's water glass.

"Brett, why don't you take tomorrow off? I'll see if Trish can show you around the area and see some of the highlights of Silicon Valley."

"Really? Wow, that would be incredible. Thanks!"

We stood up, and I walked him to the door. "I think you'll fit in very well at Parnum Fectum." I opened the door, and Trish stood up.

"Trish, do you have Brett's phone number on file?"

"Yes, ma'am."

"Good. I'm giving Brett tomorrow off and wondered if you could take the company car and show him around the area? You can charge your expenses to the company."

Her eyes lit up. "I'd be delighted. Can Raymond drive us?"

"Of course, that would be good. Unless you need Brett for anything else, feel free to let him go back to the hotel for the evening."

"Yes, ma'am," Trish replied.

"Thank you, Ms. Skyler. I can't tell you enough how much I appreciate everything."

He extended his hand, and I responded with a feminine yet firm grip. "Thank you, Brett. I think the appreciation will be mutual."

There was a hint of confusion in his smile before he walked away with Trish.

I went back to my desk, picked up my phone, and pressed the most used call button I had. "Taylor, can you come in here for a moment?"

Taylor

On my way out the door to see Grace, Brett walked past my office with Trish. "Where might you two be heading?"

They stopped. Brett was so adorable as he applied no discretion scanning my body again.

"Ms. Skyler gave Brett the rest of the day off and asked me to show him around the area tomorrow with the company car ... if that's all right with you."

"Sounds good. Enjoy your day tomorrow."

Brett smiled without saying a word. He was so delectable. I'd love to spend a day with him myself.

"What's up?" I said as I walked into Grace's office. She was standing at her fourth-story window overlooking some trees and many of the other technology companies Silicon Valley hosted.

She turned around and walked over to the chairs where I stood. We'd had countless discussions in these chairs, some company-related, but most of them about SD.

"I wanted to talk a little more about Brett."

"I thought you might." Adding a man—the right man—into the Dominae fold was new territory for us, and we needed to get it right the first time. "You asked Trish to take Brett around town tomorrow? Is there something else going on that you want to let me in on?"

After many years of working with Grace, I could tell when her mind was calculating something interesting.

"What are your thoughts about Trish helping us make Brett more confident in his sexuality?"

I shouldn't have been shocked at anything Grace said, but that was surprising. I'd always had a soft spot for Trish. She was one of the most intelligent people I knew. I pondered a moment. "She's confident but passive. I'm not sure she would go for it, and it may even be insulting to her. I don't think it's worth the risk." For over a year now, I've seen Grace double the size of her business, but with that, I was also worried that her arrogance and complacency were growing too.

We were both silent as we contemplated how to make this happen. I continued, "We could see if she would take him in for a while until he finds his own place. They're both attractive and only a few years apart in age, so they might hit it off on their own."

Grace nodded. "I thought of that, but I don't want to risk them getting attached. That might impact our overall plans with him and SD."

She made a good point.

"Make her an offer. Tell her that we want him to be more confident and see if she's willing to help him with that sexually. Offer her ten thousand dollars to rock his world for a month and teach him how to be a more confident lover."

My mouth dropped open. "Are you saying to ask Trish if she'll prostitute herself for us?" I couldn't even believe I had just asked that. "Imagine the lawsuit."

"What do you suggest?" Grace demanded.

I thought for a moment, then said, "Why not see if Trish will accept Brett moving in with her temporarily, and then we can fish around to see if it's something that might interest her. But just asking her like this would put Parnum Fectum—and us—at risk."

"Fine, but I don't want to take forever to get him ready," Grace firmly stated. She was in deep thought. Usually, I understood what she was thinking, but I wasn't sure I did this time—offering ten grand for my assistant to sleep with a new employee? This was over the top, even for Grace.

Grace leaned forward and stared into my eyes with determination. "I have four wealthy women wanting this. Each is willing to pay ten thousand; if he is successful, more will come in wanting him, so I want him ready as soon as possible.

I contemplated for a moment, not wanting to put Trish in this situation. She was a great employee, and I'd hate to risk her leaving—besides, imagine the lawsuit we'd be exposed to. "I'll ask her to find out more of what he's like, and we can compensate her for boarding him for a while. I'm not even sure she'll do that much."

Grace replied, "I'll think up a plan B for the next step. Let me know how it turns out with Trish."

I walked down the hall to a small office next to mine. Trish was planning a few job fairs we'd be attending in a few months.

"Trish, do you have a moment?" I walked in and closed the door.

She stood up, facing me. "Of course. Is something wrong?"

My tone may have been a bit alarming.

I sat in her guest chair across from her, and she sat back down as well. Her meticulously clean desk didn't have any pictures or indications she had anyone significant in her life.

"What are your thoughts on Brett?"

She smiled and tilted her head, a little perplexed. "What do you mean what do I think? From a professional perspective or personal?"

Now I was more intrigued. "How about both?"

"Well, I haven't spent too much time with him to know what he can bring to the company, but he's eager. From a personal perspective, I think he's handsome, has a nice, positive smile, and that Viking-like jawline is striking. I guess I'll learn more about him tomorrow."

Ahh, yes, the tour of the area tomorrow.

"I know this is a lot to ask, and please be honest if you're not interested, but until Brett finds a place of his own and gets his belongings moved out here, he'll need a place to stay. Would you mind hosting him? We would compensate you for your trouble."

Her eyes opened wide with surprise. "Wow, I ... I don't know. That's not something I would have expected to be asked."

"It's completely okay if you're not comfortable. We'll find him another place."

"Are you expecting me to have sex with him?"

I was surprised that she asked so directly. Perhaps she wasn't entirely the passive young woman I thought she was.

"That is completely up to you, but we would offer you a ten-thousand-dollar bonus for your troubles."

"My troubles to take him in, or more?" She leaned back into her chair, her hands clasped with mob-boss-like confidence.

Her wide smile and level stare were intriguing, not at all like the personality I'd known her to have. *Is she more than I thought she was?*

When I didn't respond, she sat straight in her chair, her arms on her desk, fingers clasped, and said, "I'll take you up on your offer for the ten thousand, and I'll treat him like a king if you like, but I also want free membership to your secret club."

One thing about human resources experience is having a good poker face. I looked inquisitively at her, trying not to show any confirmation of a secret club, but she obviously had me at a disadvantage.

"Secret club? I don't know what you're talking about."

She smiled and leaned back into her chair again. "Taylor, I've been working here for two years, and a lot of that was spent working late hours with you. Do you really believe I haven't noticed your work with the club you and Grace have going on the side? Plus, you offered Brett at least twenty thousand more than any other engineer ever hired, so something else is going on with him. I want to be a free member, and I want to be a Domina and a servus. I like to change it up now and then."

I sat back, no longer able to hold my poker face. She'd played me well, hiding her true self behind a façade this entire time. I didn't know whether to be pissed at her or proud. Unsure how to respond, I stood up and walked to the door. "I'll let you know shortly."

"Okay. And I'll help mold Brett any way you want. Just let me know how, and we can discuss our arrangement with that separately."

Amazed at the woman's gumption, I chuckled as I walked out of her office and then over to Grace's. I paused in front of her door and shook my head in disbelief. How could I have been so wrong about Trish? What else didn't I know about her?

Grace was working on her laptop at her desk as I walked in.

"How'd it go with Trish?" She glanced up at me and continued typing.

"I knew there was something about that little minx I liked," I said, grinning as I walked to the chair in front of her desk and sat down.

Grace sat back with raised eyebrows.

"Our very smart and passive Trish is not so passive after all. She said she would help mold Brett any way we want, providing we let her be a free member to SD as a Dom and sub."

Grace burst out in laughter. "That little bitch. I love her!"

I shook my head wryly, a grin teasing the corners of my mouth. "It would appear there's more to her than any of us thought."

"Bring her in here."

Grace

I turned my chair around and looked outside while Taylor brought Trish to me. Outside my window, the day was coming to a close and the sun was setting, painting the sky a brilliant, fiery orange that lit up the midtown streets below. A helicopter passed by me on its way to the Yahoo building, no doubt. I heard footsteps walk toward me. "You wanted to see me, Ms. Skyler?"

I turned around to see the seemingly sweet, innocent, twenty-something, petite woman wearing a business skirted suit that accented her stature. Standing there with her hands clasped in front of her, she could've been a poster child for finishing school. Taylor sat on the corner of my desk with her arms crossed.

"You can lay off the innocent role. You showed your hand with Taylor, so I want your true self with me now."

She smiled confidently as though she'd been called out on a brilliant lie, a lie of which she was proud. "What would you like me to say, Ms. Skyler?"

I didn't know whether I should be proud of the charade she'd held up so long or proud of how confident she was now, but I knew one thing … I liked her a lot more than I ever had.

"Sit down, Trish."

She sat down and crossed one leg over the other.

"What do you know of this secret club?"

"Well … even though the two of you have been discreet, I've overheard some of your late evening discussions about Secretum

Dominationem. Based on what Taylor asked of me, I assume you want to groom Brett for some role there."

She obviously knew enough but didn't appear to know details.

"What do you think goes on at SD?"

"I believe you have high-profile women who pay a lot of money to come and use our passive, yet horny, engineers for their sexual and sadistic pleasure."

"Sadistic pleasure?" I asked, even though I knew full well where she was going.

"Don't get me wrong. I'm all for it if everyone is consenting."

"What makes you think our engineers are involved?" I asked.

"Please. People talk. It's not hard to connect the dots between events people boast about in the lunch room and the private engagements Taylor's coordinated at the same time."

I realized I was looking at a prize employee who I never wanted to leave this company. She may be a great asset to our firm in the future.

"What is your proposal to what Taylor offered you?"

She looked up to Taylor and then back to me. "I told her I'd take the ten thousand to take Brett in for a while. I don't know what specific role you want of him, but I can groom him if you like for another ten thousand. And I want free membership to the club."

I twirled my pen between my fingers and looked up at Taylor, who tilted her head and slowly nodded. I could tell she was thinking the same thing I was. She and I were so much in tune that it was almost scary sometimes.

"I have a counter to your counter. When you take Brett out tomorrow, offer to let him move in with you until he finds his own place. Then seduce him. I want him to be one of the most confident lovers ever known. Teach him how to whisper the right words in a woman's ear and create electricity in her body with simple touches and kisses. Teach him great oral skills and how to take charge. Do this over a month, and you'll get your twenty thousand regardless of the outcome. If you're successful, we'll give you the membership you want, but you need to break up with him as soon we find him his own apartment. I don't want any attachment between you two."

She listened carefully, then stood up and put her hand out. "It's a deal."

"I think there may be more of a future in our firm for you than we previously thought," I said as I stood and shook her hand.

Her steely eyes looked into mine, and she said, "I'd like that."

I was amazed and curious at just how calculating she was. I also adored how she could go from a passive, innocent disposition to a demanding negotiator in a heartbeat.

"Enjoy your day tomorrow, and let us know how it goes," I said.

She nodded and replied, "Will do," then turned around and waved as she left my office.

I laughed. "Damn, if I don't see myself in that little minx."

I was elated. After Taylor went back to her own office, I turned around to look at the darkness over Silicon Valley. The sky was turning a dark blue, and the city's lights were sparkling through the trees. I pondered Trish's desire to be a Dom and sub. Her confidence—when she showed it—was well beyond her years. Now I had to figure out how to get Brett into the club and into the role we wanted. That could be a little more challenging.

Brett

I slipped my deck shoes on and looked in the mirror to ensure nothing was out of sorts with my gray shorts and purple polo. I went to the nearly ceiling-height window to gaze at the bright sky over this iconic city. I could hardly believe where I was and how well they treated me. When I compared my salary to other starting engineering positions, I found I was making almost twenty thousand more than most. I'd never considered myself special, but maybe they saw something in me that I didn't.

I saw the black Lincoln company car pull up into the parking lot. The same car that picked me up from the airport. I grabbed my wallet, cellphone, and room key and went downstairs.

I couldn't move after I walked out of the hotel. Trish stood outside the vehicle, looking less like a librarian than she had the day before. Her knee-length summer dress showed off her gorgeous shoulders, her slightly wavy black hair looked silky to the touch, and her smile was almost calling for me like a siren at sea. I immediately thought of Taylor and how she'd seduced me that evening a few weeks ago. I shook that thought right out of my head. I couldn't have those thoughts running through my mind today. It would drive me nuts.

"Hi, Brett. Ready for the day?"

"I am. Thanks for showing me around."

"My pleasure. I created a route with an itinerary. I'm sure you remember Raymond ..."

I nodded at him.

"He'll be driving us today."

Our first stop was a computer museum. We looked around at computers, from the abacus to calculators to large computers of the 1940s that took up an entire room and were not near as capable as my cellphone. I stared in amazement at the old, green, glowing CRT monitor as it displayed an old programming language. I was in awe of how fast everything had evolved in the past eighty years.

Trish badged us into the NASA research facility. She told me we had several contracts with them, which involved robotics. One of the program managers we worked with gave us a tour. It was fascinating to see so many aspects of space research.

While we were touring NASA, Raymond went to get some lunch. We then drove to a nature preserve to have lunch. Trish asked me to tell her about myself, and I told her the same story I told everyone.

She asked, "Do you think you're a confident man?"

I was perplexed. No one had ever asked me that before, and I took a second to think about it. "I believe I am. Well, I am with things that I know, at least."

She smiled and then stared out at the water. There were hundreds of birds flying around. Birds of all types. I couldn't get over how amazing this park was. It felt like an oasis—a strip of serenity that almost made you forget you were in a city. Trish said, "I love coming here but feel every time I do, I roll the dice by not having an umbrella."

We both laughed. I was intrigued by her fun personality.

"No girlfriends back home waiting for you to whisk them out here when you get settled in?"

I kept focus on the activity in the preserve. "Helping my mom, I didn't have time to do any dating, and then I focused on my studies. So other than some casual dating in college, I'm not attached to anyone."

As I looked at Trish, the sun brilliantly reflected off her hair. She was one of the most beautiful women I'd ever met. "How about you?" I asked.

"I date now and then, but I'm too focused on my work to get involved with anyone. For now, I just want to enjoy life without any strings."

I nodded, understanding completely. That's how I felt while studying in college.

"Where to next?" I asked.

We visited the Tech Museum of Innovation. This place was tailored toward adults and children. I enjoyed seeing the growth of technology over the years and possible future programs. Trish and I laughed a lot, messing with some of the interactive activities designed for the kids. She was a lot of fun.

By mid-afternoon, we were on our way back to my hotel. It was the best day I'd ever had with a woman. We laughed so hard at times our stomachs ached.

"I realize you don't have a place to stay yet," Trish said, "and finding a place can be quite daunting. The company gave you two weeks to stay in the hotel, but if you want, I have two bedrooms in my apartment. You can stay with me for a little while until you find your own place."

I looked at her in surprise. I'd been enamored with her all day, but I couldn't contain the urge to look at her from head to toe again. As soon as

I did it, I could have hit myself for being so obvious. "Um, I don't know. There is so much happening so fast."

"Exactly, which is why you can take your suitcase, set it in your bedroom at my apartment, and spend a month or so figuring out where you want to live without the rush. We had a great time today, didn't we?"

I enjoyed her company today, and she was very kind to me, but her offer seemed to come out of left field. We barely knew each other. The thought of not rushing into an apartment out here was appealing. "Are you sure? I can help pay for some rent or help with groceries."

"So, you'll do it?" she said gleefully. "It'll be fun, and I get bored by myself, so I usually go out to eat most nights. It will be good to have someone there with me. How about you check out of the hotel tomorrow morning? I'll swing by to pick you up. You can keep your suitcase in my car until after work."

Wow, my mind was racing. I couldn't help but embrace the positive vibes coming from her. *Is this really happening?*

We arrived at the hotel, and Trish told me she'd be back at eight a.m. to pick me up and check me out of the hotel on the company credit card.

I went to my room, grabbed a beer, and looked out my window again, wondering what I could have done to get so lucky.

Trish

On my way to pick up Brett, I couldn't help but look back at the past few years of my life. When I turned down my CIA opportunity to come out to California, I thought I was with the love of my life. As number one in my class at Yale studying Anthropology and Human Factors, I thought I would be the best forensics analyst the CIA could get. They approached me during my sophomore year in college and I couldn't have been happier ... until I met Jim. Jim was my everything during my last two years in school. He was an electrical engineer and landed a great job with Yahoo. I loved him so much that I gave up my opportunity with the CIA to follow him wherever he went.

After a year, he left me for another computer programmer. He said I wasn't mentally stimulating enough for him. I soon learned that mentally stimulating was short for not geeky enough and didn't play video games. It was probably for the best, as he preferred shooting people on his game system over having sex with me, something I craved almost every night, every day, and just about at any time.

Not knowing where to go, I had some drinks one night—okay, many drinks—and met Taylor. After listening to my woes, Taylor gave me her business card and said to come in for an interview after I recovered. Jim took his belongings a week later, and I met with Taylor. She hired me on the spot to be her HR assistant.

I was planning to re-establish my contacts to get back into the CIA when I overheard Grace and Taylor discussing their secret club one night. It was intriguing enough that I decided to stay with the firm longer. I figured if I knew more about this organization, I might be in an excellent position to make some hush money in the future. I just had to put on a conservative persona until the time was right.

With this latest offering, the time was definitely right. My goals may have changed though. Grace's use of SD to gain more clients and contracts could become lucrative to me with my own side-gig. I could see a lot more financial potential for myself with this information, And I might learn something from Grace in the process. She was brilliant, I had to admit. Besides, sexually mentoring a handsome man for a month for twenty grand seemed like it would benefit me in two ways. It had been about two years since Jim left, and the few dates I'd actually been on consisted of men from some big-tech company where most were boring and the one who wasn't boring didn't seem to satisfy my sexual needs. The more discrete work I did on the side satisfied my sexual needs, but not necessarily with a partner I enjoyed. Perhaps this would be an excellent opportunity to mold someone who knew his way around a woman's body and could take care of my needs too.

I pulled up to the hotel where Brett stood out front with his suitcase, wearing his khaki's, polo shirt, and deck shoes. *He dresses well.*

I popped the trunk for his suitcase and stepped out of the car. "Put your suitcase in the trunk. I'll take care of the bill and be right back."

I stopped to watch him effortlessly lift his bag, flexing his arm to show me his sculptured definition in his arm. *Mmmm, he is toned.*

Prying my gaze away from his bicep, I hurried inside. When I returned to the car, I beamed with optimism as I buckled in. "All ready for your start in real life?"

His gaze traveled up my bare legs, and when he got to the hem of my burgundy skirt, he looked up at me and blushed. It was cute.

"What's the matter?" I asked.

His head jerked in surprise. "N-nothing. It's just that you're very pretty."

Hooked him already.

"Thank you, but you just saw me yesterday, and I think I was much prettier then."

"I know, yes, you were quite beautiful yesterday too."

I reached over to pat his leg and replied, "Thank you, but from an HR perspective, I must advise you to use caution in complimenting people on their appearance at work. It may not be well accepted."

"Oh, I'm sorry, I—"

"No worries. We'll be living with each other for a while, so compliment me all you like. I'm just talking about work."

We pulled out of the driveway and onto the road. I'd probably just crushed his happy place—time to bring on the charm.

"We can probably drive into work together until you get yourself a car. I can write up your letter of employment for you to get a car loan."

"That would be great, thanks. But … I … don't take this the wrong way. I appreciate all you're doing for me, but I just wanted to know why? I'm a complete stranger."

"It's good that you're apprehensive. It's a great quality to have. Let's just say I've been in your shoes before, and I didn't have help. And besides …" I looked at him and winked. "You're exceptionally easy on the eyes."

A startled smile flashed across his face. The trip from the hotel to the office was only about ten minutes, so we just spent the short time getting to know each other's interests.

"You remember how to get to your work area?" I asked once we were inside.

"Yup. Thanks again, and I'll see you later."

He walked off to the stairs on the other end of the building as I went to the elevator to the top floor.

"Step one, complete!" I exclaimed, walking into Taylor's office. She sat back and smiled at me.

"So, he's moving in with you?"

"His suitcase is in my car, and he's coming back with me after work."

"Trish, can you close the door please and have a seat?"

I walked back to close the door, then sat down in front of Taylor's desk. She had a tight smile, and her eyes squinted as though she was searching for how to ask something.

"Why the façade?"

I tilted my head slightly. "Whatever do you mean, Ms. Williams?"

"Yeah ... that one. Although well executed, it's obviously not who you are. Why the act?"

"I learned long ago to only let my true self out when I need to. Everyone likes a docile woman, someone who is reliable and respectful. A strong-willed, confident, and determined woman is usually frowned upon until she works her way into a leadership role, and then she's expected just to turn it on right away."

"I must say, you impressed both Grace and me, and you don't need to fake it around us. I want you to know that."

"Thank you. I'll try to remember that."

"I also want to ask ... this request with Brett ... not many would consider it even for the money. Why?"

I didn't want to open up to her about my background or interests, but she needed something. I shrugged and replied, "Well, the only men I've ever been with were lousy lovers. I thought this was an opportunity to train someone who just might do the trick and be someone I would enjoy."

She laughed and said, "If he becomes that good, I think we all might take a turn. Just remember, don't get attached."

"Got it, no worries there. Not sure I want to find anyone permanently any time soon."

I walked back to my office and pondered on starting an organization that trained men on how to please a woman. I laughed to myself and got started with my tasks for the day.

Brett

Wow. I couldn't believe what was happening to me. I reached the engineering floor and knocked on the door to the room. My boss Steve opened the door.

"No badge yet? Trish should have that for you shortly, and then you can swipe yourself in." He welcomed me into the engineering room and walked me to my desk.

Just hearing Trish's name gave me goosebumps. She'd definitely caught me staring at her legs in the car, but I couldn't help it. Just the thought of living with her made me take in extra deep breaths.

Todd turned around in his chair as we approached my desk.

"Today, I'll have you follow Todd around to see what he does and get acquainted with how things work and the layout of our facility. When he's at the desk, you can read up on our completed studies and performance reports of our robotics programs. I think you'll find some of the projects we've done quite fascinating. I'll introduce you to the lead of that program next week."

"Thanks, Steve. I appreciate everything and look forward to working here."

"Todd, he's all yours. Don't lose him." He laughed and walked back to his office.

I sat down and placed my hands on my very first desk. Pride consumed me that I'd landed a great job doing what I'd always wanted to do. I looked in the drawer under the desk to see an assortment of pens, pencils, and blank sticky notes.

"So, have you found a place to stay yet?" Todd asked.

"Um, I found a temporary place to stay until I find an apartment." I didn't know how else to respond, and I didn't think telling him I was staying with Trish was wise.

"Yeah, it's pretty expensive around here. I'm living with another engineer in the power support section. I'm renting a pull-out sofa, and we carpool together. I'll ask around if anyone's looking for a roommate if you like?"

I wanted to tell him I'd already found one, but I replied, "I'll look around first, but if I get to that point, I'll let you know."

I followed Todd all day and soaked up everything I could with the meetings and working groups he attended. This company did a lot of fantastic things. The engineering for space programs was fascinating, and I hadn't even seen the more impressive robotics stuff in the classified rooms yet.

Todd showed me a project in a clean room, which meant we had to wear paper jumpsuits, elastic hats to cover our heads, special gloves, and sticky magnetic tags to put on the bottoms of our shoes to ensure we didn't convey any static electricity in the room. I took off my coverings and threw them in a hamper when we left. When Todd removed his hair cover, I noticed a long, red scratch behind his ear and below his hairline. It almost looked like some kind of bite mark, but I didn't want to make that assumption.

"What's that on your neck? Did you bump into something?"

He reached back to rub his hair back in place. He looked around, then whispered, "You didn't hear this from me, and don't tell anyone, but it's a really cool secret sex club I visit. The women are dominatrixes, and they use us for their sexual pleasure—no need to try to pick them up. In fact, no need to say much at all. I was at the club last weekend, and the woman I was with bit my neck when she got off. It was hot as hell. I think a few others here belong to it, but I'm not sure."

"A secret sex club?" I whispered back. "What makes you think others here belong to it?"

"No one ever talks about it, and everyone wears masks at the club, but I'm pretty sure I've recognized some people."

We walked into the hallway from the clean room. Todd looked around. "Seriously, you can't tell anyone. I shouldn't even have told you. I was sworn to secrecy and signed a nondisclosure agreement."

My eyes were probably as wide as they could be. All I could say was, "Wow." I couldn't even imagine an encounter or club like that, but California has been known for some crazy things.

Even though he said he swore secrecy, he seemed pretty eager to divulge more details to me as we walked back to our desks—stuff like being strapped to a cross and the women beating him, then having sex with him. I'd heard stories of such things but never thought it could be real. I had zero knowledge of what sex clubs were actually like, or even of the types of things he was talking about. Yet his enthusiasm had me wanting to witness such a place.

"Don't you get hurt from the beating or whipping? Do you like that?" I grimaced.

"Oh sure, sometimes I'm sore for a few days, but come on … how often do geeks like us get laid by gorgeous women? A little pain is worth it."

I sat there in awe, completely speechless. Of course, I knew of the typical stereotype that engineers were geeks who didn't know how to interact with women, but I hadn't met anyone like that until now.

"Hey, maybe I can bring you as a guest and you can watch what goes on?"

I didn't respond. Part of me wanted to see what it was like, but another part was apprehensive.

"If you're interested, I'll find out if I can take you. The first time you're usually allowed to watch with no touching or talking."

"When is the next one?"

"I think it's this weekend." He looked at his calendar. "Yup, this weekend. I'll ask … if you're interested."

I thought for a moment. "I have a lot going on right now. Maybe next time." Besides, with my moving in with Trish and having no car, I had a lot to figure out before I could do things like that, *if* I wanted to do things like that.

"Are you ready?"

I looked up and saw Trish walking up with her plum-colored, leather handbag, which she used as a briefcase.

Todd asked, "Ready for what? Where are we going?"

I looked at Todd. "She offered to drive me to where I'm staying until I buy a car."

"Hi, Todd. How are you doing?" Trish asked.

"I'm doing good. I'm nearly done with the algorithm for the new mechanical space arm we're working on for the International Space Station, it's—"

"I'm sure it's impressive," Trish cut in. "You are so smart. I'd stay and learn more, but I need to get going."

"Bye, Todd, I'll see you tomorrow," I said, following Trish toward the door.

I silently followed her out to her car.

"Did you mention to him that you were staying with me?" she asked as she started the car.

I shook my head. "No, I didn't think that would be a good idea."

Her expression made me think I had done something impressive. "Thanks, Brett. Discretion is sometimes the best path, especially when unsure what to say."

Grace

"How are we looking for this weekend's event?" Taylor asked, coming into my office.

"I have a new Dom who has already paid ten thousand for the night. The other three regulars will be there also. Do we have enough subs for them?"

"I know Todd will be there. I believe the others will also, but I'll follow up. Oh, Todd had asked if he could bring someone new. I suspect he means Brett."

"No. No, we can't do that. I want Brett to have more confidence first. And he will not be a sub. In fact, we had one more request for a confident beta. Someone more charming and attentive. Not passive, but not a type A personality either. That is what I plan to groom Brett for, for now."

Taylor nodded while running her fingers along the edge of my desk. "My instincts tell me Trish will do well with his training. My only concern is him falling for her."

"Oh? Brett is moving in with her?" At Taylor's nod, I said, "What about her falling for him?"

Taylor thought for a moment. "That was an initial concern, but Trish made it clear she wouldn't and that she'll break it off once he's trained. I wanted to test him at next month's event."

"That's quite optimistic, isn't it? Train a twenty-three-year-old to be a master seducer in a month?"

"I have faith in Trish. I wouldn't test him on a new client though." Taylor grinned. A grin that I knew all too well.

"You want me to test him?" I smiled at the thought. "I guess that's the least I can do since I hired him."

We both broke out in laughter.

Taylor asked, "What are your thoughts about Trish if she pulls through on this?"

"I was thinking about that earlier. If she is truly one of us, even though she's younger, we may want to consider training her and perhaps moving her out to DC to open another branch of the firm and another SD while at it."

Taylor stood up and placed her hands on the table. Her eyes wrinkled and whispered with a sound of doubt. "Are you serious?"

"Don't get too doubtful just yet. She's too young and inexperienced to lead the entire effort, but I think she would be of value. I've wanted to start building our firm, and with some work we've been doing here, we might have an angle with the intelligence agencies and the Defense Department ... and of course, that whole wealthy female demographic in DC that needs a release."

We laughed again.

"I plan on going Saturday night," Grace said. "No need to have a servus for me. If I find a straggler, I might take him, but I'd like to watch this time."

"Okay, I'll know what subs are attending by Friday. I'll send my private email out to them to confirm. They've been quick to respond since they found out the punishment for not responding can be severe."

"Why, Taylor, surely I don't know what you mean?" I knew all too well what she meant. I reminisced the eyes of the last man I punished as I put a metal cage on his dick and made him eat me. I could have sworn he would bust through that cage.

Taylor pushed away, shaking her head with a devilish grin and turned around to leave. "Have a good night."

I watched her walk away and pondered how well my plan was working out.

The thought of testing Brett popped into my mind again. I bit my lower lip, slowly twirling in my chair, imagining what it might be like to be seduced by him and compare it to that first time in Cancun.

Trish

"Welcome to my home. It's not too much, but it serves my purpose." I opened the door and walked in, Brett following behind.

I set my keys on the counter between the kitchen and living area and walked down the hall to the guest bedroom. "Here's your bedroom, and the bath is in the hall right here."

He walked into the bedroom, set his suitcase up against the bed, and then looked at me. "This is so generous of you. I hope I can repay you somehow."

Oh, you will, all right. I thought about how to respond but simply painted a nurturing smile on my face. Being alone with him here drove me crazy, and I wanted to take him right here—now.

"Don't worry about it. Maybe you'll do me a favor one day," I said. "Has anyone ever said that you look like Chris Hemsworth?"

"Who?"

"Never mind, just make yourself at home. How about a pizza for dinner? Is pepperoni okay?"

"Sure. Let me buy. It's the least I can do."

I handed him a coupon that came in the mail from a local pizza delivery place. "I like anything, so order what you want. And here's my address." I gave him the electric bill to see the address. "I'm going to change. Help yourself to the wine I have in the fridge. Pour me a glass too, if you wouldn't mind."

I went to my bedroom, slipped out of my work clothes, and put some jogging shorts on with a snug T-shirt that showed the contour of my girls quite nicely. I looked in the mirror, fondled my breasts to perk up my nipples, then walked out to the living room.

Brett was just hanging up. "Pizza should be here in thirty …" He didn't finish the thought as he caught sight of me.

"Thirty …?"

He shook his head. "Yeah, um, thirty minutes." He blushed and looked away.

I couldn't help but grin. "Let's sit on the sofa and chat." He sat at the end, and I sat in the middle with my legs woven together like a pretzel. "Sooo, tell me about you," I asked.

Brett talked a bit more about his background, almost as though it was rehearsed. He repeated some of what he'd said at the reserve, but his voice was just as handsome as he was, so I let him continue. I was fascinated by everything he'd done to help his mother while still being an honor student in high school and college.

There was a knock at the door. "Pizza's here." Brett got up, walked to the door, paid the delivery guy, and brought the pizza in, setting it down on the coffee table. I went to get another bottle of wine out of the fridge as the first one was only half full.

"Mmm, pepperoni and bacon. I love it," I said as I topped off our wine.

I settled into my seat again, this time with my legs crossed. I wasn't wearing any underwear under my running shorts, and I knew it would only be a matter of time before Brett noticed.

We ate and talked while I learned more about him. Then I spotted his eyes shift to my thighs and could see the embarrassment color his face as he quickly averted his gaze. I managed to keep my triumphant smile from breaking out onto my face and asked innocently, "Is everything all right?"

"Ummm, yeah, it's fine," he croaked out before downing his wine, desperately trying to avoid looking at me.

"Then why are you avoiding looking at me? And blushing?"

He swallowed hard before pointing out the obvious. "Um, you're sort of exposed."

I looked down at myself faux-surprised and replied, "Oh, I'm sorry. Does that bother you? I'm very open minded and just don't think of such things."

My response seemed to be the green light he was waiting for because he glanced down again before meeting my eyes.

"I believe nudity is natural and should be embraced. There are too many people who are uncomfortable with it. I usually walk around nude at home, but I didn't know how comfortable you'd be with that."

He sipped his wine and glanced down again. "Don't let me get in the way of how you live in your home. I'm okay with it," he replied. His heavier breathing and flushed face said otherwise.

This was going to be much easier than I thought.

"Great, I was getting claustrophobic already." We laughed as I took off my clothes and threw them in the adjacent high-back chair. "There, much better."

I finished my slice of pizza and washed it down with some wine. "So, what kind of car are you interested in getting?" I asked, trying to get him out of shock at my nakedness.

His eyes mapped out my body, trying to memorize every detail, no doubt. His glass of wine was shaking slightly. Was he still a virgin?

"Um, I was thinking of a simple car like a Honda Civic or Toyota Camry."

The wine tasted inexplicably delectable as I watched my plan take shape. "You can get more comfortable if you like, but no pressure."

His gaze shifted across my body and then met mine. The golden-green color of his eyes ensnared me; they were unlike any I had seen before, captivating and completely bewitching.

"Well, you can at least let me know how I look since you probably have my body memorized by now." I didn't need affirmation but wanted him to get more comfortable.

He laughed and blushed again. "I grew up a bit conservative, so this … this is a little new for me."

"Have you had sex before?" I asked. I internally cringed asking so pertinently, but I had to find out. It would make my task significantly challenged if he as a virgin.

His head snapped to look into my eyes, nearly spilling his wine. He narrowed his eyes. "I've had sex before, but it was usually at some frat party, and it was more private. This is the first time where I've been in an open nude environment." He kept looking away and trying to cross his legs.

He gulped down his glass of wine. I leaned over to fill it up again.

"I want you to feel comfortable here, but I don't want there to be any attachments, sooo … why don't we just have sex together?"

His wide eyes and tilted head appeared that of someone who had won the lottery—elated, yet reluctant to accept what I'd just offered. I tried not to laugh.

"What?" I asked. "You're looking at me like I'm batshit crazy or something, so why not just have a quick fix and we can relax better?"

"Oh, it's not that, but well, it just kinda seemed random. I mean, I've done random sex in college, but now … well, we work together, and I don't want to cross any lines," he murmured.

"I'm in HR, don't think you can cross any lines without my having some influence." I took another sip of wine. "How long did you date the last person you had sex with?"

He smiled and gulped more wine. "That evening."

I laughed. "What? You're going on about being conservative and here you had sex with some random fluff the same night you met her. You and I at least spent a day together."

His cheeks brightened with a red glow. I was hoping I wasn't too hard on him, but come on.

He poured himself some more wine. I grinned at him as I slowly slid closer. I reached to unfasten his pants. He didn't resist, and I looked up to an excited smile as I pulled his cock out.

I began stroking his firmness but watched it grow a little more in my hand. I looked up into his eyes. "Do you want to see my lips wrapped around it?" I whispered.

He nodded and began to breathe heavier.

"Put your hand on my neck and gently caress the back of it with your thumb, and whisper, 'I want you to put those pretty, little lips around my cock.'"

He complied, and I slowly went down to kiss his tip, swirling my tongue around his head and then along his shaft. I looked up into his eyes. His chest heaved with each rapid breath. I smiled and then let his cock slip into my mouth. I gripped him tight with my lips and slowly slid up and down his shaft while swirling my tongue around his tip. He feverishly pushed his pants down, kicking off his shoes so he could take them off completely.

"Do you want me to look into your eyes?" I asked. I kissed his shaft and made sure he could see my tongue running along his bulging veins.

"Yes," he gasped.

"Let me know what you would like us to do, don't be afraid to tell me. I'm turned on by someone who knows what they want," she said.

"Gaze into my eyes as you take me in your mouth," he softly replied. Not very confidently, but we could work on it.

She slid her lips down his shaft and looked into his eyes. His hips began to move around, and I hoped it wouldn't be over too soon.

I lifted and moved up to kiss his neck. "Would you like to taste my pussy?"

He nodded so quickly I thought he might get whiplash. I kissed his lips softly and whispered, "How do you get what you want?"

"Lay down here. I want to eat your pussy," he said with a little more confidence.

I eagerly lay down on the sofa, propping my head on a throw pillow so I could watch him. I enjoyed watching as much as being watched. He leaned in and began kissing my slit like he was kissing a balloon. He didn't use his hands. And then he licked through my center. Just when he found my clit, he left it to lick through me again. Then he kissed my thighs. I'm sure in college he was used to getting to the down and dirty, but based on his technique, I assumed he might need a little coaching, so I elected to tactfully assist.

I reached down and spread myself open, exposing my pink flesh. He smiled down in amazement. I rubbed my clit with my index finger. "Take your tongue and concentrate on my clit. Swirl your tongue around it slowly, and alternate sucking on it."

He leaned in as I held myself open for him to do as I instructed. I moaned as he enthusiastically devoured my clit. Soon I was close to an orgasm, but I needed more.

"Slip your fingers in my pussy and feel for the top of the inside and rub that gently with your fingers like you're telling someone to come here." I figured that was the easiest way to explain my G spot for now.

He followed instructions beautifully. I'm sure I gave him a refresher as he worked his tongue and fingers harmoniously. My hips began to gyrate against his mouth as though they had a mind of their own.

"Yes," I moaned and grabbed his head. "Yes, that's it, keep doing that. Don't stop!"

He kept licking and sucking my clit and pushing his fingers in deep. As I felt the pleasure building up inside me, I pressed him tightly against my most sensitive area.

Then a wave of pleasure rushed over me, more intense than anything I had experienced in quite a while. All I could focus on was the intensity of my orgasm, drowning out everything else around me.

"Wow." He popped his head up to check on me. I smiled at the sheen around his mouth.

"That was great," I said. "Remember how that works. There will be a test."

He squinted his eye, confused.

"I'm joking, just don't forget what you did."

He smiled with pride. He looked down to watch his fingers continue sliding in and out of my now soaked entrance. I smiled at his fascination and let him continue.

I sat up slightly and rested on my elbows. "What do you want to do now?" I asked slyly.

"I want to slide inside of you."

Was he serious? He could do better than that.

I smiled and kept an upbeat tone as I said, "At this point, you already know I want you, right?"

He nodded.

"So now all you have to do is take me and do what you want. Be confident and determined. Even a little aggressive. I'll let you know if it's too much."

"I've rarely experienced anything that direct before. Well, not for a long time at least," he confessed.

Geez, his cock better not get limp with that attitude. I wasn't finished yet.

He tried to climb between my legs on the sofa. This wasn't going to work.

"Position me, use me, move me as you want or need. Just take control and take me as you want." I placed my hand on his chest. "Trust me, you can't hurt me very easily."

He nodded and paused for a moment, then grabbed my ass cheeks with both hands and pulled me to the edge of the sofa, pushing my legs back to my head. *That's a little better.* He guided his cock into my entrance, grabbed my ass cheeks, and pulled himself into me with one quick thrust. *Whoa!*

I placed my hand on his chest, gasping with each methodical thrust that stretched me open perfectly. I wiggled down a little farther so he could drive down into me even deeper. I could no longer hear my pants or even the sound of moisture between our loins. His eyes were closed as he thrust himself in hard. His body tensed, and he groaned faintly. *Oh no!*

I sighed. I'd need to teach him about control.

He pulled out and plopped himself on the sofa next to me.

"I take it you're done?" I asked a tad sarcastically.

"Oh yeah! That was great!" he said proudly. His grin and euphoric glow made him look like he was anticipating a pat on the back.

I glared at him. "I'm glad one of us thought so. Perhaps we can work on pleasuring the woman you're with a little more next time."

His eyes grew wide. "I'm sorry, I … well, I …"

"How many times have you had sex?" I asked, perhaps a bit more abruptly than I would have liked.

"I don't know. Quite a few in college at frat parties, but no one complained."

I sat up with a shake of my head and put my hand on his leg. "It's a good thing I like you. We can play some more now and then ... prepare you for any future girlfriends ... if you want, that is."

His eyes lit up with eager glee. "I definitely want!"

I reached down between my legs to feel his cum leaking out of me. I wiped it and then sucked his nectar from my fingers.

"You ... you like that?" He looked puzzled.

"I love cum. I love sex. What do you think happens when you get a blow job?"

"I did get a blow job once, and after I came, she just took off. I didn't think much about it."

"Well, good girls always swallow." I laughed. "Why don't you feed some to me? It's a huge turn-on for me."

"Are you serious?"

"Of course, I am. I'm sure you've masturbated and got your semen on your hands before, and you've already been in my pussy, so just reach in, let it coat your fingers, and feed it to me."

I parted my legs; he placed his two fingers inside and pulled them out covered in his white cream. I opened my mouth to receive them. I held his hand and seductively sucked his juice from his fingers, then sucked each finger to get all of it. His mouth was slightly open as he stared in amazement.

"It's hot, isn't it?"

He nodded, then sat back down on the sofa. "Wow, I have a lot to learn."

"Well, it's a good thing you're a fast study." I smirked and reached for my glass of wine. He reached for his, and we clinked them together before drinking.

"There. Now that we got that out of the way, you shouldn't be so nervous about my being naked in the apartment. And you can be as well, if you like."

He grinned with pride. "When can we do that again?"

"Be careful. Overeating when you've been starving could be hazardous to your health."

"That is a risk I'm willing to take."

It seemed like his confidence was building already, but we still had a way to go before he'd meet Grace's and Taylor's goals.

I slid my hand along his leg and lightly floated it over his cock. "I'll make this deal with you. You can have sex with me anytime we are in this apartment. Anytime, anywhere, anyway you want, on one condition."

He looked like a puppy whose human was dangling a piece of steak over his head. I smiled at how cute he was, eagerly waiting for my stipulations.

"Only when I'm naked, which is usually always. You have to tell me what you're going to do to me seductively, and you have to make sure I have at least two orgasms before you get off ... unless I tell you just to come, like you have an urge in the middle of the night or something."

"Wow, really? So, I can just walk in your bedroom and fuck you if I want, or when you're standing in the kitchen or anytime?"

He had a look as though he couldn't quite comprehend the magnitude of the gift I had just given him.

I nodded. "Yes, to all of that, except when my bedroom door is closed. Also, there is never to be any mention of this at work. You cannot tell anyone you're staying here, and if you see me at work, I want you never to have any emotional expression toward me. Understand?"

He quickly nodded. His eyes filled with enthusiasm, and he probably still couldn't comprehend what I was offering.

He took a sip of his wine. "What if you're naked in the kitchen and if I try to fuck you, you say no?"

I almost spit up the wine after my sip. Although I enjoyed more forceful role-playing, I wasn't sure I should even bring that up to him … at least not right now.

"More than likely I won't say no, but if I do, we will address it then, and I'd make it up to you."

I could tell he wasn't grasping what was available to him and might need some coaching, but I was confident he'd figure it out soon enough.

Brett

Was this real? Was I awake? Trish was so fucking gorgeous, and I could fuck her anytime I wanted? What she'd already taught me, I would remember forever. I couldn't imagine doing those things with any of those college girls.

I sipped my wine, pretending to watch the television as my mind was in overdrive, thinking of all the ways I would want to have sex with her. Bent over the counter, in that chair her clothes were lying in, on the floor, walk in on her when I wake up in the morning … I was getting hard again, and it had only been ten minutes since we'd finished.

We watched a show for a while, and then Trish said she was going to bed. I followed her to her room. She stopped just inside the doorway and looked back at me. With a smile, she reached back and began to stroke my cock. "Does someone want more?"

I grinned back at her, my eyes dancing with anticipation. As we approached her bed, she stopped and didn't say a word. *This is a cue.* I took a deep breath, turned her around, sat her down on the bed, and lifted her legs under her knees, causing her to lean back on her elbows. She reached out and held her legs open while I gazed down at her glistening mound. I slid the tip of my cock through her slit, rubbing it gently on her clit. She had this purr-like moan, and then in one thrust, I was entirely inside. Her back arched as she moaned, "Oh yes."

The sight of my glistening cock sliding in and out of her was magnificent. I wanted it to last forever, but my body had a mind of its own. I looked down at her beautiful body, her firm, perhaps C-size breasts swaying with every plunge, the expression on her face, and my body reacted. I couldn't hold back. Her body arched in pleasure as my orgasm ripped through me, every muscle quivering beneath the sheer power of it all. I lay there, spent, locked in an embrace with this beautiful woman.

When I opened my eyes, she was smiling at me. "Something tells me you're enjoying my body. I'm tired tonight, so I'll let this episode slide, but remember the two-orgasm rule next time."

I could only nod and smile. I backed away as she stood. She kissed me on my cheek and said, "Goodnight, Brett." She walked into her bathroom as I stood there wondering again how I'd gotten so damn lucky.

I went to the hallway bathroom to wash up and then to bed. Falling asleep was challenging as the image of her and me from tonight—and my future fantasies—kept me awake for quite a while. I kept telling myself this was real, but part of me couldn't believe it.

* * *

The morning sunlight shined through the window and showed clarity of where I was. *It really did happen!* The bedroom was a spare room with a couple of simple wall hangings and a nightstand with a vase and a lamp. My morning wood was already asking for some pre-breakfast fun. I remembered what Trish said. *Let's find out.*

Her bedroom door was cracked open. I peeked inside to see her lying on her stomach in her bed. Walking up to the side of the bed, I pulled the sheets off her and caressed her ass, slowly savoring her smooth skin and perfect contour. Her legs parted slightly, giving me a glimpse of her inviting entrance.

"I told you, just take what you want," she murmured.

I caressed her between the legs with my fingers before sliding one into her. She moaned as I continued to stroke her. I climbed onto the bed and entered her from behind; her soft cries of pleasure were just as powerful as the night before.

She turned to me and said, "Grab a hold of my hair and pull it firmly."

I grabbed a bunch of her hair at the scalp and tugged back as I drove myself inside her farther.

She shouted out, "Pull that hair harder! Yes! Fuck me harder!"

So I pulled her head up off the pillow and obeyed her demand. I could feel my orgasm coming on but remembered what she had said earlier. I pulled away from her and nervously stammered, "I want you to suck my cock."

I moved over by her side, and she rolled toward me. Then, she seized my member in her hand and enveloped it with her mouth. I started pushing myself deeper inside her, making sure each movement was slow and deliberate—I could feel electricity running through my veins with every nerve ending alive with pleasure. As she began gagging each time, she still allowed me to keep thrusting until finally gripping my shaft again and taking control.

I slid two fingers into her pussy and practiced what I'd been taught. I arched my fingers and began thrusting them quickly along her inner wall. She panted and writhed, and eventually, she took my cock out of her mouth to exclaim, "I'm coming!"

She held me tightly, and I looked upon her body as it pulsed in pleasure. Her grasping movements kept me overstimulated as I felt my testicles tense up with pleasure.

I lay down on my back while she straddled me, guiding my cock inside her moistness with the skill of a seasoned lover. Once she bottomed out, she slid up and down on me. Our bodies were pressed together where they touched and squeezed against each other in ways that sent sparks through my body. Her breasts were so firm that they seemed to resist gravity—they jutted upward until the nipples hovered mere inches above my chest. With each thrust, I shoved them further away in my mind's eye, only to have them return again against me when she descended and our bodies pressed together once more.

I gripped her beautiful breasts. As I caressed them and squeezed her nipples between my fingers, I could feel that she was starting to lose control. Her movements toward orgasm caused her breasts to bounce gently off my hands. Then I slid my hands down to grab her ass cheeks and pulled her into me harder from below. She began panting and started riding faster; then panted, "Yes! Keep fucking me like that! Don't stop!" I was on the verge of a climax but used every thought possible to distract myself from coming too soon. She cried out, "I'm coming! Come with me!" in such a powerful voice that it heightened everything around us.

That was all it took. I gripped her ass and held myself deep inside as I came with a growl. She began to gyrate her hips on my cock, forcing my body to continue an uncontrollable spasm. Once I was finished and could catch my breath, I looked up at her.

She smiled and said, "Good morning," then climbed off and headed toward the bathroom. "That's how everyone should wake up in the morning."

I laughed. "I completely agree."

"Time to shower up, and then I usually grab coffee and a bagel on the way to work. Sound good?" she said as I heard the shower start.

"Sounds great." I got up and went to take my shower and get ready.

As I turned on the water, I pondered the thought that two friends—and barely acquaintances, at that—could have sex like this with little to no emotional connection and then talk about getting coffee and a bagel before going to work. It was a concept I had never imagined.

Taylor

As I walked from my car to the office, I saw Trish and Brett walking ahead. I couldn't help but grin at how envious I was of Trish. I'd been with this company since its beginning, and it had consumed me. There hadn't been time for any dating aside from a random hookup at a recruiting fair or my encounters at SD on the weekends.

I enjoyed Brett that one night at the hotel but would love to find out what he was like after Trish got him well trained. He was beyond handsome and had an excellent package. He would be like gold for us if he could eventually seduce a woman's mind.

I stepped into the HR office to see Trish logging into her computer.

"Good morning, Trish."

"Good morning, Ms. Williams."

I set my briefcase down in my office and then leaned against the doorway. "How is our young protégé doing?"

I saw her blush a little. I didn't think I'd ever seen her blush.

"I have to admit, I think it was a risk taking him on for this project without knowing what equipment he had to work with, but what he has is …" She grinned as I did earlier while reminiscing my encounter with him. "Let's just say he's impressive."

My thoughts exactly.

I smiled, not at her update, but at knowing I had experienced his marvelous body myself.

"He catches on quickly, but I think his confidence is the biggest area to work on. I have a plan for that."

"Oh? Between us girls, do you care to share?"

She smiled with a slight tilt of her head. "Well, I told him he can have me any time and any place he wants while in the apartment, but he has to tell me what he's going to do and then just do it."

My core was suddenly shocked just hearing what she was doing with him. I wanted that too. Damn, I should have trained him myself. But I couldn't run SD efficiently if I did that. For now, I'd just have to live vicariously through Trish.

"That sounds amazing. So, I take it you've already …"

She turned to her laptop and replied, "Three times already."

I bit my lip, grinned, and then turned to my office to tackle my backed-up email, hoping it would rid me of my aching core.

I took my monthly walk through the company to talk to employees and get firsthand insight into their concerns and ideas. Grace also did this now and then, and we'd made many good changes by visiting the people and listening to their ideas. I met up with Brett's boss, Steve, and asked how everything was going. He went into detail on his projects, which I tried to comprehend, but I didn't speak engineer except from an administrative perspective.

"How's the new engineer doing? I hope he's fitting in."

"Brett? Oh yes, he's going to be a perfect addition. I have him on some robotics research until his security clearance comes in. We can get him into the fun stuff after that."

"Good. Enjoy your day. I'll stop by and talk to some of your engineers for a bit."

"Stop by any time, Ms. Williams."

Steve was a nice guy. He said he was married, but his entire life revolved around algorithm development, and I couldn't see him having much more than that to discuss in a social environment. He was brought to SD once when he was a young, single, new engineer. The one client who took him sort of hurt him a little more than currently allowed, and he never returned. I wasn't sure if he knew that some of his staff were servi there, but for all they knew, SD had nothing to do with us.

"Hi, Brett," I said as I walked up to the side of his desk. He turned around, as did Todd.

"Hi, Ms. Williams."

"Hi, Ms. Williams," Todd said, quickly parroting Brett.

"Is everything going well for you? Getting settled in?"

He smiled and nodded with a sheepish grin. "Uh, yeah, everything is great!" He looked to the floor and blushed.

"How are you doing, Todd?"

"I'm very good, Ms. Williams. I'm working on this special project that does …"

I listened to Todd for a few moments, but kept glancing at Brett. He had yet to make eye contact since the conversation began. I wasn't sure if he was purposefully avoiding me or focused on what Todd was saying.

"That sounds great, Todd. I'm always happy to see so much enthusiasm from the engineers. It means we're doing something right. Enjoy your day, and let me or Trish know if you need anything."

Brett's cheeks turned a hint of pink when I mentioned Trish. I couldn't help the knowing smile that flashed across my face.

Grace

After zipping up my knee-high vinyl boots over my fishnet stockings, I adjusted my corset to make sure it pushed my breasts where I wanted them. The phone rang.

"Hi, Taylor," I said. "Are we ready for this evening? What's the lineup like?"

"We have three Dominae and five servi, so there is an extra for you if you like. Otherwise, we can see if a Domina wants two men."

Typically, I played hostess to ensure everyone was enjoying themselves. Occasionally, I took on a sub, but the men I got were not the best the last few times. They took a flogging well, but when it came time to have sex, they were inadequate.

"I'll try to take one on again. Worst case, I'll have him kneel in a corner and be at my beck and call."

"Sounds good. I'll be there in about twenty minutes," Taylor said.

"I should be there about the same time. Oh, and what about our project? How is our little minx doing with him?"

"From what she reports, he's learning well. Apparently, she gave him open sex on demand with her and she says he's catching on quickly."

"Excellent. Hopefully, we can give him a test drive at the event next month. I'll see you in a little while."

I reached into the box and grabbed one of my masks. It seemed I had a mask for every occasion; today, I chose my purple, sequin-encrusted piece with purple and black feathers to match my lingerie.

SD was located in a simple three-thousand-square-foot warehouse in an industrial section of Silicon Valley. We'd modified the interior to several themed rooms, and there was also some extra space for expanding as we grew our client base. When I walked through the door of our warehouse-turned-event-location twenty minutes later, there were four naked, masked men lined up against the wall. The collars on their necks already had leashes fastened and were hooked on wooden dowels sticking out of the wall. The placards above each leash hook prominently displayed their negative STD results, their likes … and, of course, their limits.

"Greetings, Mistress. Take me, please," they all said in unison. I loved well-trained subs.

I hung my coat on a nearby hook. The room was always kept warm as everyone had little to no clothing on. I did a quick survey of the place to make sure everything looked perfect for our customers. Separate alcoves had been built, each with its own unique design. There was a wooden cross, and another had a bed made out of wood. Other designs included chains or other restraints attached to the walls and ceiling.

"Hello, slaves. I hope you're prepared to please tonight," I said.

"Yes, Mistress," they said again together.

I saw Taylor walk in from a back room. She wore her red cloak with a black lace bra, black panties, garter belt, and thigh highs. Her mask was red and black with elastic around the back of her head. She typically blindfolded her slaves so she could take off her mask while enjoying them.

"How are we looking?" I asked.

"We're good. The slaves were obedient and came early as directed."

"Good slaves. You might get rewarded for that."

Taylor continued, "Our clients should be here any minute."

"The payments are all in?" I murmured so the subs couldn't hear.

Taylor whispered, "Ten thousand each, deposited into our account. I just checked it an hour ago."

Wealthy, sex-deprived women would pay almost anything for novel and discreet sexual encounters.

"Our newest clients asked when we might have what they want," Taylor said. "One of them offered twenty thousand to have someone for her by next month."

I couldn't believe it. I personally wanted someone like Brett too, but twenty thousand from one person to have sex with a young, vibrant man who had the skills of a fifty-year-old sex god was a motivator.

"Let's hope our trainer does well," I suggested. "If she does, I might just give her a little more than the twenty thousand we promised."

There was that special knock at the door: three knocks, a scratch, then two knocks. It was morse code for SD. Three women stood outside wearing masks and cloaks. Taylor confirmed who they were and let them in.

"Welcome, ladies. Your slaves await," I said as they approached the willing submissives kneeling in anticipation.

They hung their cloaks on the coat hooks, walked up to the subs, and took who they wanted for the night.

Taylor took hers as I reached into my bag to grab my riding crop. Let's see who was remaining.

"Stand up, slave." I slapped his arm with the riding crop. He stood, displaying his awe-inspiring package hanging in front of him. I reached down to grab his balls in my hand firmly. He appeared startled. "Why are you not smooth for me, slave? Do you not know the rules?"

"Yes, Mistress, I ... I forgot."

I stroked his shaft and ran my crop along his well-defined arms, down his ass, and back up to his hair. He was young, perhaps twenty-five, and had a body like a stone sculpture. I glided my hands along his firm abdomen, up to his pecs, and then I caressed his face. I whispered in his ear, "You have a delicious body. Do you want to fuck me, slave?"

"Yes, Mistress!"

"Good answer, but I'll have to punish you for not complying with the rules first."

"Yes, Mistress."

I looked at his status card and saw he liked ass play. *This should be good.*

I walked him to a stall with a bench made for him to lean over and secured the shackles on the bench's legs to his wrists and ankles. I ran my crop between his ass cheeks and stopped at his sphincter when his body twitched. I spit between his ass cheeks and slowly worked my finger into his ass, slowly finger fucking him.

"Hmmm. Does this sub like his ass played with, and is it clean?"

"Yes, Mistress."

I opened a wooden chest with many devices of punishment and pleasure, including several dildos and a strap-on. I climbed into the strap-on and fastened it.

LT Richards

"You're not going to walk well in the morning, but because you're respectful and have a beautiful body, I'll be kind and use lube," I said.

He strained his head, looking up at the large dildo strapped to me. His eyes opened wide as I walked up to him. "Kiss your punishment," I demanded.

I placed the beast of a penetrator in front of his mouth as he kissed the head of it.

"Are you prepared?"

He lowered his head and whispered, "Yes, Mistress."

Brett

Watching Trish's ass as she walked to the bathroom was mesmerizing. We'd just had our second round of sex for the day, and she'd already taught me so much over the past week, from gripping her hair, nibbling her ear, or even whispering what I was going to do next. Taylor had shown me some of that, but that experience was just a blur now. I was fucking Trish from behind earlier when she told me to pull her arms back and force myself into her. This forcefulness was new and more arousing than I could have thought.

I couldn't seem to get enough of Trish. The way she reacted, her little gasp when I grabbed her hair and also when I ran my teeth along her neck. Watching her ecstasy result from my actions increased my hunger even more. I discovered newfound sexual pleasure in watching her expressions of bliss; in turn, my completion was more explosive than ever.

I probably wouldn't have learned this for many years if not for Trish. Hell, who was I kidding? I probably wouldn't have ever learned most of this. I laughed to myself as she came out of the bathroom. I enjoyed the slight sway of her breasts as she walked. The sight of her gorgeous smile and the rest of her body was like a dream every time I saw her.

She smiled as she approached the bed and lay down. "What's on your mind that you're grinning like that?" she asked, propping her head upon her hand while leaning on her elbow.

"I can't believe this. I feel like I'm in a dream every day."

"Don't do too much daydreaming during the day. We pay you a lot for your mind too," she said and leaned in to kiss me on the cheek. "Time for bed, stud. Goodnight."

Our agreement meant that we slept in separate beds, but my feelings for her were already driving me nuts. I wanted to see her sleep and wake up next to her in the morning. I rolled to the side of the bed and climbed out. I took a deep breath while gazing at her naked body, her silky, black, semi-disheveled hair draping over her shoulder. Her beautiful blue eyes and long eyelashes completed the perfect package.

She tilted her head and asked, "What are you thinking about?"

I took a deep breath and exhaled. "How gorgeous you are and how you blow my mind ... goodnight." I sighed, turning to the doorway.

I walked to my room and fell asleep shortly after my head hit the pillow.

* * *

After a deep sleep, the smell of bacon and coffee was always a welcoming way to start the morning. I walked out to the living room and looked over the counter into the kitchen area where Trish had a couple of breakfast sandwiches and coffee on the small, round dining table. She looked at me standing naked while I scratched my hair.

"Well, well, we are quite comfortable, aren't we?" She smirked while wearing only an apron.

I spread my arms out with open hands and shrugged. "It would seem you're overdressed," I coyly replied.

She smiled and shrugged. "What are you going to do about it?"

I walked up behind her and pressed my cock against her bare ass cheeks. She stood there with her hands on the chair, waiting to find out what else I would do. She had taught me so much I didn't know what to do first, but I remembered she said to be confident and take her.

I moved her to the side of the chair, held her hip with one hand, and bent her over the table, pushing the side of her face onto the surface. I was already hard in anticipation and slid into her. She moaned with pleasure as I pushed myself deep into her sex.

"If I knew you preferred fucking before breakfast," she said between gasps, "I would have covered our food."

I laughed and reached down to grip her hair. She quietly yelped as I fucked her hard. Her slick inner walls wrapped tightly around my shaft, and I gazed down to watch my cock slide in and out of her.

"Yes, that's it. Fuck that pussy. Take it. I want you to come!" she exclaimed.

My core clenched as a wave of ecstasy flowed through me. I pushed in deep as I released inside of her. My shaking legs barely kept me upright as I fought to keep my bearings.

I pulled out and asked nonchalantly, "What's for breakfast?"

She stood up, laughed, and slapped my arm. I couldn't help but laugh at the playful audacity.

"When I get back from cleaning up, we can have these breakfast sandwiches I made. Here's some coffee, and here's a napkin. You make the mess, you clean it up." She pointed to my drippage on the floor under us.

She walked away, and I grabbed another napkin to wipe myself and the floor.

The coffee was delicious. She went to this coffee shop and got a unique mix of vanilla and hazelnut beans that she had ground up.

Trish came back naked and sat down at the table with a towel on the seat. I also sat down, and we began eating. She looked at me with a devilish grin and said, "You seem to be getting the hang of this sex stuff."

I laughed. "With a teacher like you, it's difficult not to get good at it."

She took a bite and chewed for a moment, drank some coffee, then said, "Just remember, while women primarily have the same body parts and similar erogenous zones, they aren't all the same. Don't assume they are. Spend time exploring, when and if you were to date anyone else in the future."

"Are you setting me up with other women already or kicking me out?" I asked, surprised to hear that from her.

She laughed with another bite in her mouth. "No, but you probably won't be living with me forever, so it's good that you know such things."

I couldn't believe how comfortable I was being naked with her. It'd only been a week and I'd learned so much, and to say I was enamored with her would be an understatement. Wait, did I love her? No, I couldn't … but I did have deep feelings for her already. I smiled at her as I chewed my sandwich and sipped my coffee.

After finishing her breakfast, she said, "I'll be gone for the day but should be back this evening. Have you looked for a car yet by chance?"

She broke the harp music playing in my mind. "I've looked online for some. If you're gone today, maybe I'll look around for one."

She stood up and walked to the bedroom. "Sounds like a great idea. I've got to get a shower and dressed." She closed her bedroom door as I sat there finishing my sandwich staring at her blank door. It might have been the first time she'd shut it since I arrived.

We weren't dating, and she was a free-spirited woman, so I didn't pry about what she was doing during the day. I shouldn't feel attached to her since I was just staying here maybe a month, but I'd never had a girlfriend before, and with the way she'd rocked my world already, I couldn't imagine not being with her more.

I walked to my bedroom and started car searching on my laptop. I heard her door open. She peeked into my room. "Have a good day. I'll be back tonight."

"Bye, enjoy your day."

I heard the door close as she left. I scanned a list of cars online but didn't see anything that caught my attention. My mind was preoccupied with the last week. So much had changed in my life in a short amount of time, and I didn't want it to end.

Trish

I made an appointment a couple of weeks ago to do some role-playing with an older man. He was a regular client I would meet every other month. My role-playing partner, who I'd been able to call on now and then, had met with me once in a while to give this old rich guy a fantasy he enjoyed. I would role-play as his daughter, and my partner would break into the house with a mask and a knife, tie him up, and make him watch his poor, innocent daughter get forced by this intruder and humiliate him while doing so.

That type of role-playing was a huge turn-on for me, but being paid ten thousand dollars for a couple of hours was even better, and I didn't have to have sex with him. We untied him afterward. I'd hug him and leave—easy!

On my way there, I thought about Brett. I didn't mind the sex—hell, I could handle as much as he could give me. But I feared him falling in love or wanting to establish something more personal with me. Living togeth- er and the constant sex could be a powerful catalyst. After a week, it was probably getting to him that he wanted more than just a friends-with-ben- efits relationship and I couldn't allow that to happen.

When I arrived at the home of my cuckold client, my friend Rob was waiting outside in his car. He got out when I pulled up. Rob was an attractive man for being nearly forty. He was great at role-playing and had a fantastic cock, but I wasn't really into him other than that. He occasion- ally provided a cock and a creative personality, and for a good role-playing experience, I gave him a cut of the take. He would probably role-play with me for free, but I wanted to keep it professional.

"Damn, you look good!" he said with his inner wolf staring me down. He hugged me and gripped my ass. "I've missed tapping into your fine body." *A real charmer.*

"Thanks ... you know the script, right? I'll go in, get into our role-playing, and look out of that living room window toward you. The door will be un-locked. You come up to the door, put the mask on, and walk in. Don't hurt him, but be a little aggressive." I placed my hand on his chest and whispered up to him, "And remember, you can be a little more aggressive with me." He leaned in to kiss me, and I pulled away, laughing. "Remember my rule ... no kissing."

"You can be such a cock tease, you know!" he called out.

I turned back to him while continuing to walk toward the house. "You'll get what you want shortly."

I could kiss him while he was forcing himself on me in a scene, but I wasn't interested in kissing him as a friend. He wasn't my type, and if I had another option who could perform the way he did, I wouldn't keep him around, but he was who I had for now.

I walked up and knocked on the door.

"Hello, Trish, come on in." Mr. Fielder was a charming man, and I liked to ensure he got his money's worth from our little show.

I shrugged off my coat, revealing the schoolgirl uniform beneath it. It was only buttoned halfway up and tied in a knot at the front, but it looked cute nevertheless. As I looked into the mirror, I realized that my sideboobs were quite visible without wearing a bra, but that was deliberate.

"Hello, my beautiful daughter. You look like you might fall out of that blouse. Let Daddy help you."

He reached inside my blouse and slid his hand over my breasts—lift-ing them slightly while running the palm of his hand over my nipples.

"Daddy, I don't think you should be touching me there," I said with wide eyes and surprise.

"It's okay, Trish. Daddy's just trying to help." He caressed each breast for a minute and backed away to gaze at me. "There, all better now."

"Thank you, Daddy," I said and kissed his cheek and realized the apparent arousal through the fabric.

We continued to do some role-playing. I got him a glass of water, and we talked about my day at school. I told him about one boy named Brett that wanted to place his penis inside of me in gym class, but I wouldn't let him. He was such a darling and advocated for me to let him do it and tell him all about it when I got home from school.

I looked outside to get Rob's attention. Once he saw me, I turned around and walked back to Daddy. His eyes shone as I walked up to hug him. "Daddy, I love you. You deserve a great day."

"It's a great day so far, daughter, but I think it's going to get better."

I screeched as the door burst open, and I ran behind Daddy.

"Do as I say, and no one will get hurt!" the intruder demanded.

"What do you want? I have no money," Daddy cried out.

"I don't want your money. I want that girl I saw walking in here. Give her to me and I won't have to hurt you."

"No! Please, don't do this to us!" I begged, the fear in my voice escalating as the intruder pulled out a knife from behind him. He threw some zip ties on the floor and grabbed me by the arm, pushing me in front of my father. My heart pounded against my chest as he placed the cold, metal tip of his blade against my throat. It was the same mock blade he always used with a blunt edge, but the metal was real.

"Girl, put your daddy in that wooden chair and begin to slowly zip tie his wrists and ankles to it," he commanded with a menacing growl muffled by his mask.

Daddy complied, sitting himself down in that chair. "Please don't hurt my daughter ... do whatever you want to me, but let her go!"

I had no choice but to defy him. Summoning up every ounce of courage that I had inside me, I met his gaze and shouted, "Stop this now! We won't tell anyone. Just leave us alone!"

The blow to my cheek knocked me to the ground, and I cried out from the pain. *That is definitely in the rough category.*

"Finish tying him to the chair! I won't tell you again!"

My heart raced with excitement as I bound Daddy to the chair, shaking my head in disbelief at what was about to occur. With knotted fingers, I slowly kneeled in front of him and searched his gaze in fear and anticipation. His eyes darkened with guilt as he whispered, "Listen to him ... please don't fight him, please ... for me."

I couldn't help but smile as I knew he was enjoying this. Through tears and trembling lips, I responded with a timid nod of agreement. The grip on my hair tightened, yanking me back upright like a ragdoll, then pushing my face down hard onto the table. He viciously tugged my skirt up around my waist and ripped my panties down until they pooled around my feet. His hands aggressively smothered my bare buttocks, then Rob taunted Daddy, "Don't you think your daughter has an exquisite ass?"

He slapped my ass, leaving a temporary sting, then slid his fingers inside me as he snarled in delight. "Mmm, she's so wet. Looks like she's enjoying this, aren't you, princess?"

Daddy begged for mercy, but Rob ignored his pleas and pulled me up by my hair. My arms hung limp at my sides as he forced me down onto my knees before him. "Open that sweet, little mouth of yours," he sneered, and I glanced over to meet Daddy's anticipating gaze one last time before submitting to Rob's demands. His shaft pushed its way deep past my trembling lips, causing an instant gag reflex. He fisted a handful of hair as his other clamped down hard on my face, forcing me to watch the eager enjoyment in Daddy's eyes.

"Tell your daughter to take me down her throat, or I'll have to hurt her."

Daddy looked at me and pleaded, "Please take his big dick down your throat, sweetie."

I knew he was enjoying the show already.

"Okay, Daddy, I'll try."

Rob's grip wrenched at my hair as he pushed his way into my mouth. I felt the movement deep within my throat, a pressure that pushed me to the edge of gagging. Tears sprang to my eyes, blurring my vision until I had no choice but to back away and gasp for air.

He ripped off my clothes with one swift slash of his blade, leaving me trembling and exposed in front of Daddy. I looked up into Daddy's eyes and knew he was watching closely as Rob reached down between my legs and forced two fingers inside me. The wetness of my arousal was undeniable, filling the room with the unmistakable sound of pleasure and desire. Even through my tears, I smiled inwardly, remembering an old saying that wet never lies. My client was finding satisfaction in this moment, but I was enjoying it too.

"Look how wet she is. Your daughter is a little slut that needs to get fucked, isn't she?"

"Please, no! She's a pure virgin!"

It was his fantasy, so I'd roll with it, but really? A virgin? Why must it always be a virgin?

"A virgin? Hmm, well then, I'll have Daddy witness your deflowering."

Rob picked me up and laid me on the table. I struggled to keep him from prying my legs open, but he slapped my ass and pulled out his knife again. He placed it on my stomach and looked at Daddy. "Tell your daughter to take it or I will leave her on your table cut open in front of you."

Daddy pleaded hoarsely through his tears, "Please take it, Trish, take his big, monster cock so you can stay alive. Please do this for me!"

"No, Daddy, please!"

He cried out, "Take it, Trish! I demand you to take it!"

Rob pried my legs open as I lessened my struggle. He had me angled so Daddy could watch as he thrust himself into me.

I cried out, pushing on his chest. "Ouch, no, it hurts. Please stop!" Of course I wanted just the opposite.

Rob brutally pounded away at my helpless body like some uncaring beast of prey. Daddy watched with determined focus with twisted pleasure in his eyes.

Rob's grip on my throat tightened as his breathing increased to a feverish intensity. The fear heightened the thrill of ecstasy, and I felt pleasure ripple through my body like electricity. I could feel every thrust deeper into me, as if he was trying to reach a place that only I could soothe. My eyes implored Mr. Fielder to witness the magnificent experience he'd paid for; I wasn't going to let him go without having every penny of his ten thousand spent worth it.

Rob roared in primal pleasure as his climax reached full intensity. His body trembled in animalistic rage at the moment, and then he pulled away, carelessly adjusting his pants before pointing his knife at us both. "Not a word, or I won't hesitate to come back here and finish you!"

He ran out the door.

I jumped to my feet. "Oh, Daddy, I'm so sorry!" Quickly, I darted into the kitchen and grabbed a knife to cut off the bonds that held him in place. I embraced his body as he hugged me back when freed.

"I hate that I couldn't stop him from violating you, Trish. Let's re-move that semen from you so you won't become pregnant."

I nodded, then lay down on the couch while my daddy caressed my womanhood with his fingertips before cleaning me out with soft licks from his tongue.

Afterward, he gently caressed my slit, savoring my soft flesh. "Once again, thank you for a wonderful time, Trish." We stood, and after giving me a hug, he walked into another room while I put on a clean outfit. Since our role-playing tended to get my clothes dirty or damaged, I brought a light sundress in my bag.

Mr. Fielder returned with an envelope containing money for me as payment for our session. He handed it to me and said, "You're worth every penny, and I appreciate your amazing performance."

I gave him a warm hug and replied, "Thank you, Mr. Fielder. I truly enjoy playing these roles for you."

I quickly scanned the envelope to see the hundred-dollar bills crammed together. "Before I go, can I ask you something?"

"Sure, what is it?"

"The time you're paying for is yours to do with me as you like, but why don't you ever want to have sex with me yourself?"

He paused for a moment before answering, "I have an issue where I don't become aroused very easily. When I'm alone, I replay this scene in my head for hours while I masturbate until I finally get off. When I forget about it, that's when I need to call you again."

"Aww, I'm glad to help."

He walked me to the door, and I gave him another hug goodbye.

* * *

On the way home, I smiled down at the envelope filled with nine thousand dollars in my purse. I ran my fingers over my cheek and realized I might be slightly bruised. I'd hate to have Brett get weirded out if I came home beaten up.

As I rubbed it, I beamed at how much Rob got into his role-playing. I fought him pretty well as a small woman getting forced by a large guy in a ski mask might. The shockwave of his backhand had sent euphoric endorphins through my body alongside the pain. When I paid him, I reminded him not to use his backhand in the future and perhaps a plastic knife. He apologized and said he got caught up in the moment. I told him I'd be looking for a replacement if it happened again.

I stopped at a bookstore to find books for Brett to learn seductive techniques and female sexual erogenous zones. Maybe he'd learn something I hadn't experienced yet. Then, as I did every other month, I went to the free health clinic to ensure I remained STD-free. As active as I was, I couldn't afford to catch anything or give anything to anyone else. I finished up with a trip to the grocery store to get some food and wine and then headed home.

Arriving home around 8 p.m., I kicked at the door as I was losing the third bag of groceries in my hands. *Come on, Brett …*

The door opened. "Help!" I begged.

Brett grabbed the bag that was slipping away from me just in time. I walked in and set the bags down on the counter.

"Oh, what happened?" he asked.

I looked up at him. "What?"

He reached toward my cheek and touched it. "Oh, that." *Time to think quick.* "When I put the groceries in the car, I turned and bumped my cheek into the corner of the door. I guess I was distracted by thinking about what sexual idea you had for me next." I smirked at him. "I found some reading material for you," I said, showing him the books I bought.

He looked at the titles. "Are you saying I still have a lot to learn? You've taught me far more than I already knew." He stepped behind me, pulled my hair behind my ear, and ever so lightly kissed the back of my neck, just gently enough to brush the soft, short hairs without touching my skin. It sent an immediate shiver down my spine, causing goosebumps to cover my body. *Wow, that's a good start.*

"This is what you want, isn't it?" he whispered against my earlobe.

I nodded. He grabbed the base of my hair and tilted my head to the side, letting me know that he had complete control. "I'm going to take you right here."

As he released my hair, I ached for him.

He reached under my dress and paused. "No panties?"

"Sometimes I don't like to wear them." *Whew.*

I kicked off my pumps as he stood up and ran his hand along my neck to my throat. The mere touch of a hand on my throat set me on fire, especially since my body was still worked up after my earlier activities.

I tilted my head back, giving him more access and showing him complete submission. He turned me around, lifted my dress off over my head, then threw it to the sofa in the living room. I stood before him naked, but he was still in his shorts and T-shirt. He grabbed my waist and lifted me to sit on the counter. I braced myself with my hands as I leaned back, watching him widen my legs and gaze at my mound.

Shit, I hadn't had a chance to properly clean up after my scene. I'd feel guilty if he were to lick another man's semen from me, and I was sure I wouldn't taste the best at this moment either. "Please fuck me. I've craved your cock all day. Fuck my aching little pussy ... please."

He quickly removed his shorts. His cock was already alert. He slipped the head through my folds and slowly entered me. I wrapped my hands around his neck and my legs around his waist as he held my ass and fucked me. Typically, when I fucked two men in one day, I'd have them both at once, but this was a little different. My engine was still warm from the previous encounter, and it didn't take as long for the pleasure to build up and near orgasm.

He slid one hand up my back to grip my hair again and slightly tilted my head back to kiss me, which I eagerly embraced; our tongues madly danced together as my body shattered. My body stiffened, and I cried out quietly. Loud enough for Brett to know I came, but not loud enough for Mrs. Miller to hear next door. She made it clear she didn't want to hear that again several months ago when I brought a date home.

As my climax subsided, I whispered, "Cum for me, Brett. Fill my body with your thick cream."

He increased his speed and intensity, his breathing getting louder.

"Give me what I need. Pump me full of your hot cum." I loved being able to command a man to come inside me at my will.

His fingers dug into my hips, pushing him deeper as his body shook against mine. The feeling of his penis spasming within me was exquisite. I closed up my pelvic muscles tightly in hopes of extending the pleasure he was experiencing.

Once he withdrew from me, I knelt before him and took his member into my mouth. It had been two men tonight who had filled me with their cum; now I wanted to savor both of them at once. The taste of my own juice blended with that of my partner post-intimacy was like a stimulant for me. My senses felt heightened while I licked him clean—the taste, scent, texture, all were like pure bliss.

I rose and gave a satisfied grin, trying to recover my breath. "That was one fantastic homecoming present! Now let's get these groceries put away."

I dodged his kiss, leaving him to look bewildered. I'd been as clear as I could that we were simply roommates and fuck buddies in this arrangement. Kissing in the throes of passion was one thing—but that's where it stopped. I couldn't afford him getting attached and not becoming the man Grace and Taylor were expecting at the end of the month.

Taylor

I went to work on Monday a little earlier than usual. Before the typical workday started, I wanted to take care of some SD business. We'd been getting more interest in the unique project we were creating with Brett. Assuming that was successful, we'd need to find another one like him soon. Trish may want more money to train another, but if she were as successful as we hoped, the revenue would be well worth the investment.

I had a separate laptop for SD work. Even though I wouldn't be questioned, I didn't want our IT gurus to know what I was doing. It was bad enough that I had to register this IP address to our network, but Grace authorized it, so they shouldn't have any reason to ask questions.

I sat back and thought about last weekend and how I wasn't as satisfied as I had hoped. I'd told my sub to take me and do with me as he wanted. I just wanted to get laid. I was a little disappointed with his inability to effectively seduce me and please me without my telling him what to do. I didn't know why I expected more. We brought them in to do what we demanded of them; we didn't recruit them to think for themselves in SD.

Eventually, I sat him on a bench and rode his cock until he came. Unfortunately, I hadn't gotten off by that point. Typically, I would discipline him, but I wasn't feeling it. I kept imagining what it would be like to be with Brett after he was ready for the role we imagined him in. I'd been a Domina for many years, and although I enjoyed it, some variety would be nice, and that just might be what I was seeking.

Someone walked into our front office. It sounded like Trish setting something down on her desk.

"Trish?"

She walked into the doorway. "Hey. Anything special happening this week?"

"Have a seat." I gestured to the chair on the other side of my desk. "How's our protégé?"

She tilted her head back and forth. "He's learning fast. I gave him a couple of books on seduction and told him to try something he learned from the book on me as he wanted."

I knew it was too personal, but I was eager to know. "I have to ask … how many times do you have sex with him? Wave me off if you aren't comfortable telling me."

She beamed enthusiastically, looked to the floor for a moment, and then looked back at me. "He's young and eager. Some days twice, some days more."

My body jolted for a moment, hearing she was getting laid at least twice a day. I was envious of her. "If this works out, and I have no doubt it will, what are your thoughts about training another guy like him?"

She pondered for a moment. "I'm not sure. I'll have to let you know after we're done with Brett." Her eyebrows merged as she looked at the floor. "There is a slight concern, which I think I'm taking care of."

"What's that?"

"I think he's developing an attachment to me, and I feel it might grow over the next couple of weeks. Will he be resentful if I break it off with him in two weeks? Will he want to cooperate with what you and Grace are trying to do?"

"That had been a concern of mine also. What do you suggest?"

"Maybe I should challenge him to test his new skills with other women. Or we just come out and tell him he's being trained to be a sex god."

134

We both laughed at the thought. "You might be on to something with introducing other women." I thought it out quickly. "Why don't we find an escort to see what he's got? Maybe you can set up some story and say she's a friend of yours or something."

"That might work, but I'd want to join them." We both laughed. She continued, "I know someone who would work out, but she's about a thousand dollars for an evening."

I was immediately intrigued that Trish would have a high-priced escort as a friend. "We don't want cheap, and we do want a specific task from her. Let me know the details, and I'll give you the cash."

A devilish grin crossed her face; she was clearly thinking of something interesting.

"What's on your mind?" I asked.

"Oh, nothing, I'm just thinking about how lucky Brett is from a man's perspective to learn so much at such a young age."

"I think we may be the lucky ones. We're going to start looking for another Brett shortly, so let me know what it will take for you to help train him. Or if you know someone else who might work out. I'm sure it's interrupting your life, and we're grateful for your efforts."

"I'll let you know by the end of the week when I see how he reacts to my friend." She walked back out to her desk.

I put a pen in my teeth and turned around to look out the glass window to watch the brilliance of green trees sway with the wind. Trish seemed surprisingly comfortable with what she was doing, and at such a young age. And how did she know a high-priced escort? I wanted to learn more about her.

Grace

The red eye was always a miserable flight, and I couldn't usually sleep on a plane. But the flight to DC and the trip in general gave me time to think about how successful last weekend had been. I received excellent reviews from my clients on how well their subs worked for them. That was another thirty thousand in cash for us. Not bad for an evening of fun.

I was excited about how Brett was coming along and even more excited about the new clients we could potentially bring on. My concern was whether we would reward Brett for his work. Would he want compensation? Compensation for the servi was a couple hundred bucks and having sex with gorgeous women, but Brett would have a more responsible role, a role that could make or break this endeavor. And what about Trish? Something was intriguing about her, but I wanted to find out more about who she really was.

I arrived at my hotel and called my favorite local male escort. I was unsure he would be available since it was still morning. Fortunately, he was. I told him to get the key I left for him at the front desk and let himself in.

Meanwhile, I sat in my tub of bubbles with some soft jazz music playing in the other room while sipping a morning mimosa. He came into the room so quietly that I didn't notice until I saw him gazing down at me.

"Are you going to just stand there, or are you going to undress and help wash my back?" I asked coyly.

Nick slowly undressed, his tanned Greek skin glistening in the soft candlelight. His abs were cut like marble, and his muscular biceps flexed as he shrugged off the last piece of clothing, revealing a monster cock that hung from his body like a fleshy tree branch. He was built for this job.

I felt my core contract as I looked over my shoulder at him stepping into the hot tub behind me. His smooth balls pressed against my back as he settled in and took up a loofa. He lathered it with body wash and started running it lovingly over my body, almost making me forget the glass of bubbly in my hand from the electricity that ran through my veins.

"How do I get you to move to the west coast?" I begged.

He nestled his lips into the back of my ear and whispered, "Ten thousand a month, and I could be persuaded."

I smiled as the heat of his breath crossed my neck; his whisper lured my head back toward his head. I did some quick assessment of what it would cost, and if Brett didn't work out, Nick just might be my plan B.

The scent of vanilla sandalwood filled my nostrils as Nick started to lather me with my favorite body wash. He lingered around my breasts, making my nipples harden before he grazed across them and sent sparks shooting directly down to my hungry sex. He poured warm water over my shoulders, rinsing the remaining suds.

I reached behind to find his cock ready to please me. Just as I was about to lift myself to sit on his marvel, he stood up and held his hand for me to rise. Well versed in the art of delayed gratification, he knew the effect it had.

For now, he reached to take the shower sprayer off the hook and slowly rinse the soap suds off me, using his free hand to gently glide the suds down to the tub and leaving a trail of heat along the way. My body was on fire for him. It occurred to me that Nick and Brett would make an excellent duo for our latest SD offering, assuming Trish developed Brett into the talent we hoped he would become.

Stepping out of the tub first, Nick held my hand to assist, drying my feet before he led me to the bed to abate my hunger.

Brett

I pulled into the parking lot at work in my newly adopted car, a two-year-old silver Toyota Camry that looked sleek and rode smoother than any car I'd ever driven. The twenty-five-year-old Ford F-150 I drove around at home was solid, but I was happy to be able to afford something like this.

I also found one available unit in Trish's complex, but the rent was incredibly high. How she could afford three thousand a month was beyond me. I may have drastically underestimated how much the human resources industry paid.

When I got upstairs to my cubicle, I realized I was the first one in this morning. As my computer was slowly churning to life, I swiveled in my chair, thinking about everything. Getting it on that one night with the HR director Taylor, and now Trish ...

The sex with her was unbelievable, and I could feel myself becoming attached. I'd like to do more with her, but she seemed distant. She was everything I could want in a woman: beauty, charm, intelligence, and an incredible sexual appetite. But she didn't want a relationship.

The girls in college were just random flings. I concentrated on my studies and was never tempted to make it more than that. Was this random sex? I mean, I knew Trish better than I ever knew the other women, and it was every day, so maybe not so random after all.

Todd walked in. "Hey, Brett. What did you do last weekend?" He sat down and turned on his computer. Before I could respond, he said, "You missed a fantastic event. Five hot women in dominatrix outfits. It was an epic time. You really need to try it. They play this dominant role, but only for a little while. Then they want to get laid."

I smiled at him in surprise. I wanted to one-up him and brag how I could have sex with Trish anytime I wanted in any position, twice a day if I wanted, but I couldn't do that. "I looked for a car and found a great Camry," I replied.

"That's great! How's the apartment hunting?"

"I've been looking around, but I haven't gotten past the sticker shock."

"Yeah, it's costly, especially around here. If you drive about thirty minutes in any direction, the prices are a little better. Where are you staying now?"

"I'm staying with a high school friend's brother who's lived out here for about five years now." The lie easily rolled off my tongue.

"Oh great, I'm sure that helps. I can show you the apartments I'm staying in if you want. Maybe you can get a roommate to save on the cost?"

"That would be great. Next weekend, maybe."

I spent the rest of the day filling out paperwork for my security clearance. The amount of information they required was daunting. I had to call my mom a few times for information. I didn't know where or when my grandparents and father were born or if they were in any political groups.

It was good catching up with Mom. She asked me a ton of questions, many of which I had to lie in my answers to, such as where I was staying, or whether I'd met any ladies yet. If I were to tell her anything about Trish, she would have kept me on the phone for an hour wanting more details. My sister was doing well, and that old Ford pickup was holding out for her. Maybe I could afford a newer car for her soon enough. I wanted to help my sister and mom, especially since my mother did so much for me.

At the end of the day, Trish walked up to our cubicle. "Hi, Brett. Ms. Skyler would like to see you for a moment before you leave today."

"Oh? Is something wrong?"

"No, she just wants to see how you're settling in."

Just the sight of her brought up flashes of the sex we'd had, starting with the freshest memory of that very morning when I walked into the shower with her and lifted her against the wall with her legs wrapped around my waist. I wanted to take her right here on the desk, and I think she knew it.

"Would you like to come with me now to see Ms. Skyler?"

"Sure." I stood up and grabbed my briefcase. I looked back to Todd, who waved with a smirk.

Trish smiled back at Todd and then her eyes locked onto mine. I could look at her smile for days and never grow tired of it.

"Ms. Skyler, Brett is here as you requested."

"Thank you, Trish. Please, Brett, sit over here on the sofa."

I sat down, and Grace walked around her desk and joined me.

"I wanted to find out how you're settling in so far."

"I just bought a car and am looking for an apartment now."

With so much sex in my life, it was impossible not to look at Grace through that same lens. Her shapely legs, deep blue eyes ... her every curve screamed at me right through her burgundy skirted suit and cream-colored silk blouse. That color on her sparked a sense of familiarity, but I wasn't sure why.

She broke me out of my train of thought as she said, "I can give you some recommendations if you like? Most places around here are expensive unless you travel outside of the city a little ways."

"Yeah, that's what I've heard."

"I'm sure Trish has been helpful while you've stayed with her."

I didn't know how to respond. Trish told me not to tell anyone. My face was unmistakably warm.

"It's okay. Trish told me she invited you to stay until you found a place. You can learn a lot from her. She's another great find … just as you are."

I didn't want to confirm what she said, but I was sure my embarrassment gave me away.

"Is there anything I can do to help you?"

I thought for a moment, but nothing came to mind other than how wonderful everything had been so far. "I don't think so. You and everyone have been so kind to me, and I can't express how thankful I am for this opportunity."

She was silent for a moment, studying me from head to toe. I couldn't help but think there was another familiarity about her.

"We try to promote confidence, Brett. We want you to be successful. There are a lot of opportunities here for the right person. I've learned in business that the boastful and boisterous people who are overconfident don't have what it really takes to help me take this company where I want it to go. You have many qualities I want. Trish and Taylor also have those qualities, but it always seems men overcompensate and those who lack confidence are too passive. I'm looking for great things from you, Brett."

"I'll get there, Ms. Skyler. I'm still learning but won't let you down."

She nodded and stood up. "I believe you. I've seen some positive change in you already. Whatever Trish is doing is paying off."

If she only knew.

I followed her to the door, thinking about what it might be like to hook up with her. She opened it. "Goodnight, Brett."

"Goodnight, Ms. Skyler."

Trish

I got home before Brett to get ready to meet my friend Megan. Today was the day I was going to present her with the offer to test him out.

I met Megan when I broke up with my boyfriend a few days before I met Taylor. I was pissed at men and wanted nothing to do with them. After a couple of long island iced teas, she walked up to me in the bar and asked, "A death or a dumping?" I laughed at her intuition and had a few more drinks with her. I was glad to have tears of laughter with her versus the sorrow I felt earlier. Megan was a year older than me, with auburn hair. I went home with her and ended up in her bed that night. I had never been with a woman before, and my encounter with her was a blur, but I had a great night from what I remembered.

She made me breakfast the following day, and we enjoyed the day in Napa Valley, drinking wine and dancing through a couple of vineyards to some tinny music out of my cellphone. She became an immediate friend and then let me in on her career secret. She was an escort, and not any type of online hundred-dollars-for-thirty-minutes escort. She catered to *private jet* wealthy men and women who wanted to act out specific fantasies. They paid a lot for someone attractive and eager to help them fulfill their sexual desires for the right price.

I was in absolute awe of her experiences. Some I wanted to act out myself and figured if I could get paid for it, that would be a bonus.

My first experience was when Megan couldn't make a trip to Jamaica that a client wanted to take her on, and she asked if I wanted to do it. He was paying ten thousand dollars for a five-day trip, all expenses paid. All I needed to do was act like his daughter and fulfill his sexual fantasies. I jumped at the opportunity. The client was in his seventies and delightful. I held his arm and adored him as he took me shopping. We went out clubbing, and I danced next to him, letting him roam his hands on my slender body as he liked, and we had sex once. Not because I wouldn't give him more, but because that was all he could take. He simply wanted to touch me and treat me to a great time. Being adored by a man like that for a week was something I'd never experienced. It was enjoyable and the fastest ten thousand I'd ever made.

Since then, I'd joined the website that Megan showed me. It was only for wealthy clients as their fee to even be a member was well over a thousand dollars. I'd probably entertained twenty clients in the past couple of years, and I had complete control of each situation. If I didn't like how a scenario was playing out, I would tactfully change it to something I would accept.

I was nearing a point where I didn't need to work at Parnum Fectum, but I was intrigued by the secret group Grace and Taylor ran. I wanted to learn as much as I could about how they were organized, maybe even start my own similar club. I never expected to be asked to train one of their future role-players. It happened to fall in my lap, and I took complete advantage of it.

I arranged to meet Megan where we always met—McFatter's Pub.

I ordered a bottle of Cakebread Chardonnay I knew she liked and took two glasses to a table in the corner so we could talk without too many ears around.

When Megan walked in, all eyes turned to her. She had an aura about her that commanded attention. I waved her over, and we hugged.

She sat down and immediately sipped her wine. "Mmmm, I needed this. Oh, a bottle, wow! You don't look depressed, so you must be asking me for something."

I laughed at her keen intuition. "I do want to ask you for a favor, but it's a paid favor."

"Oh good, those are the best kind."

I showed her a picture of Brett I had taken when he wasn't looking.

"Oh, cute. Is he a client or friend?"

"Both ... I think. I can't get into details, but I'm helping a client train him to be the perfect seducer and sex god, of sorts, for women."

"Wow, maybe I'll do him for free." We laughed. "How exactly are you training him?"

I didn't usually blush, but I could feel the warmth on my cheeks. "He's living with me and I'm trying to start with giving him confidence and teaching him some basics."

"You're fucking him at your apartment?" she asked, leaning back with wide eyes.

"He was new to the area, and the client is paying me twenty thousand for a month to train him to be a confident lady killer and learn how to please, so they get their money's worth when they whore him out to some wealthy clients."

"Oh, now we're talking. How much are they expecting women to pay for him?"

"Ten thousand a night. I heard one woman would pay twenty thousand to get him perfected in the next couple of weeks."

"Wow. Who the hell are these women? I need to promote my bi side a little more." We tapped our wine glasses together, agreeing on how lucrative this business could be. "So, how can I help?"

"I'd like you to role-play my best friend."

"Well, that'll be easy … a threesome? We haven't been *together* since that first night we met. I'm almost thinking I'm no longer attractive enough for you." She pouted.

"I'm sure your clients love that pout face, but it doesn't work on me. Besides, our friendship is great. Remember four months ago at that wedding you took me to as a plus one?"

Her eyes went wide. "Oh my God, why would you remind me of that? Thank you for saving my life, and, more importantly, my dignity."

"I just couldn't let you hook up with the groom in the closet the night of their wedding. Maybe the night prior, or the day after, but you're above the day of."

We clinked glasses. "Thank you. That champagne gets to me every time and … well, damn, he was so fucking hot."

We laughed and nodded, taking a sip of our wine while remembering that night.

I shook my head and bit my lip, gazing at her cleavage. "Stop distracting me. And as far as hooking up with you again, I'd love to, but I want you to role-play that your boyfriend dumped you and sucked at pleasing you and all you want is a man who knows how to satisfy a woman. I'll set it up with him so he knows what to expect, then you evaluate how well he does and give me some ideas on how to improve him. I have a thousand dollars for you to evaluate him."

"A thousand dollars to evaluate a sex god in training? Hell, I would think I would pay for that." We both laughed again. I loved her humor. There was a reason she was so good at what she did.

"So, you'll do it?"

"Of course, I'll do it. When do you want to arrange this?"

"How about Friday night?"

"Sounds great. What will you be doing?"

"I need to test him without my being there, but … I can come back in a couple of hours and see if a third is needed?"

"I'd like that a lot," Megan replied with a devilish grin and a wink.

"Good. I'll set it up and coordinate with you on Friday for any last-minute details. Now … tell me some juicy details of your latest clients."

She regaled me with the erotic details of a few recent engagements. For two, she was a dominatrix, and one was a forced encounter. She explained the rules and contract agreement to me with that one, so no one got in trouble outside of their little arrangement. I was intrigued. I liked rough sex, but I could see a need for a contract and thorough discussion on limits with someone new.

The bottle of wine was unexpectedly empty, and I was extremely wet. Good thing I could count on Brett to fuck me as soon as I walked in the door, because after listening to Megan, I needed it.

Brett

I couldn't get enough of Trish. She was more than I could ever ask for in a woman, and I'd only known her for a few weeks. It wasn't just her body, but her entire everything. Her looks, personality, her laugh. I'd never had feelings for anyone like this before.

I gulped down the last of my beer and set it down. I was done with the sci-fi movie and scrolled through to see what might catch my eye. Most of what was displayed on the television was a blur. In between pining for Trish, my mind drifted to projects at work. The robotics I'd dreamed of working on was now my reality. My life had gone from school to life-overload in a matter of weeks. My only concern was if it was all too good to be true.

ESPN captured my attention, and I decided to watch some highlights of the recent World Cup games. The door opened, and I looked back to see Trish come through. "Hey, Trish."

I heard her keys land on the table. She walked to me, knelt, and hastily unfastened my pants. I chuckled. "Um, I thought I was supposed to take the lead?"

"You wouldn't get there as fast as I need it right now."

Without another word, she ravenously devoured my cock, stroking and sucking on it feverishly. I immediately responded to her hunger. I'd never seen her like this before. She stood up, removed her panties, lifted her dress, and straddled me. Within seconds, she'd guided me into her warmth.

Settling herself into my lap, she began riding me. Her round, firm ass bounced on my thighs while her inner walls gripped my cock like a wet, silken glove. It was all happening so fast. Much more quickly than I was accustomed to, especially with her. She rode me as if we had only an hour left to live—rough and fast and deep. Her breathing increased as the pressure of our kiss ratcheted up. She scratched the back of my head and dug her fingers into my neck. When we broke for air, I could feel her heart in my chest pounding out of control. Our eyes locked, and there was nothing but lust and passion between us.

"I want you to cum in me and tell me when you do."

Her moans echoed with every hard thrust; she clenched herself around every inch inside and dug her nails into the back of my neck again, causing me to quickly grunt out, "I'm coming!"

"Yes! Yes! Yes!" She slammed herself down onto me equally as hard as I thrust into her.

She continued to slowly gyrate on my shaft as I slowly opened my eyes. She smiled down at me with a satisfying laugh and then stopped moving, but her inner muscles continued to clench around my shaft, causing my body to spasm. She laughed at my inability to control my spasms, which she created, and I also had to laugh.

"To what do I owe this pleasure?" I asked while caressing her smooth ass.

She repositioned herself on my lap, moving closer and keeping me inside. "I just needed a quick fix, and I knew who could give it to me."

I smiled. "That was quite presumptuous of you. What would have happened if I wasn't in the mood?"

She put her hands around my neck and leaned into my face. Her nose touched mine. "Then I'd have to go door to door and find a man who would care for my needs." She laughed, climbed off me, and went to her bedroom. I kicked off my shoes, took my pants off, wiped the mess on my lap with my T-shirt, and continued watching the soccer game high-lights. Who was I kidding? How could I watch the game when all I could think about was how wonderful she was?

Trish returned from her bedroom, naked as usual, set a towel on the sofa, and sat down. "Brett, I have a friend going through some issues right now, and I wondered if you could help her with something?"

Her words were slowly making it through my concentration on her naked body. "I will if I can."

"Oh, I think you can. She was in a relationship with a guy for about two years, and in the past year and a half, he hasn't wanted to have sex with her. She found out he was actually gay and no longer wanted her. She needs reassurance that she's still desirable."

"Wait … you want me to have sex with your friend?" I asked, surprised.

"It would mean a lot to me. She's beautiful. Maybe more attractive than I am."

"No way, I can't believe it." Trish was one of the most beautiful wom-en I'd ever met, but then again, I might be biased, having had sex with her like forty times already.

"Thanks, but she really is gorgeous. I thought she might come over here Friday evening and, well, you can use what I taught you to make her feel like a wanted woman again."

I couldn't believe the woman I was living with and having sex with every day was telling me to fuck her friend. And she was talking about it like it was as simple as watching TV. But her sincere and almost begging eyes were more than convincing. I thought about it for a moment. "So … do you see yourself pimping me out in your future?" I laughed.

"Maybe if you're good enough." She snickered. "I'll have Megan do an evaluation."

"Megan is your friend you want me to have sex with on Friday?"

She sat up. "Here is where you can see what you've really learned. Millions of women out there have never experienced how a real man can pleasure them, and what you've learned so far will turn you into a sex god."

I laughed. "I like the sound of that."

She laughed also and replied, "Just don't let it go to your head. Women like confident men, not arrogant."

I nodded. "So, you want me to seduce her and then fuck her brains out?"

"Exactly!" she said, raising her hands in the air with a proud laugh.

I stared at her and slowly shook my head, still thinking I was in some dream.

"Why are you shaking your head?"

I continued to shake my head and smiled. "I can't seem to get out of this dream and hope I never do."

She stood up and placed her hand on my cheek. "You're sweet … how about frozen pizza and wine tonight?"

"Sounds great!"

Grace

My return flight last night didn't have Wi-Fi working, so I came in early to catch up on my email. I was trying to deliberately sip on my grande caramel macchiato after each email, or it would get cold before I finished typing.

The sun slowly brightened my office as it peered over the trees. Taylor walked in. "Welcome back," she said cheerily.

I looked at the clock on the computer—seven a.m. "Hey, I still have about fifty emails to go. I'd like to catch up before the day gets started. Any fires around here?"

"No, no fires. I have Trish testing our protégé, though."

I leaned back in my chair and clasped my hands together. "Oh, I can put my email on hold to hear more about this."

Taylor smiled and sat on the edge of my desk. "There's a lot more to Trish than we thought, but she seems to be doing well. She's getting a high-paid escort *friend* of hers to give Brett a midterm test."

"A *friend* of hers, you say?" I laughed lightly and shook my head. "That little bitch has got a lot more going on than we were led to believe." I stood up and walked around my desk, staring at the floor while thinking. "I think we have more with her than we thought. If this works out, I want to give her a raise."

Taylor laughed. "Okay, will do."

"Oh, oh," I said excitedly. "I have a backup plan if Brett doesn't work or if we need an extra for later. This male escort I've seen a couple of times in DC. He's older but exactly what we're looking for. Unfortunately, the ten thousand per month, plus expenses, would be quite painful to bring him out here."

"Ouch. Is any man worth ten thousand?"

"This one is. Especially if we have a client willing to pay twenty thousand, maybe we should invite him out here for our new adventure. He's thirty-nine years old and holds a lot of experience, and he might give some additional tips to our young Brett?"

Taylor stood up and walked toward the door. "That might be worth it, but damn, girl. You pay ten thousand for a man when you can get so many for free?"

"If you experienced him, you'd pay ten grand too," I replied defensively.

"Okay, catch up on that email. I'll have some more coming your way shortly."

As Taylor left, I grabbed my coffee and walked to the window to scan over the Silicon Valley sunrise, visualizing what SD could become. Maybe I'd just open an east coast location.

Taylor

I'd always been more partial to being a dominatrix. Men's efforts to seduce me, as Grace was trying to find, had brought only disappointment in the past. Being in control allowed me to have them do whatever I pleased and satisfy me however I desired, but that could all change if Brett turned out to be even more spectacular than the first time I had him.

From a financial perspective, I understood what Grace was trying to do. If there were women out there who wanted to pay for Brett, I was all for him providing a service, but I preferred my men to be obedient to my every demand.

I looked at my list of emails to address and sighed as I sat at my desk. I didn't want to read any of them. A few seconds later, another one popped onto my screen. My thoughts were more focused on this guy Grace saw in DC and whether I could get into one of those men—or, more importantly, if they were good enough to give me what I needed. I didn't think I could easily give up that control I'd gotten used to over the years. Hell, I might even hurt the poor guy.

Then I thought of Trish. She intrigued me even more. The way she was so calculating—and willing—in her negotiations to train Brett, I was convinced she wasn't new to this. I powered up my SD laptop and began searching. Most of my searches for SD revolved around dominant women and submissive men, so I changed my search criteria to see if Trish might be in there somewhere.

I searched around on many websites, including the sugar daddy sites, but I couldn't find a profile that had a hint of her. There were other sites, but I wasn't about to pay the fees they demanded as a client to search.

Then it dawned on me that some of these websites allowed me to set up a free profile as a woman. Perhaps I could search the high-cost ones that way.

I established quick profiles on some of the sites, doing reverse searches for other women, but still no luck.

"Good morning, Taylor."

I panicked as Trish popped her head in my door, but I calmly closed my laptop, making sure nothing showed on my face. "Good morning. How's everything going with Brett?"

She walked in closer to my desk. "It's going well. My friend is going to test him out tomorrow night."

"Is there anything you can tell me about your friend?"

"Funny enough, she found me the same way you did. Sulking in a bar after my fiancé left me. I found out later that she's a high-paid escort. I asked her to pretend she'd gotten dumped and needs a man to make her feel wanted again."

Damn, she's good. "Sounds great! You said high-priced. How much does she normally charge?"

"Well, she told me her clients typically pay between five to ten thousand for her."

As our clients paid the same amount, I wasn't too surprised, but I wanted to fish. "Wow, good for her. That's a lot of money. Surprised you haven't tried it yourself. It's definitely a lot more than we're paying you."

"What makes you think I haven't?" She smiled, raised her eyebrows, and walked back to her desk.

I knew it. I got up and walked out to her desk as she sat down. I immediately found the humor in her sitting back, clasping her fingers as though she was in the driver's seat. She knew I wanted more answers, but I needed a discreet approach.

"If your friend typically charges so much, why only the one thousand we're offering?"

"She's doing it as a favor, especially when I told her what he's learned so far. Also, her typical clients are a lot older, and she wanted the taste of a young man again."

I sat down on the edge of her desk. I wasn't sure how to ask, but since she already knew about SD, I decided to take the chance.

"You don't have to answer if you don't want to, but I'm curious what you've explored with your earlier comment."

"I've met some clients who pay a lot of money for a woman who wants to role-play with them."

I looked at her in amazement. What were the odds that I'd found another woman who dabbled in a similar world to me and Grace? "You mean like schoolgirl outfits or daughter role-playing?"

She leveled a look at me, obviously searching for how she wanted to answer. "Those might be a couple options, but it's typically much more than just performing those roles. Some men feel the need to discipline their girls, and let's just say I give them everything they're looking for."

I was speechless. I would never have expected the girl I'd met, crying over her boyfriend in a bar, to be ... this.

When I didn't respond, Trish asked, "Are you all right?"

"Um, yeah, you sort of threw me off ... I'm quite impressed, actually. Your façade was brilliantly applied since I've known you."

She had her hands clasped on her crossed legs, and she looked at me head-on as though she was an open book; all I had to do was ask. I wanted to continue our dialogue but knew more details wouldn't be good to discuss at work.

"Perhaps I can meet you and your friend on Saturday to get her feedback on Brett?"

"She likes to keep her life private, but I'll find out."

"Thanks." I returned to my office and looked out of my glass wall at the trees waving with the breeze. The sun was getting brighter, but my mind was becoming foggier. I couldn't help but think about that entire fantasy fulfillment concept. We'd been successful catering to women all this time, but if we delved into her world, we might get many more clients and potentially more lucrative contracts. The question was would Grace go for it, and could we combine it with SD somehow?

Brett

I was getting more and more nervous as the day progressed. I was supposed to have sex with Trish's friend tonight. Or rather, romance her first, seduce her … hell, I barely knew what I was doing, and I was expected to be some type of professional gigolo? And how was Trish so open and free about sex? I'd already caught feelings for her despite her warnings and distance—or maybe because of it? Then again, I had sex with her before I had these feelings. I was so preoccupied thinking about my evening that I hardly accomplished any work all day.

When I got home, Trish was already there getting ready for something. "What are you up to tonight?"

"I'm going out to dinner with a friend. Megan should be here around six. Just be your sweet self. Don't be nervous. Pretend she's me if you have to, but make her feel beautiful, wanted, lusted for, then fuck her brains out."

Trish grabbed her purse, walked up to me, and kissed my lips. "That's for confidence. You'll be fine, just enjoy. I'll be back a bit later."

She walked out the door, and there I was, stunned with a racing heart. She just kissed me, and we weren't having sex. Did she slip with her no kissing rule, or was the success of her friend tonight that important?

I took a shower and groomed myself down below. Trish called it man-scaping when she told me how much a woman loves a smooth cock and balls. I got dressed in nice slacks and a polo shirt, spritzed a little cologne on my neck, and then went to the fridge to see if we had some wine ready.

Fortunately, we did have a nice bottle of chardonnay. In need of a little liquid courage, I opened it and got an early start. I sat in the chair to watch some hockey on ESPN and waited.

The subtle knock at the door hardly warranted alarm, yet I was startled. Nearly losing my breath at the sudden adrenaline rush, I leaped to turn the TV off.

I opened the door and wanted to say, "Hi, Megan," but I froze. Trish had said her friend was good-looking, but that hadn't prepared me for the stunning beauty in front of me. She had shoulder-length, red, wavy hair and green eyes, and she was wearing a short black dress that hugged every curve.

"Hi, I'm Megan. You must be Brett?"

My embarrassment was obvious to me and probably her, but I was able to shake out of my hypnosis and reach out to hug her. "Yes, yes, Megan. I'm sorry, Trish told me you were beautiful, but I underestimated her definition of beauty."

"Awww, you're too sweet," she responded, hugging me in return.

"Please, come in. Can I offer you a glass of wine? I have a nice bottle of chardonnay opened."

"Yes, please, that would be wonderful."

I slipped a few feet into the kitchen to fill her glass and paused to calm my nerves with a deep breath. When I returned, Megan stood at the bar between the living room and kitchen. I smoothly walked up close and handed her the glass of wine.

"Trish told me about your recent breakup. I'm sorry, but I can't believe any guy could ever leave you."

"Thank you again, but it's his loss. So, you've known Trish for a while now?" she asked.

"Yeah. I was a new hire, and she offered her apartment for a little while until I found my own place."

We engaged in some small talk, but I couldn't help but stare at how beautiful she was and wonder what chapter of my books or what approach Trish taught me I should take. I was getting a little more comfortable as we talked, but Trish wanted me to do more, and from what she told me, Megan wanted more too.

I'd never been this bold in my life, but I took a leap of faith based on what was expected of me. I slowly placed my hand on her cheek and glided my fingers gently along her skin just under her ear, my thumb resting on her cheek. "You are so beautiful."

She leaned her head into my hand. I slid my thumb to her succulent lips, which she parted, her tongue flicking out almost reflexively against my finger.

Seeing her perfectly pink tongue dart out and taste me sent an electric pulse straight down to my manscaped area. Unable to help myself, I leaned in closer and brushed my lips gently along hers. I wanted to feel that tongue against mine, but I held back, just barely gliding our lips together. My hand remained cupped around the back of her neck, and my fingers gently caressed her earlobe. I figured I'd start with what Trish had dubbed my signature collection of smooth moves.

Her breathing hitched as my lips followed where my hands had just been. I gently kissed her neck, trailed my lips back to her mouth, and slid my tongue along her lips. She opened to kiss me harder, but I wouldn't let her.

"You have me so hard right now," I whispered.

Her leg expertly glided along mine, confirming my claim. Just as her leg brushed along my erection, she reached behind my neck and pulled my lips firmly into hers. Our kiss became more passionate. I continued to caress her neck, tearing my lips from hers to brush them across her cheek to her ear, then I ran my teeth along the length of her neck down to the neckline on her dress.

I kissed the tops of her breasts, pulling her dress down slightly to run my tongue over one of her nipples. Her hands held my head there, and I bit her slightly. When she moaned, her fingers clenching my hair, I whispered, "I want to get you out of these clothes. Follow me."

I took her hand and led her to my bedroom. She kicked her heels off as I put my arm around her waist. Pulling her in tight, I reached one hand along her neck to grip the back of her head and brought her lips to mine. My hands slowly glided down to undo her zipper and gently slipped her dress off.

It fell to the floor, and there she stood in her matching black lace bra and panties. I leaned back to gaze at the gorgeous lingerie that perfectly fit her curves. I looked into her eyes again and said, "You're amazing."

Stepping up to kiss her lips softly, I reached behind her and snapped her hooks, releasing her bra and letting it fall to the floor, exposing her voluptuous breasts. I couldn't take my eyes off them, but I remembered my lessons and tried to ensure my look was one of admiration without being too eager or lewd.

The skin along her neck was smooth as silk against my lips as I dragged them down her body, kissing her breasts along the way, stopping momentarily to tease her nipples with my tongue until I felt her breath catch. Lowering myself slowly to my knees, I glided my hands along her legs, cupping her ass with a firm but gentle squeeze.

My mouth trailed kisses down her stomach, to her hip, and then her inner thigh before I turned my lips to the lace covering her mound. I reached for the elastic of her panties and gracefully pulled them down, remembering a moment too late a tip from one of the books to remove them with my teeth. *Next time!*

I was already hoping there would be a next time as my pleasure started to cloud my feelings for Trish. Megan stepped out of her skimpy panties as I dragged my lips up one thigh, straight to her warmth, letting my breath touch her more than my lips. I exhaled onto her slit and continued the same process with her other thigh.

After what I hoped seemed like just the right amount of time for her, I stood up slowly, my lips retracing their path from where I knelt until I found her soft, full lips again.

"Open your mouth," I said. I wet my fingers on her tongue as she kept her mouth open wide for me and then reached down to slowly swirl them around her clit as I leaned in to her partly open mouth and slipped my tongue inside. Her breathing increased as I pressed more firmly against her clit in a circular motion. When I left her clit to slip my fingers inside her, she gasped, then tensed as I brought them back to her clit to circle around again.

Her cries echoed through the room as my fingers moved in rapid circles around her most sensitive spot. She could barely stand, her slender body shaking with pleasure beneath my touch, and I reveled in the sensation of her nails pressing into my shoulders like claws.

I looked into her eyes, filled with an aching want that only I could satisfy. Taking her hand, I guided her backward until she rested against the edge of the bed. My mouth hovered above her ear as breathy words escaped me, "I need to taste you."

She gasped, soft skin rising in anticipation as she nodded and gave herself entirely to me.

She sat at the edge of the bed and lay back.

Not knowing her tolerance for force, I chose to gently part her thighs, lifting her by the inside of her knees, and expose her beautiful bald mound. I paused, waiting for her to open her eyes so she could see the desire in mine. *Time to test another one of my signature moves.*

I glided my lips up her leg, pausing to give extra attention where I got the most response. I had versed myself in erogenous zones, and the back of the knee was supposed to be a pleasure point for most women. I had a flashback to my frat days and realized how clueless we all were to how surreal sex could feel. Hell, I was still beginning to understand. There was so much more to discover.

I worked my way up her thigh, all the while planning out my oral strategy on her. In my head, I continued to repeat to myself, *Keep it slow until she urges you otherwise, and even then, prolong it just a little more.*

I finally reached her mound and gently kissed her warm folds. My efforts were rewarded as I tasted her wetness and felt her radiating heat on my face. I had played a game with Trish using my tongue to form the letters of the alphabet on her clit. While we never came close to getting through the entire alphabet, I learned some techniques as she directed me on what felt best for her. Now, it was time for me to figure it out on a new canvas.

I started with slow, circular motions, with an occasional flick of my tongue, and then back to circles.

My confidence grew with every arched back and moan. I was finding at least some of her spots. That wasn't the only thing that was growing. I was so hard I ached, but this wasn't about me.

I rapidly slid my tongue down through her slit to her entrance and then back up to her clit, randomly changing it up again as I tried to keep her on the edge of an orgasm. Every time I saw her grip the comforter, I knew she was close and would change my technique to prolong the effect. I slowly removed my clothes as I concentrated on her pleasure.

Her scent and taste were like an addictive drug. I slipped my tongue inside her, slowly thrusting it in as deep as possible, then licking her up through her inner pink, back to her clit. I slipped my middle and index fingers inside and slowly massaged her as I continued tantalizing her clit with my tongue.

Having learned how she reacted, I continued to back off whenever she gripped the sheets, bringing her to the brink of an orgasm, but not allowing her to complete it. Edge play was one of the techniques I'd learned in the books, and it was paying off.

I stopped the fifth time, slightly backing away, caressing her thighs, but she was too far over the edge. She was determined to have an orgasm regardless of my actions. She gripped the sheets and arched her back. She was at the point of no return, so I dove back in and sucked on her clit and mercilessly fingerfucked her. I thought her pelvis would take out my front teeth as she bucked herself into me.

Once she relaxed, her breath still coming in pants, I moved along her body, gliding my erect cock up her thigh, brushing it slightly against her mound and up her stomach. She remained breathing heavy while watching it come closer. She nodded as I brought myself toward her mouth. She opened wide as I passed by and leaned down to kiss her. She gasped with a hint of laughter, then reached for it and began stroking me. She pulled me toward her mouth, closed her eyes, and devoured me.

Her lustful hunger was evident as she savored every inch of me. Rolling her tongue around my head, down the shaft, and then ran her cheek alongside, only to suck on it again. Her enthusiasm for me was amazing to watch.

I reached down and grabbed a fistful of her hair, holding her head firmly in place. She let go with her hands and opened her mouth wider, inviting me to fuck her mouth as I wanted. I grabbed her head with both hands and thrust myself as deep as possible.

When she gagged a bit more intensely, I stopped and quickly slid off the bed. I grabbed her ass and pulled her to the edge with her legs on either side of me. The tip of my cock slipped through her slit, rubbing over her clit. I pressed it firmly against her clit and rubbed it, slipping it just inside for lubrication and rubbed her clit again. Her breath was shallow, and her hands grabbed my ass and pulled me closer to her heat, wanting me to fuck her. Her stomach clenched with anticipation. I found her entrance and plunged myself inside.

Her back arched, and she gripped my ass harder. Her inner grip had me on the edge in mere moments. I let her legs go and grabbed her breasts, caressing her nipples with my thumbs, randomly pinching them between my fingers before leaning down to suck on them. I had to use every ounce of self-discipline I had, saying a silent thank you to Trish for her *I get two orgasms before you can come* training. I slowed my thrusts to avoid coming too quickly as I tried to maintain my focus on Megan.

Her panting grew louder, and this time when she came, she let out a cry just as liquid splashed between us and ran down my legs. I was momentarily taken aback. Neither Trish nor Taylor were squirters. In fact, I'd only ever been with one woman who squirted—my very first time in Cancun.

"I want you to fuck me from behind." She broke our silence as I closed my gaping mouth and shook my head to help clear my mind. I hoped she hadn't noticed my eyes bulging out of my skull at the surprise shower. I had gotten more comfortable with Trish prompting me to speak to her during sex, but I was shy about vocalizing with Megan.

Still surprised by her eruption, I tried to ignore it and pulled out as she turned around, her ass up high, her legs spread wide, and her face turned deep into the mattress. I knelt between her legs and pushed myself in. Moments later, she cried out, "Fuck that pussy, fuck it hard!" She let out a squealing noise, and then the water spray covered my legs again and saturated the comforter. Making a woman orgasm so intensely suddenly gave me a sense of euphoric triumph.

She turned around and seemed to take over, pushing me onto my back and climbing on top. She positioned herself over my cock and slowly slid down. I watched my shaft quickly disappear into her sex, and then she began to ride me. I could feel the tip of my cock rubbing against her inner walls as she maneuvered to get me in the right spot. She held onto my chest while looking down into my eyes, fucking me slowly, then faster, moving from side to side. Then she whispered, "I want to feel you come inside me. Fill my pussy with your cum."

Her whimpers and writhing were in concert with my ravenous plunges into her. I finally groaned, "Here I come!"

She began to buck on my hips even harder and cried out as I released. Her cum sprayed all over my hips and onto the comforter again. My bed was beyond saturated—the sound of splashing synchronized with her movements sounded like we were fucking in a wading pool.

We both regained our breath enough to look at each other and smile.

"Damn, you don't know how much I needed that. Thank you."

I felt too new to be thanked for doing so well, but maybe I knew more than I gave myself credit for.

"So, he did good?"

My head snapped toward the door—there was Trish.

"Hey, girl!" Megan called out with a grin on her face. She was still sitting on top of me with my recovering limp cock inside her.

"I hope he treated you well. If not, I'll have to spank him." Trish and Megan both laughed while I tried to determine how long she'd been standing there.

"Don't let me stop you from giving him a good spanking, but he did very well," Megan replied while caressing my chest.

I remained quiet, not knowing what to say. Both Megan and Trish seemed entirely too cool with Trish seeing us fuck. I know that Trish was the one who instigated this, but it still seemed bizarre to me that Megan was okay with Trish watching us.

Trish walked over and sat beside me. She combed her fingers through my hair and looked down at my continued union with Megan. I felt like my brain had frozen and wasn't sure what to do. Before I could say anything, Trish said, "Does she feel too good to pull out?"

I followed her gaze, shaking my head a little in confusion. "We both just came and were resting when you walked in."

"Oh really? Megan, do you mind if I have a little taste of him?" Trish asked coyly.

Megan lifted and rolled over, and my cock slapped down on my stomach in a sloppy mess. Trish slid her hand through our mixed cum and licked it from her fingers.

"Mmmmm." She went down on my cock and began sucking. I writhed with ache as the sensation of just coming mixed with getting aroused again by Trish was intense.

My balls suddenly began to receive attention. I looked down to see Megan sucking on them as Trish sucked my cock. Holy hell. This was beyond anything I could ever imagine and certainly beyond any frat party threesome conversation. I'd never even thought something like this was possible for someone like me.

Trish grabbed my shaft and began stroking it. I was thinking about the contrast between my growing feelings for her and the excitement of a sexual encounter with someone new when Trish jolted me out of my thoughts.

"So, how long before it gets hard again?" she asked.

I shrugged. "I guess that depends on how attentive you two are."

They both laughed. Trish said, "Well, let me get naked and help accelerate this process."

Trish took off her clothes and climbed on the bed, leaning her pussy back to sit on my face. I loved her scent and taste. I licked through her slit, then swirled my tongue around her nub. She moved her hips, positioning her clit where she liked while they both sucked and fondled my cock and balls. The two of them going at me simultaneously was unlike anything I'd felt before, and I never wanted it to end.

Megan climbed up and slid herself back down onto my semi-firm shaft. She began moving on me as I continued to eat Trish. I couldn't see anything further as my face was buried. I could hear Megan have another orgasm as her cum splashed over my lap again.

"Damn, girl, you have my bed soaked," Trish said, laughing.

"He knew how to get the job done. You're so damn lucky, girl." Megan continued her slow motions up and down my shaft.

"You hear that, Brett? Megan is going to write you a testimonial." Their laughter made me even more bewildered that they were so comfortable having sex together.

Megan rolled off, and Trish sucked on my cock again.

Then Trish repositioned herself over the top of my cock and lowered herself down. She began riding me as Megan knelt alongside, kissing her and caressing Trish's breasts. I had the best view in the world. Watching and experiencing this was something I'd only imagined, and it was right out of a porn video.

Trish continued to fuck me long and slow as she kissed and fondled Megan. Then Trish asked, "Do you want to taste his cum together?"

"Mm-hmm," Megan eagerly replied.

Trish moved off me and stroked my cock with a firm, slightly twisting motion that took me closer and closer to the edge.

"That's it, Brett, come for us. We want to share your cum," Trish said in a yearning tone and then she spit on it, allowing her saliva to slide with her hand as lube.

Other than porn movies in college, I'd never seen such things before. My hips began to churn more, and I exclaimed, "I'm coming!"

The sensation of their lips and tongues slowly sliding along my shaft was mesmerizing. I couldn't see but clenched the sheets and embraced the pulsating sensation as I let go and groaned. I could hear them moaning as they didn't stop their mouths on me. I was much more sensitive now and couldn't bear it any longer. My knuckles had to be white, gripping as I grimaced and grasped a handful of the wet comforter.

"Okay, stop!" I gasped.

They continued to kiss each other, licking some of my cream from each other's chins. All I could do was breathe heavily and stare in awe at how incredible the two of them looked. *No one I know would ever believe this.*

They turned to look at me, and their breasts connected as they embraced each other.

"So, Megan, how did he do?" Trish asked as she smiled down at me.

She tilted her head to the side and placed her finger up to her mouth. "Hmmm, I'm not sure." She tried to hold back a smile, but it was there. "It was a little slow to start, but he *finished* brilliantly." She emphasized the latter words with her hands in the air and a wide grin.

My face got warm, but I smiled with pride. "I didn't know I was being evaluated."

Megan leaned down, grabbed my cock, and kissed the tip. She looked at me and said, "Brett, dear, everyone is always being evaluated."

The girls climbed off the bed and went to take a shower. I toweled off, put my boxers on, went into the kitchen to get my glass of wine, and thought about what I had just experienced.

Going back into the bedroom, I looked down at the messed up and soaked bed. I pulled the comforter off and saw the sheets were wet too.

I took them off and realized the mattress was a little damp. I laughed a little at how insane that had been. It had been three weeks now, and I wasn't sure I wanted to find my own place anymore. Being with Trish, and all that entailed, was way better than anything else I would find. I was certain of it.

Trish

Once Megan had left, I grabbed what I assumed was her half-empty glass of wine from the kitchen, took a sip, and looked at Brett. "So, how did it go? I want details."

"I was nervous at first, but she helped me feel more comfortable by talking. Then I heard your voice in my head telling me she was there to have sex, and I didn't want to disappoint you."

I rolled my eyes and laughed. "That didn't look like guilt fucking to me as I watched you thrust that meat stick into her shoulder blades."

Now he looked guilty.

He continued, "I walked up to her, set her glass of wine down, and began kissing her ..."

As I sipped my wine, he told me the rest of the details up to when I walked through the door and joined them.

Getting turned on by his comfort in telling me graphic details of their encounter, I said, "So, if I were to bring another woman over wanting the same thing, you would be more comfortable?"

He raised one eyebrow and squinted with the other, trying to find out if I was serious, and then laughed, "Are you pimping me out?" He laughed harder. "I better get a cut if I'm doing all the work."

I couldn't help but laugh also. "I didn't pimp you out, but it does sound like you have a talent to make some money. Many women in Megan's situation would pay a lot to have what you can give."

His mouth fell open slightly. "Are you serious? I was joking … you're kidding, right?"

"No, I'm not kidding, especially in Silicon Valley. So many wealthy women often don't have a man in their life to please them. They're willing to pay a lot for what you just provided Megan."

Brett went quiet as he seemed to think about my words. After a minute, he burst out laughing.

"What's so funny?"

He replied, "I'm just thinking about telling my mom that I went through four years of college to be a male escort."

I joined his laughter. *If only he knew what I was training him for.*

Grace

I pulled up into my parking spot at the office, my mind on the amazing weekend I'd had. I met one of my subs from SD in a hotel room Saturday night, where he waited on me and massaged my feet, and then he slept on the floor like a good sub. I would have let him sleep on the sofa if he asked, but he didn't. This one didn't work for my company, so I didn't mind him seeing my face.

I kept thinking about what Nick gave me in DC and how much I was looking forward to test driving Brett. He would a great fit for us if he was anything like the tidbits I'd heard.

As I got out of my car, I saw Brett walking into the building, more at ease with himself than he was when he first started. I hadn't received a detailed report from Taylor or Trish yet, but I was hoping he would be ready for our next SD event. I had set up a room in our facility just for that role-play and had our first client tentatively lined up. I planned to test our young protégé myself, and if he satisfied me like I hoped, I'd book the appointment.

I walked up to my office, logged into my laptop, and saw the new emails rolling in. *Some mornings never change.* I went to get coffee, then decided to make the rounds. Showing face to the employees was important to me—I wanted them to know I was here for them if needed—but more importantly, I liked to remember who they were. We had a lot of employees at Parnum Fectum, and as CEO, I rarely got a chance to interact with most of them. I stopped in the engineering section and saw Brett working on a robot we were putting together for the Army. He had a control panel in his hands while his colleague, Jim, worked on the object.

Brett looked up as I approached. "Ms. Skyler. What do we owe this pleasure?"

Jim stood up and turned to look at me also. I'd had him as a servus several times. There was something infinitely satisfying about knowing my employees so intimately when they had no idea who I was. "Hi, Ms. Skyler."

"Hi, Jim. I was taking a stroll through the building to catch up on what everyone was working on. What are you two doing?"

Jim replied, "We're calibrating Project Mule for the Army. Brett is helping with the limit testing while I move the legs to calibrate to the software."

I nodded at Brett, and he smiled back easily. He didn't seem as embarrassed as he once did. "How are you settling in, Brett? Have you found a place to live yet?"

"I've been looking, but it's expensive around here. I plan to look at the surrounding areas this weekend."

I looked him over from his feet to his head and back again, trying to remember what he was like in Cancun and how much better he was likely to be now. Thinking about this handsome young man having his way with me caused my core to twinge slightly. I could faintly hear Jim's voice and realized he was still talking to me.

"I'm sure it'll come along great. Let me know when you're ready for testing. I'd love to see it."

"I will, ma'am. Thank you for visiting us," Jim replied with a smitten look.

That look had me thinking of all the ways I'd had Jim before, and I just barely contained my smirk. I nodded at them both, then walked to the HR department and into Taylor's office, where I found Trish sitting with her.

Closing the door, I said, "So, how's our protégé coming along? I saw him walking into the building with a spring in his step, so it seems something is going well."

Taylor replied, "Good. Trish just walked in to give me an update."

Trish turned her chair to look at both of us. "He seemed to do quite well with his test run on Friday. My friend Megan said he was exceptional. He may have a slight confidence issue, but that will get better with more experience."

"Great! When can I take him for a test run?"

Taylor and Trish smiled. Trish replied, "When do you want to? I sort of tossed out the concept of being his pimp. He laughed and wanted to make sure he got a cut."

"No, he didn't," I said, taken aback.

Trish nodded. "He absolutely did. I'm sure he thought I was joking around. Well, I was partly, but I think he would do it. I could set it up to meet you somewhere and you could check him out."

"How would he react to wearing a mask, or if I were wearing a mask?"

"That's a good question. I honestly don't know. I think your eyes would give you away regardless of the mask, but I can prep him for a mask; explain how you're a prominent CEO in a major Silicon Valley firm and don't want anyone to know your identity."

I couldn't help but laugh at her sarcasm.

"Let's set it up for Friday night at SD. I have a room there which I plan to use as his lair, and I'll try some colored contact lenses."

Trish laughed. "A lair? Let's not let his ego get too crazy by telling him that. I'll try to prepare him for Friday. I think you'll be happy, but I don't take responsibility if he finds out it's you."

"I agree." I turned and walked toward the door. "Ladies, enjoy your week. I look forward to Friday."

I walked into my office and up to my glass wall. The morning glow of the valley was always inspiring. I sipped my coffee, hoping Brett was just what we were looking for to grow SD's clientele—and make even more money than we now did and potentially more contract opportunities.

Brett

I got home from work a little later than usual. Trish was home already; she came out of her bedroom naked. "I ordered Chinese from around the corner. They should be delivering it shortly. Would you mind getting it since you're still dressed?"

Even after all our sexcapades, I couldn't stop looking at her amazing body. I stared at her as she walked up to me, slapped my arm, and laughed. "Hey! Focus. Are you okay with getting the door when they get here?"

"Uhh, yeah." I laughed and rubbed my arm from her slap. "How can I help but stare at you when you walk around like that?" I walked up behind her as she stood by the kitchen counter. I reached around with both hands to caress her breasts. Then I slowly kissed the back of her neck ever so softly. I moved my mouth to her ear, nipping it playfully with my teeth, and followed the firmness of her neck to her shoulders. I could feel her goosebumps form on her skin beneath my lips.

Knock, knock, knock.

"A shame … you were doing so well, too." Trish smirked as I walked to answer the door.

I set the food on the counter, then went to my bedroom and stripped down. Trish was digging into the cashew chicken when I returned to the kitchen.

I helped myself, sat back, and looked to Trish, who tossed her silky black hair over her shoulder. She looked at me and tilted her head with her eyes wide. She shrugged and then swallowed. "Stop staring, or I'll get dressed."

We both laughed. She asked, "So, you remember after that night with Megan?"

I eagerly looked up. I could never forget that evening.

"How could I forget?"

She smiled. "Remember when I joked around about pimping you out?"

I nodded. "Yeah, I said I wanted a cut, but I'll do that for free with Megan and you again."

"I talked with Megan and she was delighted with how well you turned her on at first and how passionate you were. She said she has a wealthy friend that needs an evening with a man who can make a woman feel as good as you made her feel."

"Are you seriously considering pimping me out?" I stared at her, no longer lustfully but with disbelief. And I hated to admit it, but a hint of intrigue too. The setup with Megan was much hotter than I'd expected, and I couldn't help but wonder about another.

"Well, it was a suggestion from Megan, and you could make a lot of money. Not many men are like you."

I stared at her, tilting my head, and ran my fingers through my hair. "How much would someone pay for something like that?" I put some more rice and chicken in my mouth, waiting for Trish to finish her mouthful.

She swallowed down. "You could make as much as one thousand for an evening."

I nearly choked on my rice as I gasped. "One thousand for one night of having sex? Do women make that much? There's no way."

"I'm serious. Some of these women are super wealthy, and a few thousand for one night of bliss is nothing for them. They just want attention and quality. Someone who knows how to please them."

"You're serious about this?" I knew prostitutes or escorts existed, and had even seen some on the streets, but to think of myself in that category was almost ridiculous.

There was a pause for a few moments while we ate, and I contemplated what Trish had just told me. Trish stood up. "Want some wine?" she asked.

I nodded and continued to stare in front of me, not focusing on anything in particular, trying to think of myself as a prostitute.

Trish returned, set my glass of wine in front of me, and sat down. "What are you thinking about?"

Warmth flooded my face as she caught my attention from imagining my new life as a prostitute. "Sooo, what you're saying is I could meet a stranger like Megan, she pays me a thousand dollars, I seduce her, have sex with her, and that's it?"

Trish tipped her glass of wine. "That's it. Maybe some role-playing, who knows, but you're giving them a fantasy experience."

"Why me? There have to be many men out there. Why would anyone be interested in me?"

"You're terrific at sex and a lot more confident than when I first met you. You're handsome, young, and not an ass like many men and ..." She paused and had a sincere look on her face. "You're a genuine person who wants to please a woman versus be with a woman to please yourself. That, Brett, is very rare."

I pondered for a few moments as I continued eating. Damn, If I could make a few thousand dollars for having an hour of sex with some rich woman, that would be incredible and help my mother and sister even more.

"What does this friend of Megan's look like?"

Trish looked surprised. "Really? You'd do it?"

"Well, if she's some seventy-year-old hag, then probably no, but if she's attractive and rich, I wouldn't mind too much older. Someone like Grace would be great."

I thought Trish was going to choke on her wine. "Grace, our boss?"

I laughed. "Yeah. I mean, she's definitely attractive." I thought about how she'd stopped by earlier that day, and the way she'd looked at me, like she was imagining my clothes off …

Yeah, I definitely wouldn't mind getting with someone like that.

Trish stared at me so hard I thought she might be trying to look into my soul. I asked, "What's the matter?"

She shook her head. "Nothing." She took another sip of wine, continuing to analyze me. "Most of these women want to wear a mask. They don't want their identity known. They simply want to be seduced and then leave without anyone recognizing them later. But most are attractive with nice figures."

I pondered it a few moments. "Okay, I'll do it. When do we set it up?"

"I'll ask Megan and find out, but I think she wanted to try for this weekend."

I finished the last of my chicken and rice and washed it down with some wine. I was trying to decide whether I should ask Trish a question or if it wouldn't be well received ... but I had to know. "You're a lot more comfortable with all this sex stuff than I'm used to. Especially with encouraging me to have sex with other women even though we have sex all the time. It seems a little strange."

"Sex is just sex. It's something that everyone should enjoy. Love is a commitment of souls who are bonded regardless of sex. If everyone simply opened up about sex, the world would be a much happier place."

I tipped my glass toward her. "I'll toast to that."

She clinked her glass to mine and smiled as we both took a sip.

Taylor

It had been a hectic and frustrating day. I recently had to let a couple of people go for trying to sell proprietary information. Now, trying to find their replacements had been a challenge. Sales reps for an engineering firm were not easy to come by. I'd had Trish working on our few recruiting booths coming up while I was also trying to work on the next SD event. Grace wanted me to plan for Brett to debut at that event and wanted our deep-pocket client to be his first. I was a little hesitant about using him for this client still. Someone willing to pay twenty thousand dollars for an evening better get everything she was looking for, and I wasn't convinced Brett was ready. But then again, I'd only experienced him once.

I logged onto my SD laptop and sent some reminders of an event night coming up. I liked to know how many clients we were expecting so I could line up the servi for their pleasure.

I wrote to our ever-so-eager client, Heather, to let her know we had a young man who we believed was just what she'd been seeking, then coordinated with some of my other subs to see who was available for the weekend to keep the other side of the event running as usual.

Before I closed my laptop, I received an email back from Heather.

I'll forward the 20k to the usual account today. And if you have more like this in the future, I might consider a regular occurrence. I'm looking forward to the next event. Heather.

I lingered over her email for a few minutes. The first test with Trish's acquaintance, Megan, had gone well and Grace would give him a shot this upcoming weekend, though I couldn't help but feel there was much on the line with this idea.

I shut down my computers. It was nearing closing hour, and I thought I'd take a walk around to see how the company was doing. Well, I ultimately wanted to see how Brett was doing.

I walked into his work area to find him sitting at his desk. He was shutting down his computer and looked up, surprised. "Ms. Williams … hi."

"Hi, Brett. How are you doing?"

"Uhh, I'm doing good, thank you. I'm working on a new—"

"Why don't you tell me over a drink for happy hour? I know a great place I think you'll like."

"Sure, just text me the address and I'll meet you there."

I looked at him in his newly acclimated clothing—plaid shirt, Dockers pants, and Sperry shoes. He had a youthful face but was undeniably handsome with his intoxicating eyes and broad shoulders.

"Ms. Williams?"

I snapped out of it. "Yeah, I'll text you the address and meet you there in, say, twenty minutes?"

"Sounds good."

I grabbed my briefcase and walked to my car. What was I doing? Everything seemed to be working as planned. Why risk messing everything up?

I sent Brett the address of a bar a block away from my condo. I drove home and changed into a more casual dress, then walked down to the bar where I saw him waiting for me at a table with a beer.

"I'm sorry I'm late. I live just next door and thought I'd change into something more relaxing."

"No problem. I didn't know what you wanted to drink, so I just got myself a beer until you arrived," Brett said as I caught him with a glance at my cleavage. He was far more subtle than that first night with him, but I exposed them purposefully, so it was expected.

The waitress stopped by to see what I wanted to drink. "I'll take a chardonnay please, and another beer for my friend." He was nearing the end of his pint, and I wanted him loosened up a little. Or perhaps he no longer needed liquid courage for what I had in mind.

"The last time you took me out and bought me drinks, we did a lot more than have drinks," he said, taking a slow slip of his beer.

His confidence and demeanor were far better than I remembered, and I winked at him. "We did indeed. I'm glad you hadn't forgotten."

"How could I forget? I'm only sorry I was so nervous." He took a long drink of what remained in his glass, then set it aside just as our server brought us the new round.

"Were you expecting the same end to your evening tonight when I asked you to meet me here?"

His face reddened, and he didn't seem to know how to respond other than a gaze into the copper blend within his pint. I suspect he didn't want to disclose that he was shacking up with Trish.

"Trish told me you were staying with her. She's quite generous and, of course, beautiful."

He seemed surprised. "Oh. She asked me not to say anything about that."

"It's wise you didn't tell anyone else, but she told me." I took a sip of wine as he did the same with his beer. A smile slowly formed on his face. "Why the smile?" I asked, placing my hand on his forearm. His devilish grin told me it was something worthwhile.

"I just imagined how much better I might have been with you had I known what I know now."

Wow, it would seem he wants a redo.

The buttery taste of my wine perfectly sweetened my desire to take him home with me, and I said, "Well, as I said, my condo is a block away. Perhaps you'd like to show me some of these newfound talents?"

He looked into my eyes, setting his beer down. "I'd like that a lot. Care to lead the way?"

I placed twenty dollars on the bar. We both slid off our barstools, and I said, "Right this way."

My core tightened that very moment as he took the initiative. I thought back to our first encounter, where I practically taught him everything. I was looking forward to finding out what he knew now.

We walked into the condo, and I heard the door shut behind me as I set my purse down on the table. I kept my back to him, waiting, and was surprised as he gripped my arms and spun me around to face him. His hungry gaze down at my cleavage only fueled the burning flame inside me. His firm, soft fingers confidently slid along my neck under my hair. I didn't even notice I was walking backward until my back met the wall. *Damn, he's good.*

"You're so beautiful." His hand softly gripped my throat, pushing my head against the wall, just hard enough that the sudden rush of adrenaline immediately turned the furnace in my core up to extreme heat. My breathing became rapid as he leaned in to kiss me ever so softly, like the touch of a feather. As I opened my lips to receive his kiss, he only brushed along them lightly, running his tongue around the rim of my lips while keeping my head firmly in position.

His other thumb caressed my cheek and then my lips. I opened my mouth as he slowly slipped his thumb inside. I began sucking on his thumb while he kissed my neck. "I'm going to fuck you mercilessly," he whispered.

My stomach tightened and I began sucking his thumb harder as my desire grew. He stared into my eyes, replacing his thumb with his two fingers, pushing them in deeper. I concentrated to not gag, while I stared into his eyes as he pushed his fingers to my tonsils. Then he released my throat, stepping slightly away from me to pull my dress up and over my head. With a snap of his fingers, he had my bra unhooked. Damn, he was so much more than when we first met.

"Wow, you *have* been practicing."

He sported a confident grin, his gaze taking me in from head to toe. The desire in his expression alone turned my want to need, and my nipples puckered under his lustful stare.

He caressed one of my breasts and then slowly brought his fingers around my aching nipple. He closed his warm lips around it, and I gasped as he bit tenderly.

My hands moved eagerly to his head, gripping firmly as I encouraged him to explore with more intensity. His tongue laved hungrily against mine, and I felt the heat spread through my core, my need for more of his touch growing rapidly. As our kiss intensified, he effortlessly guided me backward until I felt the bedroom wall meet my back. One hand lingered at my breast, teasing the tip until a shudder passed along my skin, then glided lower, slipping easily into my panties and over my mound.

With a powerful gaze that demanded attention, he asked me to look into his eyes as his fingers toyed expertly between my legs. A fire of pleasure built up inside me as I felt myself melting into the sensation. His other hand caressed my throat as a wave of shock sent my heart racing. He had an almost supernatural power over me—I wanted him deeper within me than I'd thought possible. Everything in me longed for his touch, and yet he continued to tantalize me further.

He looked into my eyes as he slid his fingers down and pushed them inside me. His grip on my throat was intimidating as he began to aggressively fingerfuck me. I squirmed, pressing back into the wall as the heat inside me built to a crescendo. Holding me immobile, he continued to mercilessly fuck me with his fingers until I was sure I would explode.

And then he whispered, "Come for me."

I couldn't help myself. I nodded and could hear my own panting while my muscles clenched as a wave rocked my body. The sound of water against his fingers as he continued to fuck me sent me past the edge all over again, my entire being shaking with release. If he weren't holding me up, I was sure I'd be on the floor.

Finally, he relaxed his hand on my throat and led me to the bedroom. "I want to see that pretty mouth around my cock."

Licking my lips, my gaze went to his pants. He hastily removed his shoes and shirt as I pulled his pants down and tossed them aside. His thick shaft jutted out toward me, and I grabbed it like a lifeline. I needed this. I had never been so hungry for a cock in my life. I'd had a lot of sex, but nothing had exhilarated me the way Brett was. Not even those weekend subs who I could do what I wanted with. Something about how Brett took control had me ravenous, and I sucked on him feverishly, licking along his shaft and his balls. When he grabbed the back of my hair, I froze.

"I want to fuck you. Hard." And then he pulled me up by my hair.

Holy shit. He was much more than I was expecting.

He pushed me onto the bed facedown, then took down my panties and spread my legs apart. I lay there with my face against the comforter, my ass in the air, just waiting for whatever he was going to do next. When his cock teased my entrance, I couldn't help the gasp that escaped my lips. I wanted him … all of him, but he entered me slowly, stopping when just the tip of his cock was in, then pulling out and doing it all over again. I panted and whimpered at his teasing. The sensation of his large head along that part of my inner wall was driving me insane.

I tried to back into him, but he kept me in place, pulling one arm behind me to keep me pinned to the mattress.

The sharp pain, with immediate pleasure, sent a shockwave through my body as he suddenly forced himself in. I cried out, gripping the comforter, only for him to follow up by fucking me halfway again.

"Please, Brett. Fuck me harder … just use me." I was beside myself at what I had just said. I'd been a Domina for years, always in control. *Please* was never in my sex vocabulary, and here I was begging for him to fuck me.

His thrust filled me immediately. I cried out again as he continued to plunge himself into me hard and deliberately. I tried clenching my muscles around his cock, but I didn't need to. He stretched me out just right, and I gladly endured every bit of him.

He pulled out of me, turned me over, and set my ass on the edge of the bed. Before I could flick my hair out of my eyes, he was inside me again, fucking me mercilessly. I couldn't believe how hot it was to be used however he wanted.

I answered each thrust with a cry of pleasure. He gripped my throat again. An intensity in his eyes caused me to embrace what seemed like a bit of fear, again an emotion I was only versed in giving. "I'm going to come deep inside of you."

"Yes!" I cried out; my body erupted and clenched around him. "Yes! Come for me! I want it!"
He grunted hard as his cock jolted inside. I glided my hands along his well-sculpted muscles and could feel the waves of his eruption pulsing deep within me. Once relaxed, he kept his cock inside and leaned down to seal my lips with his.

"A lot better than last time, wasn't it?" He smirked.

I laughed. "Wow, you can say that again."

He pulled out and climbed up behind me, connecting our bodies as one. His hand slid up to my breast and gently caressed it. "Just out of curiosity, you weren't wanting to meet for a drink, were you?" he asked as though he already knew the answer.

I chuckled. "I guess you got me. I enjoyed our last encounter, and to be honest, I had a hard day and needed to get laid. I wasn't expecting you to be *this* good."

He kissed my shoulder. "Thanks. Can I get a testimonial?"

My burst of laughter even surprised me. "Building a new resume, are you?"

"Maybe."

It seemed Trish was doing a much better job than I had expected. Grace should be happy with how he'd evolved.

Trish

Fortunately, I didn't need to stop anywhere after my client engagement. It would have been a little embarrassing to stop for gas with ripped clothes, but that was the least of my worries. The lacerations on my dress were large enough to reveal areas best left hidden. Without a bra, my chest dared to peek from beneath the torn fabric. I had to use my hair clip to keep the top of my dress together; it was makeshift, but it would suffice.

I typically kept a bag of clothes with me when I visited a client, but this one was short notice, and I wasn't prepared. This particular client enjoyed interviewing young babysitters, like myself, and I was just what he was looking for. My role was to resist his advances before he forced himself on me. This was one of my most enjoyable role-playing scenarios, providing the client didn't get too carried away. We discussed rules before our first encounter and explained that with any violation of the rules, I would leave without a refund. But I'd enjoy the five thousand for the past hour even more. The fact that he was an attractive, fifty-something businessman didn't hurt either. I could easily replace this simple sundress with that kind of money.

I laughed, realizing my pigtails were still in my hair. I pulled the hair ties out and tried to blend it all while driving, but it was no use. Disheveled was the best it would get.

Brett said he was out for drinks with a colleague, so I should have enough time to get home, shower, and change before he got home. I'd hate to have him see me like this. He would ask a bunch of questions, and I wasn't ready to answer him. I didn't need to answer him, but I still wanted ed to avoid an awkward situation.

I walked to the apartment door and put my hand on my cheek. It was a little tender from some of the slaps I'd received for resisting earlier. I needed to incorporate some type of training in my clients before these rendezvous.

I walked in the door to find Brett standing at the kitchen counter, pouring a glass of wine. He smiled at me, but his expression turned to wide-eyed panic when he saw my clothes. Wine splashed onto the countertop as he overfilled his glass.

"What happened? Are you all right?" He walked up to me and took my purse to set it down, and the envelope fell to the floor. "Were you attacked?"

I wanted to say, "You could say that," but thought better of it.

I smiled. "Yes, I'm just fine, but I need to take a shower."

"Did someone hit you?"

Ha, did he ever.

"I'm fine, Brett." I picked up my envelope but couldn't shove it back into my purse before he got a look at the cash stuffed inside.

He squinted at me and slowly backed away. "What's going on?" His voice expressed an almost psychological pain. He gestured to the money and then to my ripped clothes.

I sighed. "Let me take a shower and change. Pour me some wine, and I'll let you know."

I drifted into my bedroom, mind racing. What would I tell him? Should I be honest, or fabricate a story? I had to send him to Grace tomorrow – it wouldn't be long before he found out the truth. I turned on the shower and stepped inside, hoping the hot steam would clear my head and help me with an answer.

I walked back to him, cleaned up and with my pajamas on. He had a glass of wine waiting for me in the living room. I grabbed the glass and sat in the chair with my legs crossed, still unsure what to say. I took a long drink and then a deep breath.

"I'm a high-paid escort. I think you already know that I like a little rough play, but I like extreme role-playing also, and I have clients who pay a lot of money for me to do that with them."

His eyes widened as he asked, "They pay to beat you?" Fear laced his words.

I placed my hand on my cheek, contemplating a response. I hoped some intelligent replies would come with my next sip of wine. "I do like a little rough play, but the client I was with hit me a little harder than I prefer. He apologized, and I will remind him in the future."

Brett shook his head as though he didn't believe a word I'd just said. I gulped down the remaining wine, then grabbed the bottle to refill my glass.

"What type of role-playing were you doing?" he asked me. I wasn't sure how much further to take this explanation with him.

"I was role-playing a babysitter who was interviewing for a job, and then he forced himself on me." Short, sweet, and direct.

"Damn, Trish! That's something you're into? You like to be raped?" He shook his head and looked everywhere but at me for answers that could better explain the rationale to him.

When he said it like that, it did sound irrational.

I glared at him, my words vibrating with anger. "Let me be absolutely clear: You have no right to judge me. And don't even think of judging any-one else unless you fully understand a situation. I truly enjoy extreme scenes, and clients who are properly vetted and pay an exorbitant amount for discre-tion—it's a professional business relationship based on fantasy role-playing that is consensual and strictly within pre-determined boundaries. Have no doubt about that. I am an expert in creating a secure atmosphere."

My voice was cold and brittle like broken glass. He looked down at the coffee table like he had been gutted and gulped down the last of his wine in one swallow before raising his head again slowly, eyes accusing. "Was this what you were talking about the other day? You've been doing this all along and now you want me to join in too?"

My heart sank. He'd figured it out and suddenly, I felt like shit. I was usually much quicker in answering any question, but I didn't know how to answer this one.

He stood up and walked toward his room. "I need to think." I heard the door close behind him with a loud thud.

Shit! Did I just fuck this up for Grace? I drank the last of my wine and poured another glass. I thought about it a moment. How I'd snapped at him, and yet I was deceptively trying to turn him into a prostitute. I could either let him come up with his own understanding of what was happening or lead him to an understanding by talking to him.

I knocked on the door. "Brett ... can I come in and talk?" There was no response. "Brett?" I opened the door, and my blood froze like ice in my veins when I saw him packing his clothes.

"Brett, what are you doing?"

"This entire time I've been here was for you to teach me to be a male prostitute, wasn't it? Some whore for you to make a profit on!"

I sat down on the end of the bed, trying to find an answer that wasn't a lie but also wasn't the truth. "I stumbled on this world of wealthy people who want to throw their money at people who are smart, young, attractive, and confident. I've made over two hundred thousand dollars in cash in the past two years. I've never been put in danger and could refuse anything I didn't want to do. I enjoy sex, and I enjoy role-playing. So, I offer a unique service to those who want to pay for this."

"And you just assumed I would want to also?" He paused and stared at me, waiting for an answer.

"I was hoping …" I said, looking down at the comforter. "I wanted a partner I could trust and understand me. Someone I could confide in, and maybe even work as a team with some clients. You are deliciously handsome, have a deep sexy voice, and your body is … well, it's wonderful. All you needed was some confidence and additional coaching on pleasing a woman. That's the part I was trying to give you."

His one eye squinting at me showed that he was contemplating my words. "Were Megan and Taylor in on this plot?"

"Megan is a good friend, and I wanted another opinion on how good you are. Why do you ask about Taylor?"

"She's who I had drinks with earlier, and then she took me to her condo. She wanted to see if I was any better than when she recruited me at school. Was that another test?"

I was stunned. "I had no idea about that. At all. That was all her." I didn't know whether to be surprised or pissed or both that she would do something like that. She could have also influenced the emotional meltdown he was having right now.

"Brett, don't go this way." I wiped a tear from my cheek. I wasn't sure if it was the potential to lose my deal with Grace or whether I genuinely had feelings for him. Either way, I was forming an attachment to him, which I didn't want to happen.

"Why shouldn't I? Was the entire act of hiring me a setup? A plot?"

Damn! He was much smarter than I thought.

"I don't know anything about that. I just know that when I met you, I found you attractive, and I thought you might be interested in working with me, making a lot more money than you could ever imagine. That's what I've been trying to do, and I'm sorry you found out this way."

He rolled up the polo shirts in his hand and threw them at the dresser. They bounced off and unraveled on the floor. "Damn! I …"

He sat down next to me, silent. Then he took a deep breath and said, "I'm sorry. I developed feelings for you, Trish, and you made it obvious that you didn't have the same feelings, and then … this!" He paused with his hands open, expressing the enormity of what he had just learned. "I can't help but feel used and deceived this whole time. I don't know what to believe."

I didn't have good answers for him because, in reality, he *was* being used and was about to be used a lot more.

It had been a long time since I'd had any attachment to a man, and I always vowed I would just treat them cold and without regard. I took on Brett because I was getting paid to and he was an attractive man and my instincts told me I would like him. Now that I knew him better, I couldn't help but feel guilty about what we were doing. Brett was caring and kind, and I'd just hurt him.

I placed my hand on his, happy that he held it. I usually didn't do silence very well. I was never at a loss for words but now found myself speechless. I wiped another tear from my cheek.

"Brett, when we talked about the concept of having sex for money, and when I say money, I mean thousands of dollars, you seemed excited about it then. Was that just acting, or were you interested in it?"

He stared at his suitcase for a moment, then clenched my hand a little tighter. His thumb caressed the back of my hand. I hadn't felt that endearment from someone—someone I cared about—in a long time.

"I thought it would be intriguing. The thought of you making over two hundred thousand in a couple of years in cash ... well, I'm intrigued with that, but it feels like the entire reason I'm here was to be exploited as some sex novelty ..."

"You were recruited because you're a good engineer, top of your class in college, and any firm like ours would die to have you. Don't throw that away," I pleaded while caressing his arm. Was I afraid of losing him? I didn't want to go through that again.

He stared at the dresser against the wall, then looked into my eyes. I smiled sincerely back at him and was getting lost in the gold within his emerald green eyes when he brought his hand up to my throat.

Goosebumps covered my body in alarm, but I remained still, showing a little fear even though my inner exhilaration had switched on.

"Is this something you like too?" he asked, gripping more firmly. I was scared because he was upset and not too experienced with choking, but I wanted to see where he would take this.

My heart raced, embracing his firm grip as a new side of Brett emerged. His grip was tight, and he could take me right here if he wanted, but I wasn't going to seduce him while he was emotional like this.

He removed his hand and looked at me.

"Did you like my reaction when you grabbed my throat? My look of fear and anticipation?" I asked.

His eyes darted to his hand, my throat, my eyes, and finally over my body. He had complete control of me. He nodded.

"I did, actually. I read how to do that in one of your books and did it for the first time with Taylor. She had the same reaction."

"That's good, I'm glad those books helped." However, I wasn't crazy about Taylor getting involved.

I caressed his leg. "This is what I've been trying to help you better understand. This is the nirvana sex that many women will never experience. The wealthy ones are willing to pay a lot of money to experience it, but it needs to be someone who is also respectful, caring, and confident."

"Do you really think I have what it takes to be this?"

"I do. You have it all, but if you want out, I'll cancel the rendezvous with the client I have set up tomorrow, and we can forget about all of this. If you're still interested, you get a thousand dollars to simply rock her world for an hour."

"I thought you said five thousand. Are you cheating me already?"

I looked up at him, surprised by his comment. Then I saw the smirk on his face and pushed him to the bed, laughing.

He sat back up and continued laughing. He caressed my leg and nodded. "I'll do it tomorrow, but I need some time to consider additional clients."

I sprouted a wry grin, rubbed his leg, and seductively whispered in his ear, "So if you had a chance to make five thousand dollars to have sex with me in front of another man, would you be interested?"

"Are you serious? They do that?"

I nodded. "There are many kinky people out there with a lot of money. Some just like to watch a young, hot couple have live sex in front of them, or maybe put on a show for their perverted guests at a party."

He looked dumbfounded. Then he smiled. "That would be kinda hot."

"I know, right? Now, you know why I'm involved in it. I'm very selective, and the money is incredible."

"Let's see how tomorrow night works out," he said as he pulled me in for a hug. "And thanks for coming in to talk to me."

Grace

Taylor gave Trish the address for SD. I went early to ensure our new room was set up as I wanted. When I walked in, I saw the door was closed to the main BDSM section, leaving another door to the left, which led to our new seduction room.

I walked into the room and was impressed. The furnishings were a rich burgundy with large pieces of fine furniture scattered around to create a cozy space where one could lounge in comfort. In the middle of the room was an oversized leather sectional with a matching chair at one end, a coffee table in front of it, and an ottoman.

A warm bed—with a soft headboard—sat against the wall opposite the door, within arm's reach of yet another piece of fine furniture, a polished wood desk. I walked up to the bed and ran my hands along the smooth surface, felt the coolness of the metal rings attached to the wood, and imagined all that they might be used for.

To my right stood a private hot tub large enough for four people. The temperature was ideal: 99 degrees. Perfect for relaxation but not so hot as to cause discomfort or injury. Across from me on the other side of this bit of calm luxury was a small bar complete with everything needed to whip up some amazing drinks.

I pulled out two flutes, carefully popped open a bottle of champagne, and poured myself a glass. Taking a moment to enjoy it before setting about touching up my makeup and hair, I surveyed my surroundings once again. A giant bear skin rug rested on top of a layer of soft padding placed on the floor while delicate scented candles perfumed the air.

We constantly evaluated and fine-tuned our rooms based on client feedback and the evolving needs of our participants. I took great pride in creating the perfect setting for carnal desires to be fulfilled. I enjoyed these memories while walking through the facility alone, remembering the origin of a particular item, especially those that elicited rave reviews and became client favorites.

I took a few sips of champagne and paused to reminisce on one evening with twelve servi in a circle, their heads bowed down toward the center and asses up to form a clock.

Several of our Dominae took turns selecting names of random implements from a Viking helmet and then choosing which servus to use it on. I wasn't surprised that the man who ended up with the giant studded alien dildo never returned.

Shaking off those mental images, I made my way to the bathroom, which had a spa-like feel and a shower big enough for six people. The bench in the shower was a nice addition. Though my schedule didn't always permit it, I had ensured I would have ample time to unwind and prepare for the evening. If it went as I envisioned, it would expand our offering and open a new outlet for our kink-minded community.

Sinking myself into the soft texture of the bench, I lifted the flute, allowing the bubbles to tease my nose before hitting my palate and tickling my throat. My mind quickly went to what else may tickle my throat later. I began to play the scene I had planned in my mind as I disrobed and headed toward the shower.

While it was still business, I had every intention of enjoying the evening, and I was going to start with a little self-indulgence. One thing the BDSM world had taught me was that something as simple as the right fabric and softness of a bench, along with the perfect lighting and ambiance, could mentally invite those willing to open their minds to explore.

Scent was also integral to the experience, which I incorporated into the candles, body wash, and hand lotions. The scent, my own personal concoction, included a touch of eucalyptus to awaken the spirit and was finished with a slight undertone of sandalwood. Thanks to my local essential oil shop and a lot of experimentation, I landed on a scent that appealed to both men and women and created the allure and mystery I wanted for the brand I was creating.

Turning the shower on to a setting as hot as I could stand, I stepped in, lathered up my loofah, and ran it across my skin, reminiscing on my evenings in DC with Nick. The mind was such a powerful aphrodisiac. When properly provoked, it held the keys to extraordinary sexual adventures. Tap the mind, and the body would follow. I had even progressed to giving myself mental orgasms, though that was not on today's agenda. For now, I just took the time to inhale the aroma and enjoy an extended steamy shower as I continued to run through tonight's scene in my mind. The heat opened my pores and allowed for the extra smooth shave I wanted for Brett's evaluation. I hoped Trish had taught Brett to do the same. Once a woman sucked on a smooth cock, she'd never want a hairy one again.

Stepping out of the shower, I finished my ritual with some body oil scented the same as the shower wash. Then I turned my attention to hair and makeup before putting on the black, skintight, formal dress I had chosen specifically for this encounter. The mirror showed off my curves nicely, and the length hit just the right place on my leg to show off my calves. A finishing touch to add some green contact lenses. With the deep blue contrast behind them, my eye color was fabulous. I stared intently at the color combination and wondered why I had never thought to do that before.

I selected a mask that covered my face well. It might shock him if he found out who I really was. Then it dawned on me … my voice. He would recognize my voice for sure. Damn! I usually thought everything through so well. How could I not have thought of that?

He should be here any minute, and I didn't know what to do. I mulled it over while I placed my mask on, ensuring my hair was accessible without the risk of my mask coming off. I just wouldn't talk and see how good he was with a challenge.

I looked in the mirror for one last check when the doorbell rang.

I walked to the entryway and opened the door. There he was, wearing a nice button-down linen shirt. His rolled up sleeves showed off his well-defined forearms, and he wore nice, black dress slacks, leather shoes, and a bandit mask like the Lone Ranger. A wave of cologne hit my nose, creating an impulse to take a deep breath. I couldn't determine what brand, but it complemented him well.

"Hello," he said in a deep and confident tone. I saw his eyes grow wide for a moment, and then he scanned my body and took a deep breath. He must have figured out it was me.

I opened the door and gestured for him to walk in and through the door to our room. He walked in as I followed. He turned to look into my eyes, but when our eyes connected, he tilted his head in thought. He paused, looked me over, then placed his hands on my hips and pulled me close. "I must say, you look stunning." He deliberately gazed at my entire body and then looked back into my eyes. "I'm going to enjoy ravishing your fine body." I placed my hands on his chest and looked into his eyes. I wanted to say something but couldn't risk it.

"Is everything okay?" he asked.

I nodded, then pointed to my throat.

"Oh, you can't talk?"

I shook my head as I slid my hand up his chest and behind his neck. I found it difficult to restrain myself from taking charge, but I wanted to see him take the lead. My not talking made it a little more complex.

He dragged his fingers through my hair and gripped it tightly, sending electricity down my spine. Our eyes locked as he kissed along my exposed throat, tracing patterns with his tongue while biting down on me intermittently. Trish had trained him well; he knew exactly what to do to make me feel vulnerable in the best way possible.

His hands glided down my shoulders and stomach, caressing every inch of me before stopping at my hips. He guided me toward the mirror, and I watched in awe as he towered over me with confidence.

I glanced up at him standing tall over me, commanding power over my body with a newfound confidence as his mouth kept exploring every bit of exposed skin. The view of his hands caressing me was so intensely erotic that I gasped for air.

"I want you to watch me undress you," he breathed against me in a husky voice, and I shivered again from anticipation. Other than Nick, no man had ever taken control of me like this before—and I reveled in it.

He slowly unzipped my dress from behind, his mouth following the zipper's trail down my back. When the dress fell to the floor, he placed his hands on my bare hips, slid them forward to my stomach, and then up my body. My breathing grew heavy with expectation as he approached my breasts, only for him to slide his hands to my back. He unfastened my bra, easing it off.

My body was on fire. Perhaps more so, given the stark contrast to our first encounter. This was far from what that spontaneous evening had provided in Cancun.

I kept catching myself holding my breath as I awaited his next move.

My body was heating up, but the silence was deafening. I moved away and put my index finger up to indicate a moment of time. I leaned down to grab the remote from the coffee table and turned on some music before returning to my position in front of the mirror.

Goosebumps burst up from my skin at his delicate touch on my breasts. He squeezed hard then let up and caressed my nipples with the pressure of a feather.

He concentrated his mouth at the back of my neck, each kiss raising my hair with titillation. He slowly ran his teeth down to my shoulder. A light bite on my skin sent even more shivers through my body. My core was on fire, and it had dire needs.

"Keep watching in the mirror," he whispered as one hand moved down my stomach. His fingers disappeared into my panties. He lubricated his fingers with the abundant evidence of my arousal before gliding them around my clit. I didn't realize how turned on I was until my inner core began to pulsate with desire. My hips gave me away as they began to move under him. His pelvis rubbed against my ass, where I could also feel his apparent arousal.

We made eye contact in the mirror, and he whispered, "Come for me."

I nodded and panted out loud as he hit the right spot. I felt the pressure inside me building, and I moaned. I wanted more—needed more. I reached down, placed his fingers where I wanted them, and pressed more firmly against my clit. Electric tingles shot through me, radiating from my center, and I arched into him, holding his hand where I needed it most. My body shivered as I finally came. My desire to take some control overcame me. My voice was so thick with lust I didn't even sound like myself when I whispered, "I want you to fuck me right now."

He gripped my hair from behind and tilted my head into submission. His firm control paralyzed me. "You'll get fucked, all right, as soon as I think you're ready for me."

I whimpered and nodded to him. I'd never been this submissive, yet all I could think of at that moment was how much I wanted to be taken. It had been a long time since any man but Nick had turned me on like this.

His pants dropped to the floor, and I turned and knelt before him. As I took him in my hand and ran my lips and tongue along his smooth shaft and balls, my pussy clenched in needy anticipation. I ached for him. I lifted my mask slightly, wrapped my mouth around him, and began sucking and licking. I sucked on one ball gently while stroking him. He continued to look down at me with a smile. I could just see his face through the eye holes of the mask; I hoped he couldn't see mine.

I vigorously sucked on his cock, but I craved more. He grabbed my elbow, and I reset my mask as he guided me in front of the sofa. He laid me down on the ottoman and took his shirt off, showing his fabulous muscle definition ... much more built than I remembered five years ago.

He knelt between my legs when his eyes immediately grew wide ... almost horrified. He stood up and backed away, scratching his hair while staring at my thigh.

"I know you," he said in a dull tone of disbelief. "The woman from Cancun. That tattoo on your thigh, I recognize it. Vicky?"

He sat down in a chair and removed his mask. "Wow, I thought I'd never see you again." His eyes got wide with anticipation and enthusiasm.

He did remember, but thought I was Vicky. It was a rare moment in my life when I didn't know what to do. I sat up and removed my mask.

"Grace? You're Vicky?" He sat back with a tilted head, trying to rapidly put puzzle pieces together in his mind. "Did you stalk me all these years?"

He shook his head and looked for the door.

"Brett, please let me explain."

"Was Trish behind all of this too? Of course, she was. She set me up with this. Is your entire company in on this? Taylor, Trish, and you … oh my God, the other engineers are in on this?"

He breathed heavily and stood up to walk around, scratching his head.

"I hired you because you were the best in your class with the education we wanted. I learned about Taylor's evening with you, and that's when we thought about introducing you to something like this."

He snapped his head up, his gaze burning directly into mine. "Did you have Trish take me in to do some type of training on me to make me part of your sex cult?"

"That wasn't the plan." Damn! I always knew this could be a risk, but I wasn't prepared as I should have been. "We just asked Trish to take you in until you could get a car and apartment."

"If Trish wasn't involved, how did she know about tonight? She set me up with some client, and it happened to be you! She comes home with her clothes ripped and beat up, but with an envelope full of cash. I can't help but think you're all in this together and were grooming me to be part of it."

At this point, I didn't think there was a lie I could come up with that would satisfy him, so perhaps some truth would be best.

"Brett, you want the truth?"

He nodded.

"Would you like me to be dressed when I tell you this truth? Or perhaps you'd prefer me to stay naked?"

He looked me over, and then he shrugged.

"Let's be adults and discuss this openly, but I want some champagne. Would you like some?"

He shook his head. "No, thank you."

I went to retrieve and refill my flute, collected my thoughts, and sat down in a lounger near Brett. He was sitting back in his chair, trying not to look at me.

"Remember our time in Cancun?"

He nodded.

"I was married then, and my company was just taking off. I wanted more attention but wasn't getting anything from my husband. You happened to be at the right place at the right time when I needed a fix. You were just the fuck I needed. I go by a different name when I travel so people don't know who I am. When I met you at your school's industry day, I recognized you immediately and remembered how fantastic you were. It wasn't appropriate to remind you then, now, was it?"

A faint, sheepish smile curved his lips before he shook his head.

"I had built a great company, a company you're happy to work in, aren't you?"

"I'm thrilled to work for your company."

"I'm not going to lie to you. I have some wealthy clients who need to feel wanted again, feel alive, vibrant, and beautiful. They will pay thousands of dollars to have what you were in the process of giving me. These women are busy businesswomen with a void in their life, and someone like you can give them that little boost of self-esteem and improve their lives. They are all beautiful and successful women who want to be discreet. Could you see yourself making a few thousand dollars to make a woman feel alive again?"

He looked at me again and then to the floor, and then his gaze slid over my body. "I don't know, I ... I need some time to think about this."

I stood up and walked to the bar to refill my champagne glass. I knew Brett was watching my naked saunter, and I turned to catch him gazing at me.

He blushed as I took a sip. He was curious; I knew he was.

There was more at stake than simply pimping him out for cash. Some of these high-powered women had landed me millions in contract opportunities, and having someone like Brett onboard could bring in even more based on the interest we'd received.

"Brett, many of these women lack affection and lust in their lives. They want a man to want them, crave them, for an hour or two. What they pay varies, but you would get fifty percent."

"Fifty percent of what? How much do these women pay?"

"Some pay ten thousand dollars. We have one woman who is eager, right now, to pay twenty thousand dollars."

His eyes widened as he leaned forward, staring into mine. "I would get ten thousand dollars to have sex with another woman right here like I did with you?"

"You mean like you almost did with me."

I caught his lips twitching in a smile before he returned to a straight face.

I took another sip and nodded. "There is one catch, though."

"Of course, there is."

"If you've calmed down now, perhaps we can discuss over some champagne in the hot tub. There's no point in letting fantastic bubbly go to waste. Besides, something tells me you enjoy looking at my body."

He shrugged and nodded reluctantly. "I'll stay for a little while to hear more, but it doesn't mean I'll do it."

"Of course. I don't want you to be angry and leave my company. I'll respect any decision you make."

I stepped into the hot tub and motioned for Brett to join me. He stood up and walked over but just sat on the edge. His legs parted, allowing a clear display of his cock to hang down along the spa wall. I took a deep breath, realizing I probably wouldn't have that in me as I had hoped.

"I realize I should have come clean with you earlier, but I wasn't quite sure how it would play out. We asked Trish to take you in and give us some insight into what you were like. She was not part of our group. In fact, I'm still learning more about Trish."

"Yeah, so am I," he murmured.

He continued to run his hand along the back of his neck, and his eyes darted everywhere for answers. I didn't know how to cure his troubled mind other than maybe offer him a way out if he wanted, but I needed a decision.

"Brett, here's the deal I'll make with you. You can have fifty percent of the proceeds from each lady you're with. You can have a fantastic time here and continue thriving in my company in a career field you truly enjoy, or …"

"Or?" he replied.

"Or, I will pay you twenty thousand dollars and have you flown back home to Virginia to try a career elsewhere. No questions asked, but I would ask that you sign a nondisclosure agreement, of course."

His eyes lit up at the twenty thousand to go home. I sipped my sparkling wine, thinking how I had just lost my investment in him, and all my effort was for naught.

"How often do you have these women come here?" he asked.

"We usually have an event here twice a month on the weekends. You can come here every weekend if you like, and we can arrange a new woman every time. That would be perhaps an additional twenty thousand dollars of cash in your pockets every month. Think about what you could do to help your mom and sister."

Now, his eyes lit up.

I let him have the time to think about it. The music was just enough distraction not to make our situation more awkward. He scanned around the room, pausing to study a few artifacts I had for decoration, then looked back at me.

I smiled up at him and sipped my drink, waiting for him to tell me he wanted out.

"Can I try it once and make my decision afterward?"

I sat up with enthusiasm. "Of course, you can. That first client wants to pay twenty thousand, so you will get ten thousand from your first encounter."

"I'll do it, but make sure she's attractive."

I stood up in the spa. Water ran down the contours of my body, and Brett stared. "Do you think I'm attractive?"

"You're very attractive."

"Almost all the women who come here are just as attractive as I am, or better."

He nodded, stood up, and walked to get his clothes.

I sighed. "Are we not going to finish our little session tonight?"

"I'm still pissed at how everyone deceived me. I need to think everything through, but I'll take you up on your offer for that first encounter where I make ten thousand."

"That's fair. Think it through and enjoy the rest of your night."

He walked out, and I sat back down in the spa, gulped the last of the champagne in my glass, and contemplated how I could have done this any better.

Brett

I woke to the smell of coffee. I'd gotten in late after driving around to clear my head. How could some engineering graduate from nowhere Virginia become the primary focus for some secret sex group in California? I didn't know how to talk to Trish either. I was still piecing together what had happened, as well as my feelings for Trish and whether she actually had feelings for me. If all of this was simply to lure me into being some man whore, I might take Grace's offer to return home and start over.

When I'd gotten in last night, I was too disappointed to do anything but go to sleep. And now it was morning, and I still had to figure out whether to give everything up and move back home with twenty thousand or become this high-paid gigolo that Trish and Grace believed I could be.

With a sigh, I slipped on my pajama bottoms, which I had never worn while living here, and walked out to see Trish sitting in a chair naked with her cup of coffee in her hands. She looked up at me and smiled. "Sorry if I woke you. How was your evening?"

"Oh, with Grace? I haven't decided yet how it was or how it will be in the future."

She blinked slowly, her mouth slightly open. "So, you know?"

I poured coffee into a cup and sat on the sofa, letting the silence stir her mind a little longer. "I'm still a little foggy on some details, but I know about the overall campaign to groom me for a role as a man-whore. Apparently, she thinks you did a great job."

It was one of the only times I'd ever seen Trish blush. She took a sip of her coffee. I could tell she was searching for the right words, so I sipped my coffee too, letting her squirm.

"When did you put it all together?"

"I began putting it together last night as I connected the dots between Taylor, seeing you come home from your client, and what you told me. But then when I recognized Grace last night and realized she was the woman who fucked me in Cancun when I was eighteen, all the dots connected to give me a clear picture. She tried to get away without talking, but I recognized her tattoo on the crease of her leg." Trish sat there listening and looked reluctant to say anything further.

"What more did you discuss?" she asked.

Realizing she was still playing me, my irritation heightened, but I would probably be doing the same thing if I were in her shoes. "The entire satisfying her clients thing. You know, the thing you've been training me for this entire time?"

"She told you that?" Trish snapped.

"She said you initially agreed to help me find a place, stay with you, and evaluate me."

She sipped her coffee. A pregnant pause filled the room.

"So now what?" she asked while staring at the floor. She wouldn't even look at me. I let the silence continue for a few moments. I debated whether to hate-fuck her right here on the sofa or leave her and go to a hotel. My mind was all over the place. Her naked body had always been irresistible, but right now, I just couldn't.

She groomed me to be a prostitute with total disregard for whether I was interested or not. Still, I couldn't discount what she did for me by teaching me so much. And, of course, the sex was mind-blowing, her personality and wit were intoxicating, and I had fallen for her. How could I ever be mad at her?

I sipped my coffee and tried to keep a straight face. "Well, I think at a minimum, you should be punished."

She laughed. "Punished? How do you intend on doing that?"

I tried to maintain a serious expression, but my mouth twitched into a smile despite my efforts. "I'm going to force you to wash me *thoroughly* in the shower and then take me out shopping to find some good clothes for my new sex god role."

"What?" She squinted and shook her head, confused with a slight laugh.

"Grace provided me a choice. She would give me twenty thousand in severance and let me go home, or give me half of what the women pay, and I seduce them for an hour or two every week or every other week. It was up to me."

"And you decided to go for it?"

"I decided to give it a try. Knowing how much you made in a couple of years, and how much I could make from Grace every month … it's hard to turn down that much money. I mean, I enjoy sex, and I could use that kind of money to help my mom and sister."

She laughed, rolled her eyes, and stood up to slap my arm. "I can't believe you had me squirming all this time. I was truly ashamed for putting you through all that, and then you accepted the role anyhow?"

"Oh, I'm still pissed off at all the deception and scheming, but I'll probably get over it. Especially since I don't think I'd want to leave you."

She set her coffee on the table, took my hand, and tugged me up. "Well, let's get my punishment over with."

I set my coffee down and followed her to the shower.

* * *

I enjoyed our time together as we shopped around Santa Clara and the Silicon Valley area. She had me try on clothes I never thought I'd wear, but they looked great. I also had never paid more than fifty dollars on a pair of shoes, but the two-hundred-dollar Aldo's did give me style I hadn't had before. We had a great time spending the day together, goofing around, and holding hands. At one point, we walked by a country western boot store playing some slow music. We dropped our bags and began to dance. A small crowd of a dozen people gathered around us to watch. I surprised Trish with a couple of twirls and then a dip at the end that I'd learned from my mom. We laughed and bowed at the round of applause when the song finished.

Her personality and her laugh were exhilarating. The way her silky, black hair shined in the sunlight and her long eyelashes enhanced her gorgeous, brown eyes drew my need for her even closer. I couldn't deny it any longer. I was falling for her. I knew she had her life, and it didn't involve being romantically involved with anyone, but my feelings were what they were. I didn't care who she fucked. Hell, I'd love to even join her in some of those role-playing scenarios she described. But I wanted what they wouldn't get—her heart and her soul.

We went to dinner at a nearby bistro famous for its tapas. I ordered some pinot noir and asked, "We've spent a month together and I don't know anything about your background."

She took a sip of wine, pondered a moment, and then looked at me. "Perhaps it's better that way."

Our entire day of laughter and smiles suddenly shifted. I could tell she was holding something back, and her eyes were getting watery as she stared out the window. Best not to push any further.

The rest of our dinner was a little quieter than usual. Trish asked, "Do you know what they'll pay you for your first client?"

"Grace said I'll get fifty percent, and the first client is paying twenty thousand. So, ten k in my pocket for a couple hours of sex."

She smiled. "Well, you seem quite confident in yourself. That's a lot of money. Imagine doing that once or twice a month. You could retire by the age of thirty."

We both laughed.

"I wanted to ask you about that. I want to learn to role-play more, and I would like to maybe role-play with you … perhaps with your clients or new clients."

"Do you think you could put on a sex show with me in front of a hundred or two hundred people?"

I sat back and looked at her in amazement. "What? Are you serious?"

She laughed. "There's a gig once a year where wealthy people get together for a Roman bath party. They come dressed in ancient Roman attire and hire escorts to do their bidding while role-playing as sex slaves. To start the event, an attractive couple has sex on a large mattress while they all stand around watching. They might suggest things for the couple to do, but it would be about a thirty-minute show, and it's ten thousand dollars."

"Holy shit!" I yelled out, then realized where I was. The elderly couple in a booth nearby furrowed their eyebrows at me. I whispered, "Ten thousand dollars for the two of us to have hot sex on a mattress in front of a couple of hundred people?" Wait, what? When I said it out loud, it seemed a little more intimidating. That old couple shook their heads.

She nodded while sipping her wine. I sat back in disbelief. Then I thought about all those people watching, wondering if I could get hard under that kind of pressure.

"It gets better. After that thirty minutes, you can make even more by having sex with the guests. You wear a wristband that will monitor your tips, and at five hundred to a thousand dollars a person, the amount of money you can make could get ridiculous."

Then I panicked at the thought of rumors from ancient Rome. "I don't have to do any guy-on-guy stuff, do I?"

"There is this large, stone dildo ritual with a cat shape on the tip." My eyes got wide as she laughed. "I'm kidding. You don't have to, but with your fine, young, sexy body, you'd make a killing."

I shook my head and thought for a moment. "Okay, but I don't receive."

Trish spit out her wine and barely reached the plate to not get red wine everywhere. All eyes in the restaurant turned their attention to us as we formed tears in our eyes from laughing so hard.

Taylor

My morning never started until my first cup of coffee, and Sundays were no different. My laptop was always open when I was home. It was the last thing I saw before I went to sleep and the first thing I would look at in the morning … after my coffee, of course. I woke it from its sleep and saw forty-two new emails. *How can people send messages on the weekend?*

I looked at my phone and saw a text message from Grace.

Can you meet for brunch? Café Louis? 10 a.m.

I'd learned over the years that if Grace made a request with this type of specificity, it wasn't a request. I replied, *See you there.*

I assumed it was to tell me how her evaluation of Brett had gone. I know my assessment of him went better than anticipated.

I walked into Café Louis and saw Grace at a table with a mimosa in her hand and one waiting for me. I sat down.

"Thank you." I raised the glass as she did the same to make that all too familiar clink. "I assume you want to tell me how the evaluation went last night?"

"I do, but I wanted to let you know your little romp with him Friday evening almost jeopardized everything."

I was about to take a sip of my mimosa but set it down as a hot flash of guilt flowed through me.

"You did fuck him Friday after work, didn't you?" Grace whispered.

Damn. "Yes. I had a stressful day, and we met for drinks. I asked how he was settling in, and then he turned on his charm. I needed a fix and asked him to my place. What happened?"

"Apparently, Trish is much more cunning than either of us thought. She's a high-paid escort on the side as well."

"I know. I suspected such and called her out on it. She didn't even deny, but she's in the same price category as we operate."

"And you didn't tell me?"

"I only found out a few days ago. Besides, I wanted to learn more from her."

"So, between her and you, he was on to our scheme and called me out last night."

"What did you tell him?" I asked, then took a sip of my drink.

"I told him the truth. The whole truth. And offered him fifty percent for his contribution."

I raised my eyebrows. "What made you offer him so much?"

"Do you think he's worth it if he can please the clients already waiting for him? Besides, I'm hoping it'll bring in more contracts."

"He made my toes curl, and the fact that he knows and will do it willingly, I guess it's worth it."

"Exactly what I thought. He was sold when I told him he'd make ten grand for a couple of hours of seduction."

I couldn't help but laugh. Grace had already ordered our meals, and we began eating a fantastic smoked salmon with capers and a fruit salad.

"What do you want to do about Trish?" I asked.

She picked up her mimosa and took a sip. "I don't know. What she's doing isn't much different than what we're doing, and she knows too much to let her go." She took another sip. "I'd like to see if perhaps we couldn't harness her clients and expand what we have."

I looked at her, surprised. "You mean we bring male clients in?"

"Why not? We can expand to role-playing scenarios with men one night and our standard clients another. Why limit ourselves to two nights a month?"

"Um, because I wouldn't be able to keep up and run the HR department," I replied with uncertainty.

"Perhaps Trish could be your assistant in both?"

We paused for a moment to think while eating a little more. The room was filled with women our age, all leaning in to spread gossip, no doubt, or conduct some scheming as we were doing.

"What would you offer her?" I asked.

"I don't know. She would be bringing her own clients, after all. Perhaps let her keep sixty percent? What do you think?"

"That would only be three to six thousand a month. I don't think she would settle for that, but we can make the offer to see how she counters."

Grace sipped more of her mimosa, staring intently at the purple and pink floral centerpiece. "I think I'll take her out for a drink this week and learn more about what makes her tick."

The rest of brunch consisted of work-related stuff, how we were looking for recruits, and which colleges we were setting up interviews at, but I couldn't get Trish, or how she would react to Grace's offer, out of my mind.

Grace's actions strayed from our initial plan, leaving me unsure of what she was doing. I knew that if we pursued the development of SD too vigorously, it could have a negative effect on her business which I was trying to avoid at all costs.

Brett

Sunday afternoon, I spent some time glancing through apartment catalogs while watching a hockey game on TV. Trish was at the gym. I found a few apartments that looked reasonable and were close to Trish.

I had no idea how this would play out. There was no denying my feelings for Trish, but she hadn't given me any sign that she was interested in me other than the sex. We had a great time and always laughed when we were together. I knew she had feelings for me; I'd sensed them. But she was putting up a wall.

I couldn't think straight with what was running through my head—meeting Grace in Mexico, hiring me here, becoming a prostitute, my career, and how everyone had deceived me, but I could significantly help my mom and sister with the money I'd make.

One thing I did know was that I needed my own place. With what I was getting paid plus the side jobs—if I could even call them that—I'd have plenty to afford rent in this area.

I narrowed it down to five apartments at three thousand dollars a month with a world-class gym and pool. *Women like a well-chiseled body on a man.*

I stared at the hockey game but wasn't really watching it. At this point, it was stuff moving on a screen while I thought about what it would be like to perform with Trish in front of hundreds of people. The thought of being watched was scary. And what if I was too intimidated for my cock to work? That would be devastating.

I thought about making the extra money on the side, the role-playing, and simply being a man-whore. What would my mom say if she ever found out? *Damn, why am I worrying so much?*

Trish came in panting as though she had run back to the apartment. "Find anything you like yet?"

"Yeah, I found five of them to look at this week."

"I can go with you if you like?"

I looked at her shoulder-length, black, silky hair in a ponytail. Her sweat glistened on her shoulders and face, and her workout clothes hugged every curve of her body. I couldn't get enough of this woman.

"Sure, I'd like that."

"Cool. I'm going to take a shower. Does Chinese sound good for dinner?" she asked while walking toward her bedroom.

"Sounds great! I'll call it in."

I called our favorite local Chinese place. As much as we'd ordered from them, we should get some type of loyalty rate.

I reviewed more apartments, wondering if Trish's *fuck me whenever you want* rule still applied now that I knew what was going on.

The knock at the door instantly reminded me of my hunger. I went to get our food and had just set it on the coffee table when Trish came out wearing only a towel in her hair. She walked by me to her chair with her breasts swaying and lightly brushing against me as she stepped past to sit in a chair. *Did she do that on purpose?*

"Smells good," she said as she opened her Szechuan chicken and fried rice containers.

We ate and talked about some of the apartments I found. She recommended I not consider two of the five as it wasn't safe to walk around outside in those areas.

"So … are you interested in that Roman party I told you about?" she asked. "It's next weekend, and I need to let the coordinator know what roles I'm interested in playing out."

"Oh, you're going regardless?" I was a little surprised but realized I didn't really have a say. I almost felt embarrassed that I believed I would have a voice in what she did. Despite my feelings for her, we weren't in a relationship, and if I wanted to have one with her, I should probably learn more about her life.

"Of course. It's a lot of fun, and where else would you make that kind of money in one evening while enjoying sex?"

I thought about it while eating my General Tso's chicken and fried rice. How had my life gotten to this point? And was this where I genuinely wanted to go? I knew I wanted to be with Trish, and if this was what she wanted to do, I was willing to try.

"It's okay if you're not interested. I just wanted to offer it as … well, I'm turned on at the thought of you using me *Roman style* in front of many people."

"What do you mean, *Roman style*?"

"You would be a Roman elitist and treat me as your slave girl to use as you like. You would be aggressive both physically and verbally to me. Some people would shout out what they want you to do to me. I would plead for you not to, but you'd comply to their desires and put on a show. Then at the end, you ask everyone where they want you to come, and you do it. Some might even offer a tip to pick their choice."

"Damn! I'm not sure I can do that level of acting."

"Sure, you can. You've already shown how you can be a little dominant—gripping hair, choking, slapping my ass. And you can be a little verbally dominant. Besides, it will be the fastest ten grand we could ever make, and then we can do other things afterward and make even more."

I had to admit, the thought of treating her as my slave girl was a turn-on. I still wasn't sure I could do that type of role-playing in front of everyone else.

"If you like, I can invite a guy I know over and he can help you learn a little more. Maybe get more comfortable?"

"You've done this before?" I wasn't sure why I was surprised.

"I have for a cuckold client. The partner I have isn't nearly as attractive as you, but he's more experienced at role-playing."

"Cuckold?" How many more terms did I have to learn?

"It's where a man gets aroused by seeing his woman having sex with another guy. Sometimes I role-play as his daughter, and then another guy comes in like a home invasion, ties the client up, and has his way with me in front of him, forcing him to watch his little girl getting violated while I resist."

I cringed at the thought, yet the brief description was creating arousal. I never thought I would be interested in something like that.

She smiled as she saw my erection growing under my sleep pants. "I see the concept turns you on. Many men are, whether they admit it or not."

My cheeks became warm as I looked down to see a tent pitched in my loose-fitting pants, then looked back at her naked body. "I can imagine how exciting it might be."

She stood up and took my food, placed it on the coffee table, then straddled my lap, pulled my cock out, and guided it into her. "We can't let a good hard cock go to waste, now, can we?"

She fucked me while talking about what role-playing might be like. "You would tell my daddy how tight I am and how you're splitting my little virgin pussy wide open, and you would move me to display your cock penetrating my tight little flower."

She leaned forward, pressing her breasts against my face. "You would suck on my young titties in front of my daddy and bite them to make me squeal."

I took the cue and bit into her nipple she had in front of my mouth. I looked up at her to see her bottom lip between her teeth. Once I saw her eyes grow wide, I realized I was at her limit.

"I would plead with Daddy to help me, but he would be tied up and couldn't move. Then you tell him how you'll fill his little girl's pussy with cum. He begs for you to stop, she begs for you to stop, but then you grunt your load into her proudly."

I lost control. I gripped her ass cheeks with my hands and let out a groan. She continued to ride me, her inner muscles gripping my shaft like a clamp, driving my sensitive cock into a frenzy.

I opened my eyes to her kissing my lips, and she asked, "What do you think about that role-playing scenario?"

My breathing was still heavy, and I nestled into her breasts. "I'm sold!"

"So, you want me to invite my friend to help prepare us, and I can call the organizer and let him know we'll be their main event?"

I was hesitant to commit, but she wanted this, and it did sound exhilarating. "Let's do it."

She kissed my lips again, stood up, and went to the bathroom. I picked up my chicken, took a bite, then looked down at the sheen on my cock and shook my head, thinking about how exciting she was. I wanted more of her, even if I had to share her with others.

Trish

I knew I could convince Brett of how erotic it was to role-play. I just needed to get a little creative. The only potential issue would be his ability to keep his cock hard in front of an audience. I texted Rob to come over this evening to help prepare Brett for the event. I'd never been the main attraction at this Roman party, but I'd always wanted to. The thought of being used as a sex slave while everyone watched made me wet every time the scenario came to mind.

Brett was a little hesitant about meeting Rob. Probably because he'd never seen me with another man before, and other than Megan, he'd never had anyone watch him. Rob should be good at helping coach him, and besides, it had been a long time since I'd had a threesome with two men, and it was something I craved.

I showered and shaved myself bare. When I walked out of the bedroom, Brett walked in the door.

"Hey, Brett. Rob should be here shortly."

"Okay." He looked a little apprehensive.

"Are you okay with this?" I asked.

"Yeah, it's just another thing I've never done, and I'm a little uncomfortable about another guy involved."

"No worries. Rob is a great guy. You'll be fine, and besides, you'll get to fuck me. How could it be better than that?"

He laughed. "It would be better if it was Megan instead of Rob."

I laughed back. "Oh, so it's okay for two women, but not two men?" I tilted my head and waited for a response.

"I guess it'll be fine. It's just that the thought of another guy fucking you in front of me is a little strange for me."

I walked up to him, took his hand, and placed it on my bare mound. "Trust me when I say you'll find it hotter than you think." I guided his fingers through my slit, and he slipped his fingers inside. I gasped and smiled into his eyes.

I took his hand and placed one finger at a time into my mouth, wrapping my lips around them, sucking my moisture from each one. His mouth fell open with amazement.

I turned away. "Okay, gotta get dressed. He'll be here shortly."

I glanced back to see he was still stunned and smiled at the connection we'd formed. When I broke up with my boyfriend, I vowed I would never be hurt like that again. I was growing fond of Brett, but I knew I couldn't let myself get too close. I didn't want to be emotionally devastated like I was before.

I went into the bedroom to put on my short, silk robe. I rarely wore it, but since Rob was coming over, I thought I'd first have something on before letting them take it off me. Brett wore shorts and a T-shirt. We listened to some soft rock music with wine in the living room while paging through apartment rental magazines.

Knock, knock.

I looked at Brett and raised my eyebrows. "Game on!"

I opened the door; Rob walked in and hugged me. "Hey, gorgeous!" He slapped my ass and backed away.

"Hello, handsome. Rob, I'd like to introduce you to Brett. Brett, this is Rob."

Brett walked up and shook Rob's hand.

"So, he's your new partner in crime?" Rob said jokingly.

"You're still the master role-player, but a girl needs options," I said, caressing his arm.

Rob clapped his hands together into a grip and smiled. "So, how do you want to play this?"

"Well, I thought you would watch as Brett had his way with me. I'm supposed to be his sex slave, and he's a dominant Roman. Give him some pointers to act out, and then the three of us can have some fun together."

Rob stared down at my body and tugged on the loose knot holding my robe closed. It fell open, exposing the front of my body. He shook his head with a devilish grin. "Mmmm, I missed that body." He slapped Brett on his shoulder as a comrade. "You are one lucky son of a bitch. Let's get it on!"

I looked to Brett to make sure he was okay. He smiled as we turned and walked to my bedroom. I dropped my robe as Brett hastily took off his clothes. I stopped at the foot of my bed, and Brett walked up and kissed my neck.

"Whoa, what are you doing, man? You're a fucking Roman! Take your slave girl and take her hard."

He looked at Rob and seemed confused. Rob walked up to us. "Like this."

He slapped my face with his open hand, gripped my hair, and pushed me down to my knees. "Suck my cock, slave!"

Brett's eyes widened in shock.

"There, now you do it."

My goosebumps were as large as a freshly plucked chicken, and my inside clenched like performing a Kegel. A man taking control of me like that was my kryptonite. I stood up again as Brett looked at me, and I nodded, letting him know it was okay.

"I'm not sure I can hit her," Brett confided.

"It's okay," Rob said. "Do it with your hand open and your fingers loose. It won't hurt her as hard. Just a little sting on the cheek. It sounds worse than it is. Besides, this little minx loves it … don't you?"

I bit my lip and nodded.

"Here, try slapping my face first. Just like I told you." Rob turned to face Brett.

After a moment of hesitation, Brett slapped Rob's face.

"There, just keep your fingers a little closer together. Otherwise, you won't get a good sound, but that was good. The sound of the slap is more important than the physical hit, along with her crying out to maximize the effect."

Brett looked at me and took a deep breath. I nodded, and he slapped my face. I gasped and cried out, giving my best look of despair.

He immediately recoiled. "Oh no, was that too hard?"

"I was acting, Brett. It's all part of the role-playing. If it's ever too hard, I'll say 'limit' so you know to lighten up."

He nodded and paused for a moment, then gripped my throat, nearly lifting me by his hand. "Now suck my dick, you little slut!"

Holy shit … he caught on quick!

He released my throat, and I knelt before him, taking his cock in my mouth.

Rob grinned. "There you go. With time, you'll get smoother at it. Keep in mind, it's just role-playing. Not everyone's into it, but those who are enjoy it a lot. Now, use that whore of yours. Show her who's the master."

Brett grabbed my hair and began thrusting his cock into the back of my throat.

"That's it, slave, open that throat, or I'll force it open!"

He gripped my head and held it in place while using my throat for pleasure. I gagged with every thrust, and my eyes watered. I could feel my saliva collecting around my lips and dripping to the floor.

"There you go, good job," Rob coached. "Now, it's not for everyone, but you're doing this for an audience who has specifically requested it. Forcing her mouth open and spitting in it is a sick turn-on for many."

Brett whispered, "Are you okay with that?"

As I nodded, Rob said, "Don't ask your fucking slave if it's okay, just do it! Trish will let you know what she won't do, but don't mess up the role-playing by asking. Also, I know her hard limits from our role-playing, but make sure the two of you discuss it. It's easy to get carried away when you're in the role."

Brett pulled his cock out of my mouth, yanked my head back, and spit in my mouth. He redirected my mouth back to his cock and began fucking my throat again.

"That's it! Good job. Don't do it all the time. It's a humiliation thing people get into, especially those voyeurs who pay to watch."

Brett pulled out of my mouth, and I looked up, breathing heavily, ready to do whatever he had in mind. He picked me up and pushed me onto the bed, forcing me to bend over the edge. He pried my legs open, and I cried out as he shoved his cock into my depth.

"Good job! Trish is great at that cry. The voyeurs eat it up while you're fucking her. They'll want to see your cock fucking her pussy, so try to keep that in mind and position yourself so they can watch you slide into her."

I couldn't see what Brett was doing as I was lying there accepting every thrust, whimpering in my slave role.

"I guarantee you someone will tell you to fuck her ass."

"I've never done that before," Brett said.

It just dawned on me that after all the sex we'd had, he never once fucked my ass, nor asked to.

"For the event, I'll have a plug in my ass to keep me loose. There's some lube in my nightstand," I said.

I heard the drawer open and close. The cool lube drooled down my ass and flowed to my entrance.

"Now, slowly take your finger or your thumb and work that lube into her ass," Rob said.

I relaxed with my face in the comforter as he stretched me open.

I wasn't a big fan of anal sex, especially with more well-endowed men like these two, but I'd prepare and role-play it appropriately for a special occasion, like the Roman party.

I looked back. "Brett, during the party, when you fuck my ass or most any other time, just remember, my crying out and pleading with you is all acting. Just take me and do whatever, and I'll be fine."

"There you go, she's ready. Now fuck that tight, little ass," Rob said like a football coach encouraging him to make the winning touchdown.

Brett pulled out of my pussy and pushed the head of his cock against my asshole. I relaxed as he pushed harder. His head lurched in.

"Oh no! Please no!" I cried. "That hurts. Please, Master, don't!"

"Perfect. Now how do you react to that?" Rob asked Brett.

The crack sound of his hand slapping on my ass sounded like a whip, and the sting soon followed, sending my endorphins into a frenzy.

He pushed himself farther into me. "You'll take my cock wherever I put it, slave!" He slapped my other ass cheek. The warmth of the sting spread across my skin. I loved being used like this.

"Good, good," Rob said.

Brett continued fucking my ass as Rob continued his coaching. "Now you need to fuck her in other positions so your audience can see your cock sliding into her. They love to see you move her around like a rag doll, like some wanton whore who's yours for the taking. So, put her on top, fuck her from behind, and each time, position yourself so new people can see. If you can manage it, pick her up without pulling out, put her in a different position, and continue fucking her."

"Damn, this is a lot more like work!" Brett chided.

"You're getting paid a lot of money to do this, so yeah, it's work, but it's a lot of fun for work," I replied.

Brett pulled out of my ass and then laid on his back, pulling me over him.

"Whoa! Don't fuck her pussy after you fuck her ass unless she cleaned herself first. Here …"

I looked back and saw Rob throw Brett a towel I had on the nightstand.

Good call. I hadn't thought to douche back there beforehand.

After the brief pause, Brett pushed his cock into me and began fucking me again. I leaned down next to him, allowing the best view of his cock sliding in and out of me from behind.

"I'll pay a thousand dollars to fuck your slave's ass while she's riding you," Rob asked. "It could be asked of you."

Brett looked up at me, and I gave him an approving grin. "Go ahead and fuck this whore's ass! Let's split her open!"

I gasped as Rob slid into my loosened ass while Brett was fucking my pussy. The movement of both their cocks sliding in and out of me with only a thin membrane separating them sent electricity through my body. My gasping was erratic, and I leaned down to let Brett suck on my tits. The feeling of fullness was intense but also exhilarating, as though my body was on fire. My thighs trembled, and the two men using me, their cocks filling me simultaneously, pushed me toward the brink. "I'm coming!" I exclaimed.

A sharp tug on my hair snapped my head back. It was Brett.

"You won't come unless I tell you to come, slave!"

My gasp echoed in the room, and my eyes widened at his demand. It wasn't like him to catch on this well, but I forced myself to hold back. I desperately wanted to climax. They both pulled back and thrust in simultaneously, filling every possible inch of me. I had to grit my teeth to keep my climax from arriving.

"Please, Master, please let me come."

"Not until I say!"

I might burst into flames if I didn't come soon. They continued pumping into me, breathing heavily now, and I moaned with each new thrust. I'd never withheld from having an orgasm this much. I desperately needed release.

"Where should we come on her, Rob?" Brett asked.

"Good. Remember that the audience likes to help you make those decisions. Let her come first and let's have her swallow both of our loads. Lots of people like watching a pretty face getting loaded with cum. Just avoid her eyes. It can cause a nasty infection."

I looked into Brett's eyes, pleading silently as though my life depended on his approval. "Please let me come," I begged.

"You may come now."

My body shuddered, and I cried out as the orgasm ripped through me. From my head to toes, I spasmed uncontrollably. The guys continued fucking me through it, heightening the intensity and prolonging my euphoria.

Eventually, my climax subsided to some gentle aftershocks. They both pulled out of me, and Brett grabbed my hair.

I followed along with weakened limbs. He forced me to my knees, and knowing what they were doing, I lifted my face to them.

"Open that pretty mouth of yours and take your reward, slave."

I opened my mouth and stuck out my tongue while looking up into Brett's eyes as he and Rob vigorously stroked their cocks over my face. Rob groaned first as waves of his warm semen spurted over me. I tried to catch it in my mouth, but much of it landed on my cheeks.

I kept my mouth open, waiting for Brett. I stared into his eyes as his face became red. He was vigorously stroking himself. This was new for him, and I thought I'd help a little. I leaned up to put my tongue under his head and fondled his balls. He immediately groaned and shot himself into my mouth. His body spasmed slightly as his load didn't seem to stop flowing. I displayed their pool of white in my mouth and then grinned at their expression of awe as I swallowed.

"Goddamn! That was the hottest thing I've ever done or seen," Brett exclaimed, reaching down for my hand to help me up. "Fuck, that was incredible!"

I held onto his hand for a moment after getting to my feet, still a bit wobbly after my orgasm. "Just think about how much more creative your imagination can be with sex and how exciting it can be."

Rob sat down on the bed. "Damn, Trish. You are the hottest woman on this planet."

I smiled and sat down next to him. "Well, it takes more than me to make the experience hot."

Brett sat down on the other side of me and caressed my back.

"Well, do you think you can perform this well for the Roman party?" I asked.

"Absolutely! I'm all in," Brett answered confidently.

"I suspect you will be for sure." I laughed, then got up and went to the bathroom to clean up. I looked in the mirror to see cum on my cheeks. I loved its taste, but I'd already drunk enough to impregnate a horse. I washed my face and then went back out to the boys.

"There we go, all pretty again."

Rob looked up at me. "I don't know. I think you looked better with our cum on your cheeks."

I slapped his leg and laughed.

"I must say, that was one of the hottest threesomes I've had in a while." I looked into Brett's eyes as he looked back into mine. Not many men would be this understanding. Despite my best efforts, I might be falling for him.

Grace

Another contract signed. Fortunately, Taylor and Trish were heading out to do some recruiting soon. We needed some engineers for the company, and I couldn't help but think about hiring more like Brett for more nefarious purposes.

Last weekend with Brett could have backfired, and I was glad he seemed okay with what we were offering him.

My thoughts turned to Trish. Brett had let it slip about her being an escort. Perhaps she had some other intentions with Brett, intentions that could jeopardize my goals.

To take my mind off the mysterious Trish, I walked through the company as I sometimes did to see how the corporate engine was humming. I loved what the sales and marketing department did for our company, but they could be my biggest suck-ups. I appreciated honest people, people like Taylor and Trish. Well, I thought Trish was honest, but now I didn't know.

I walked to the engineering department and spoke to Brett's supervisor, Steve.

"How are the programs coming along, Steve? We have another contract signed to start another robotics effort next month."

"Um, we're doing great, but I don't think we have the manpower to take on another project right now."

"It's okay, we're looking to hire more engineers in the next month." I looked across the room to see Brett working on something with a couple of other people. "How's Brett coming along?"

"Brett is doing great! He's quickly learning and comes into work energetic and ready to go. I can't say that for many others. He's great to have on my team."

If these other guys were getting laid as much as he was, perhaps they would also have a cheerier disposition.

"Thanks, Steve." I walked over to where Brett was working. He was holding some piece of equipment while the other two engineers were looking at something within the robot.

"What are you guys working on?"

Brett was startled for a moment, then he blushed. One of the other engineers said, "Careful, that's a ten-thousand-dollar RF sensor you almost dropped."

"I'm sorry I snuck up on you," I said.

"It's okay, ma'am. How can we help you?"

"I'm just walking around to see how everything is going." I smiled at the others and then at Brett, who didn't say anything. He didn't have to. I knew what he was thinking, and I couldn't help but think about having him again.

The other engineers were quietly concentrating on the task, and I caught a glimpse of a mole on one of the engineers. A distinct mole that I remembered from one event a while back. I tried to determine if I had him or just saw him in the lineup one night.

"Keep up the good work." I walked off, and as I stepped through the door, I looked back at Brett, who was watching me walk away. I winked at him and left to see Taylor.

When I walked into the HR office, Taylor and Trish were discussing their recruitment plan and the potential candidates they were interviewing.

"We locked down the next contract. How are we doing on getting the engineers?" I said gleefully.

"We're putting the finishing touches on our recruitment strategy right now," Taylor explained. "We're going out to Virginia Tech tomorrow and MIT on Thursday. The schools said they would send emails out to all the recent graduates. Not everyone left after May graduation. We have twenty-one applicants."

"Have we considered Georgia Tech, Texas A&M, or others?"

"We plan to attend those in the next couple of weeks. We anticipate hiring ten engineers for the ten new positions, but we'll get two more strategic hires for any additional task orders that might come up."

"Good, good. Now, as for our other endeavor ... is Brett ready to go next week?"

Trish looked at me, narrowing her eyes and crossing her arms as though she were a police interrogator. "Maybe you should tell us. You did the final analysis. Actually, you both did."

I looked to Taylor and then back to Trish. "You've accomplished exactly what we hoped you would. Taylor, go ahead and pay her the full twenty thousand we agreed to, and she can be a member of SD."

Trish would be an excellent addition to SD, not only because she was beautiful, but she also had a mind for the business. Or so it seemed.

"Brett is on for the weekend after next. We have one big client eager to have him. What do we have for other clients so far?"

Taylor responded, "Currently, we have three Dominae lined up and three wanting Brett. Or a Brett-like guy."

"A shame we can't divide him in three," I said with a slight laugh.

"I might have a guy who could fill in, but he's nearly forty years old," Trish said.

"Thanks, but our clients are looking for younger men, and I think even thirty would be too old," Taylor said.

There was a moment of silence. I smiled at Trish. "So, Trish, I'm just going to come right out and ask. You don't have to answer if you don't want to, and it won't leave this room, but what are you into with your escort business?"

She looked down briefly and then looked back up at me. "Let's just say I reach out to fulfill the ultimate fantasies of the wealthy. Probably in the same category as what you do, but my clients are men."

Impressive. I hadn't expected a direct answer.

"What are your thoughts on bringing your clients to SD? A secluded location for them to act out their fantasies?"

"Well, the way it's set up now, I keep one hundred percent of the take. How do you imagine it working out if they come to SD?"

I looked to Taylor, who also seemed intrigued with where I was going. "We would create the fantasy environment in our location and perhaps split the take fifty-fifty."

Trish painted a contemplative smile on her face. "I'll think about it."

I could tell she wasn't interested but was humoring me. My low offer may have insulted her, but I was a businesswoman; it's what I did.

Taylor added, "Trish, why don't you come by next week as a Domina? I'll have an extra male servus lined up for you. You can check out what we have going on and decide afterward."

Trish smiled. "That sounds great. I look forward to it."

I nodded in approval. There was a reason I'd kept Taylor on so long. She was astute and calculating and always seemed to know what I was thinking.

"I need to get back to my never-ending email inbox. Go get our engineers, ladies."

As I walked into my office, I thought about how I'd like to tap into Trish's market somehow, with or without her.

Brett

The week was a whirlwind of activity; there was barely any time for leisure while Trish was away at work. I managed to learn a great deal and gain my interim security clearance. The backroom projects were mesmerizing – it was truly remarkable how small one could make robots. I especially found the slithering snake-like robot, consisting mostly of just battery and micro communications hardware, ingenious. I planned to explore further into that area of robotics.

Trish got home late Friday night. I had been a little concerned she wouldn't get back in time for the Roman party Saturday afternoon. There was no way I would go alone, and I didn't know anyone to attend with me.

It was near noon on Saturday, and I was waiting for some returns on apartment applications. I'd narrowed it down to two of them nearby.

Trish walked out of her bedroom. Even with her messy, morning hair, she looked amazing. "Is the coffee still hot?"

Her firm, bare ass was mesmerizing as she walked to the kitchen. I could watch her ass move every hour of every day, even with her hair snaggled like it was.

She walked by me and sat in her favorite chair. "Remind me never to fly through Philadelphia again. The layover there is brutal." She sipped her coffee. "How was your week?"

"I got my interim security clearance, was read into the job I'm working on, and got to see the cool things in the classified vault."

"Congrats! I thought I saw something about that come through my email, but I was too busy to check the details. Good for you." She sipped some more coffee. "I got in around three in the morning, and I might need a nap before this afternoon's party."

I got up to get some more coffee, gripped the back of her hair, and whispered, "How much sleep do you need to be a slave?"

"Ha, ha, very funny. Regardless of the role-playing, it's only as good as the actor, and if I'm to be good, I need a nap. Any responses to your apartment applications?"

"Not yet."

"I'm sure you'll get something on Monday. You're not much of a risk."

As I poured coffee into my cup, she asked, "Did you tell Grace I was an escort?"

I had to think about it before I answered. "I guess something like that might have slipped out when I found out about Grace. I was angry about being used and not thinking. I'm sorry. I shouldn't have said anything."

I could tell from her silence she wasn't happy about that, but I wasn't going to grovel. They used and deceived me. I had a right to be pissed, but I shouldn't have called her out like that.

"Grace asked me the other day, and I gave a benign answer, but she wanted me to bring my clients to her club. I was just wondering how she knew."

"Are you mad at me?"

"I wish you hadn't told her that. I don't like those surprises, but I'm not mad at you."

I could tell she wasn't happy about it either.

"You can make it up to me by getting me a breakfast burrito at the coffee shop next door—extra salsa and a large latte."

I leaned down to kiss her cheek. "I'll be right back." I went to my room to get dressed and oblige.

* * *

Later that afternoon, we arrived at the event location. It was a large mansion near San Francisco. A guard at the gate checked our names and let us drive toward the main house. Trish did a great job finding legitimate Roman attire for us to wear. She had her hair down to her shoulders and wore a slave tunic with a rope belt and leather sandals. I had a nice, white robe with a purple sash and a brooch holding it all together on my shoulder. I also had some sandals.

We were about thirty minutes early when we walked inside and saw many Roman-looking guests already there. Trish looked around and found the coordinator.

"Greetings, welcome," he chirped.

"Greetings. We're your *main event* … Brett and Trish."

"Ahh, yes." He looked both of us over. "Yes, indeed. You two will make for a beautiful opening to our event. And you know the role-playing aspects of what we expect?"

"We do," Trish answered.

"Very good. You'll receive the ten thousand at the end of the evening. You can get your wristbands in the room around the corner. We plan to have your show at five o'clock. Come find me before then."

We walked to the next room and received our wristbands. They were registered with our names and an account. Those guests who planned to spend money were given what looked like a digital watch. They could establish the amount to transfer to someone, confirm, and transfer it to the other account. It seemed pretty straightforward.

A beautiful brunette slave wearing only several layers of beads that didn't come close to covering her breasts came up to us with a tray of wine. We each took a chalice of wine. She smiled at me before she walked away.

"You can tap her after our gig. Once we get that done, you can do whatever or whomever you wish."

Was that a hint of jealousy in Trish's tone? She was usually all business.

Truth be told, I just wanted Trish. I couldn't care less about having sex with anyone else, and I was here mainly to experience role-playing in front of other people. The way Trish explained it to me was intriguing.

I smiled at Trish's cavalier attitude toward sexuality; I could never have thought of it this way before I met her. We both scanned the room to see people of all shapes, colors, and sizes. They all drank wine and laughed while wearing togas or some type of slave outfit. Some slaves wore leashes held by who I assumed were their masters.

We walked around and socialized with several people. One older, bald man we met was actually from Rome, with ancestors who lived in ancient Rome. He had a rounded belly and looked exactly how you would imagine a Roman senator in a movie to look. He seemed to flirt a little with me, and I wasn't sure how to take it. Trish went along and humored him with simple pawing of his arm and making him feel like royalty. He talked about his large yachts, properties all over the world, and boasted of the royalty he knew in many countries. He loved to talk about himself, but I was getting a little suspicious that he was more interested in me than Trish.

"We have to go for now, but maybe we can find you later," Trish said.

"I'd like that." He placed his hand on my shoulder and winked at me. "I'd like that a lot."

Trish took me aside and said, "Just remember, you can slap me around a bit. I'll act out in pain, but just carry on. I put an anal plug in before we left, douched my ass, and used a lube shooter to pre-lube myself, so it should all be clean for whatever you want to do to me."

Wow, she was prepared. I couldn't help but beam at how much she turned me on.

We saw the coordinator motion us his way as it was near five o'clock.

"Are you two ready?"

Trish looked at me, and we both nodded. My heart was racing, but I convinced myself I would calm down once we got into our role-playing.

"Excellent. That round mattress being put in the middle of the floor right now is your stage. You are acting as a Roman elitist." He pointed to me. "And you, a new slave girl who will get initiated. So put on a good show, and as attractive as you are, you just might get an invite to do this again for the next event."

We thanked him and walked toward our *stage*.

The coordinator got everyone's attention and made some announcements. "Are you ready?" Trish whispered.

I smiled. "Too late to ask that now."

She smiled back, and we heard, "Let the show begin!"

I pushed Trish onto the mattress so hard that she lifted off the ground and landed in the middle. She appeared surprised at the suddenness, then cried out, "No, Master, not again."

I fought myself not to laugh at her acting, but it was funny.

"Yes, again. You're mine to use, and I will use you as any proud Roman would." She resisted as I leaned over, pulled her rope loose, and threw off her tunic. She lay on her back, completely naked, trying to cover herself with her hands. Her gorgeous body glimmered under the bright lights focused on our display. Everyone crowded around the mattress to watch.

"You're going to learn to please a Roman one way or another." I took off my robe, exposing myself. There was chatter in the background. I grinned when I picked out the word "nice" from someone in the crowd, but I couldn't tell from whom. I tried to block out the voices of the voyeurs as much as possible, it was obvious they were enjoying what they'd seen so far.

I reached down to grab the base of her hair, yanking her head to my groin. "Now suck my cock, whore, and convince me you like it."

She opened her mouth and began sucking me. She sucked it like a hungry whore. She had never sucked me with such aggressive desire before. She spit on it, stroked it, and was like a starving lioness trying to devour a fresh lamb.

"Take it down that pretty throat of yours," I directed. She positioned herself on her knees and leaned into my cock with her mouth wide open. I gripped her hair with both hands and fucked her mouth, pushing my tip to her throat. She gagged, and the audience loved it. Drool began to fall from her mouth, and tears formed in her eyes, making her eyeliner run slightly down her cheek. *Fuck, that was hot.*

The whispers among the voyeurs were hopefully a good sign. I let her take a breath and then pushed my cock into her throat again. She leaned forward a little more, and I could feel my cock penetrate deeper into her throat. She gripped my ass cheeks and pulled me in deeper yet. The tightness of her throat around my head sent shivers down my spine. Her gagging was more of a struggle as her whole body spasmed. I continued as though she was acting while some of the audience clapped. She pulled off and caught her breath as even more people clapped.

I picked her up and positioned her in front of me, then reached down to finger her and grope her breasts. There were smiles everywhere as I rotated her around, aggressively fingering her pussy as she whimpered and pleaded for me to stop.

I pushed her down. "Get on your hands and knees. Time to get that little pussy of yours fucked."

She was slow to comply, begging and resisting the whole time. "Please, Master, that hurts. Please don't."

I pulled her up to face me … my slap across her face echoed through the room. She cried out; gasps came from the audience. I wasn't sure if I actually hurt her or not, but she complied, and I rolled with it. Leaning down, I forced her face to the mattress, then tilted her hips up to me.

Kicking her legs open wider so the audience had a good view, I said, "Show that pussy, slave!" I stood just to the side so I wouldn't block anyone's line of sight as I reached down and slid my fingers through her crevice. Many people were leaning in to see my fingers split her lips open and slip inside. Though I'd been with her numerous times, I couldn't help but gaze at the beauty of her sex.

"Fuck her!" someone yelled out. I was pulled out of my hypnotized state and returned to my role.

"Fuck her in the ass!" someone else shouted.

I got behind her and buried my cock entirely in her drenched pussy with the first thrust.

"Whoa!" she cried out while white-knuckling the mattress. Her warmth was intoxicating no matter how many times I'd entered her. She might have prepared her ass for the scene, but I didn't think she'd done anything else before we left—she was this wet just for me. Well, me and the audience.

I began fucking her slowly, positioning myself so that others to the side could watch my cock slide in and out. I intermittently gazed down to see myself sliding into her slickness. I could never have enough of her.

"Damn, that's hot," a voice called out.

I leaned in the other direction to let more people see my shaft slide in and out of her. Then I leaned in and fucked her hard, grabbing her hair and pulling her head back for everyone to see her face.

"Fuck her ass!" someone yelled out.

"Yes, fuck her ass."

Rob hadn't been kidding about people wanting to see that. I was grateful Trish had thought ahead with her lube preparations. I removed her anal plug with a ruby-red jewel at the end.

"I see you wear the jewelry I give you with pride."

The audience roared with laughter. I tossed the plug aside, stood, and squatted down into position. I paused with my cock pressed against her sphincter and waited for her to relax and stuck my cock into her back door.

"No, not there. Please, Master, it hurts." She gripped the mattress as she cried out in pain.

When she finally opened up for me, a wave of cheers and lusty moans came from the audience. Once in, I paused to give her a moment, and then, with a slap to her left ass cheek, slowly began fucking her ass.

"Take it, slave. Take it all." I slapped her ass several times, leaving a bright pink handprint on each cheek. I looked down to see myself bottomed out in her gorgeous ass. I could scarcely believe this was my life.

Once warmed up, I fucked her ass hard for a few minutes. Her whimpering was realistic, as though she was in pain. I pulled out of her and lay on my back.

"Ride that cock, girl! And make sure you go down on it slowly. I want to watch my cock impale that gorgeous body of yours."

Her hair dropped down, covering her face. She smiled and whispered, "Good role-playing," before slipping back into character.

She squatted over my cock, tilted her head down, averting her eyes, so she didn't make eye contact, and whimpered, "Master, this hurts worse when I sit on it. Please don't make me."

"Put that cock in your cunt, or I'll whip you into compliance!" Without thinking, I grabbed the rope from her tunic, wrapped it around her neck, and gripped it firmly. Her eyes lit up, and she bit her lip. I think she actually liked it.

I grinned as she squatted down, pausing as her pussy touched my head. She winked at me and slowly lowered herself, letting everyone watch her swallow up my entire cock. She hit bottom and lifted slightly.

"It hurts, Master. Please don't."

"The whip will hurt worse." I grabbed her hips and thrust my cock into her. "Now, take it all, I said."

She cried out as I began driving into her. She leaned forward, allowing everyone behind her to witness every thrust. I looked around to see many moving closer to get a better view of our display.

She then positioned her legs forward and leaned back, allowing them to see my cock slide in and out of her while also getting a full view of her gorgeous body. I caught myself out of character, amazed at the view.

"Now go down and lick that sweet nectar from my cock!"

She got off me and knelt to suck my cock. I grabbed her face with one hand and waited for her to look me in the eye before instructing, "I said lick, not suck. And do it slowly. Show me how much you appreciate me."

Her smooth tongue sliding along my shaft caused my muscles to clench. Instead of looking into my eyes as was her typical practice, she kept them averted to stay in slave character. Looking out to the audience, she moved around to let them all see her eyes as she practically savored my cock. I caught the look from the side once and was impressed with her ability to pull off half fright and half hungry sex slave with her facial expressions alone. At first timid with her hands and mouth, as though it was something she didn't want to do, she shifted into a full-blown slut when I prompted her to prove she wanted to please me.

After giving the crowd a chance to enjoy her oral talents, I got up to show the firm results of her efforts. I had been worried the atmosphere would be intimidating, but I found myself feeding off the growing sexual frenzy around us. Trish remained on her knees, head bowed, waiting for my next move. I lifted her to her feet before pushing her until she fell back and bounced slightly on the mattress. Then I was struck with an idea that hadn't occurred to me before. Grabbing a leg in each hand, I nodded to a man on each side to come closer. "Hold my slave's legs open wide. She needs to learn to present her pussy to her master properly."

They were only too eager to indulge, grabbing her calves in both hands as I began to toy with the folds of her pussy, bringing my hands up her thighs so they could inhale her scent. I realized the look on their faces added to the crowd's entertainment. Although tempted to engage them a bit more to twist her nipples, I had already stretched my luck by soliciting two unknowns, so I resisted. Then I noticed Trish squirming and lifting her ass off the bed and realized just how turned on she was.

"Beg your Master to fuck you," I demanded.

She looked me straight in the eyes and cried out, "Fuck me, Master. Please, I beg you! Fuck me mercilessly. I need to feel your hard cock deep inside me. Please, Master!" I could tell by the desperation in her voice she was no longer acting but truly in need. Grabbing her ass cheeks, I brought her to me and thrust myself in, giving her the pounding we both wanted. For a moment, it was just me and her... and the two volunteers. And it was fucking amazing! It was exciting on a level I had never even imagined. I could feel my adrenaline rush through my body as the crowd chanted for me to fuck her. Our eyes connected and then it was just the two of us for a few seconds, until the crowd's roar got louder.

I pulled out and waited for her to look at me again. Her eyes pleaded with me as her ass squirmed in my hands. "You want more, don't you? You're lucky I'm here to give it to you." I thanked the men for their service as I reclaimed her legs and wrapped them around me so I could shift her to the other side of the bed. Then I slid my cock into her from below and started fucking her standing up.

My orgasm was building, and I could probably come at any time. I didn't know how long we'd been at it, but it had to have been nearly thirty minutes. Regardless, I thought it had been a great show so far.

I tossed her back on the bed and followed, putting my cock next to her face. "You've been such a hungry little slave. It's time for a treat. Lick your sweet nectar off my shaft."

She quickly got on all fours and complied, playing to the audience as she licked her lips and spread her legs so those behind her could see her dripping wet, swollen pussy.

"That's enough for now. There will be more rewards if you continue to behave." Moving her ass around ninety degrees, I positioned her on her side, straddled her bottom leg, and pulled the knee of her top leg into her chest to expose her bare mound once again. "Such a pretty pussy needs to be shared. I bet there's plenty of men eager to enjoy your pussy now that I have it nice and stretched and…" A few hands raised in the audience, and I heard a few enthusiastic affirmatives.

I thrust into her pussy once again, one hand keeping her knee to her chest while the other reached down to choke her. "That's a good slave. Take every inch in that little fuck hole." From this position, I could fuck her pussy from different angles. I explored her with my cock, shifting slightly to feel my way around like I was going spelunking. Finding a spot that felt particularly good on the tip of my cock, I fucked her harder, changing it up to have my balls slapping on her ass.

She gripped my hand around her throat. I made sure I wasn't choking her hard. Her role-playing was so natural that I thought I was choking her out as she gasped for air. I lifted my hand away at one point, but she pushed it on her throat again. I laughed down at her when she struggled.

I exclaimed, "She's a fantastic slave! I ask you, guests, where do you want me to finish?"

It seemed like everyone wanted to help with this decision. "Come in her ass! Come on her tits! Cream pie her pussy! Make her swallow!" These were repeated requests throughout the crowd.

"I want to swallow it!" There was a pause as that older rich man we'd talked to earlier walked up to the mattress in his purple and gold Roman attire. "You fuck her from behind, and when you're about to nut, pull out and I want to swallow you." I looked to Trish, who provided no other answer except for a shrug. *Great help.*

"I'll pay you an additional five thousand to swallow your cum." Now Trish nodded.

I wasn't sure about this. I'd never done anything with a man before, and I didn't care to try it, but if he wanted to pay five thousand dollars to swallow my load, I decided to comply. Besides, I was so built up he'd probably gag.

Trish shifted to the edge of the bed and got on her hands and knees, face down, ass up, legs spread. The man laid on his back with his face underneath her pussy. *He definitely had the best view all night.* I stood at the side of the bed and slid inside of her.

I fucked her hard and fast. There was a wet sensation against by balls as I continued to fuck her, and I realized it was the man's tongue. I tried to block the thought of him licking my balls, but my body reacted oppositely, as my inner volcano was about to erupt.

I couldn't hold out. I pulled out of her, and a hand pulled on my cock, followed by warm lips wrapping around my shaft. I was getting sucked by another man. I stared at Trish, who looked back over her shoulder smiling at me. I gazed at her glistening body, while holding onto her hips.

I was at a point of no return and exploded into his mouth as he continued sucking on me. I gripped Trish's ass while my body continued to spasm.

Once he got every drop, I picked my leg up and let him slide out from under us.

"Let's have an applause for our feature show of the evening." The coordinator walked out to us, clapping as I helped Trish stand beside me.

We took a bow and thanked the coordinator for letting us put on the show.

"We definitely want the two of you again," he leaned over to say as he transferred the ten thousand in credit to Trish's wristband.

The older man came up to me. "That was a fantastic show. I know not every guy is into men, but thank you for humoring me. Here's your five thousand I offered." He placed his wristband next to mine and transferred the funds.

I looked to Trish, who walked up and gave me a gleeful hug. "You were great! That was hotter than I had expected. Let's go get cleaned up."

We walked to the massive coed bathroom where men and women were open about sharing it. Guests congratulated us along the way. We laughed while talking about our role-playing experience and how much fun it was. Trish said, "When that guy offered you the five thousand to suck your cock, I almost died. I'm glad you didn't freak out about that. You did great!"

"I wasn't sure how I would react to a man sucking me off. I'd never been attracted to men, and for a moment I thought I'd go limp."

"A mouth is a mouth. Just enjoy the sexual experiences as they come to you. You never know what you might like."

Trish ran her fingers through her freshly fucked hair as if to comb it and asked, "How do I look?"

I gazed at her beauty and sighed. Then I reached up behind her neck to pull her lips to mine. I kissed her passionately. She first met my kiss with a passion of her own, but then it faded away.

"What was that about?" she asked.

I smiled. "I just wanted to. Honestly, I prefer you to sport your freshly fucked hair. It brings out the savage in me, and I'm sure others would agree."

She laughed and slapped my arm. "That's funny. I like how comfortable you've become about this. Now, let's see what more we can get from these rich perverts."

We went out to the ballroom area, where several people came up to us with praises for a great show. I had never been so popular. Trish was bombarded with requests by men to go with them.

"I would love to help all of you," she said. "We can do this one of two ways. Gladiator style, winner takes me as their slave, or diplomatic, and I go with the highest bidder."

"One thousand!" a man yelled out without hesitating. "Two thousand...Three...Four."

Then a woman spoke out. "If you spend an hour with my husband and me, we'll give you ten thousand dollars."

Trish's eyes lit up. "Sold!" She came up to me. "I'll be all right, but try to look for me in an hour, Okay?"

I nodded as she walked off with the attractive older couple.

I meandered through the throng of people, taking in all the carnal activity spread before me. A mattress was draped with two women entwined in pleasure, and around them lounged couples in various states of undress on replica furnishings from some long lost civilization. Two young men were busy lavishing attention on a well-dressed Roman who held up his cup to me and gave an arrogant smirk before returning his attention to them. Across the room, a brunette slave girl winced at each hard thrust her Roman benefactor drove into her body against the pillar. It was erotic to watch, especially when she looked at me and displayed her euphoria. As I watched, mesmerized by the scene, a voice whispered from behind me.

"Hello, handsome. Are you ready to go again?"

I turned to see a woman standing behind me wearing a mask, but her disguise only fooled me for an instant. *I won't forget those eyes again.*

"Holy shit!" I exclaimed. "Grace! What are you doing here?"

"I came here to indulge in some male slaves, but all I see are Roman diplomats. That was a hot show you and Trish put on."

She was wearing an elegant toga with what looked like a jeweled brooch and a gold necklace, and her mask was gold with blue and purple to match her brooch.

"So, what is the going rate to fuck the star of this event? And where is Trish?"

I quickly gathered my scattered thoughts. With a steady voice, I said, "Trish went off with another couple for a little while, and the last person paid me five thousand dollars to suck my cock dry. What are you offering?" After our last encounter in her sex den, I had thought I gained more confidence around her, but she caught me by surprise.

She grinned. "That was pretty hot. I didn't know you went both ways. You may have just opened my client aperture."

"No, no. I don't go that route, but five thousand to suck my cock for a minute didn't seem too bad."

"I was hoping to get both of you for a little while, but that wine slave by the pillar seems to be finished. Perhaps you and her could join me."

She pointed a manicured finger at the other woman by the pillar, who smiled serenely at me as her wealthy client walked away with a satisfied smirk on his face.

I asked, "How much might you offer for the two of us? I am sort of a star now."

Grace laughed. "Okay, star ... how does two thousand sound, one thousand for each of you?"

"Let me go ask her."

I walked up to the other woman just as her partner left and introduced myself.

Once we exchanged names—hers was Evelyn—I pointed at Grace and said, "That woman in the purple mask would like you and me at the same time and offered one thousand to each. Are you interested?"

"Come, let's talk to her."

Evelyn spoke with a thick, foreign accent, but I couldn't place it as being either French or any other Western European language. As we walked back toward Grace, I heard her ask, "Hello, Domina. How might I serve you?" It was apparent that she had a lot of experience in this setting.

"I want him to force himself on you while I watch and perhaps join in." I couldn't believe my ears and looked at her in horror, but then Evelyn shocked me further by replying, "How extreme would you like this scene?"

"Personally, neither of you could handle as much as I'd like to see, and we are somewhat limited to the rules of this establishment. What are your limits?" she asked.

"No fists to the face, light cutting is fine on areas that don't show. As far as other activities go, I'm okay with fist fucking, floggers, ass hook, humiliation and clamps ..." She kept going down her list of possibilities.

My heart sank at the level of forced sex they were discussing. Light cutting? That alone was enough for me to decide that maybe I was out of my depth with this kind of role-playing. As they talked about their plans, most of what they said sounded like a blur to me. "My fee is ten thousand dollars plus whatever extra fee you will pay him separately. But judging by how nervous he looks, it seems like that fee should be pretty high."

"Are you doing all right, Roman?" Grace asked calmly, placing her hand on my arm.

My heart was racing, and I couldn't believe what they wanted from me. *Does Grace really want me to cut her? Punch her?*

I was nervous, not knowing if refusing would be frowned upon. If I said no, how would that affect me at work, or my new role in her sex club? Hundreds of thoughts ran through my mind, most of which were to walk away from this and find Trish. I was surprised that this gorgeous woman would take such abuse from someone, but then again, I remembered Trish coming home bruised up one time.

"Will five thousand work for you, Roman?"

I looked to Grace. Holy shit. Ten thousand for her and five thousand for me? I didn't mind her getting more since she was taking the pain, but ... could I actually do this?

"Okay, let's find a room," I said before I could overthink it any longer. I shook my head in disbelief that I was going through with this. I wished Trish was here.

"No need. I have a private room reserved upstairs," Grace said.

"The Chamber?" Evelyn asked.

"Oh, you know it?"

Evelyn smiled. "I know it quite well."

The curved staircase and ceiling were painted in a deep green color with dark brown molding around the walls. Grace led me up the stairs to a heavy wooden door with carvings of Roman gods and goddesses cavorting all over it. The figures on the door writhed in sexual positions while others drank wine and laughed out loud. It was like something from a medieval history book.

On the other side of the door was another world, one that looked like some strange medieval torture chamber. Racks and torturous devices hung from hooks all over the place, and wooden beds with wheels flanked either side of a long hall. The door at the far end had a thick bolt locking it into place. Below each device was a placard describing what it was for. Whips of every shape and size lined one wall. I had a slight fright just being in the room.

Trish

"Fuck that slave! Fuck her hard," the other woman demanded. We'd enjoyed a lot of foreplay earlier. They both used toys on me and used me as their human sex toy to do with as they wanted. I enjoyed women, but at the end of the day, I needed dick.

The wife wanted to watch her husband fuck me, and he was doing great. I sat on his cock while facing his feet, in reverse cowgirl, and rode him while his wife lay next to him and watched. I lifted slightly as she reached down to caress me and then massage his balls. I was enjoying these two immensely.

"Can he come inside of you and let me lick his cum out of your pussy?" she asked.

"I would enjoy that, Domina."

The husband was a little older, perhaps mid-seventies, but seemed to have fantastic stamina.

"Come for me, Rex. Come in this virgin slave's little pussy! You want him to fill your little cunt with his cum, don't you, slave?"

"Yes, Domina," I cried out. "Fill this filthy slave's cunt with your seed, Master."

He let loose a feral growl as his hands fiercely gripped my hips, anchoring me in place. His cock quivered within me, sending shudders of pleasure through my spine as I looked back to see his face contorted in agonizing bliss and his eyes screwed shut. The intensity of the moment was palpable, but they weren't done yet.

His wife stepped closer and pulled him away from me, her lips greedily lapping up the cum dripping from his shaft. With a gentle gesture, she guided me to recline, then spread my legs with wanton intent. Her tongue caressed every inch of me as she plunged her finger deep within to extract more of her husband's seed, licking it from her fingers while gazing into his eyes—an erotic act I knew all too well.

"Your combined cum tastes incredible. Would you like to taste it?"

"Yes, Domina," I eagerly replied.

She leaned toward me and kissed me deeply, her cum-covered tongue giving me a taste of her husband. We embraced for several moments before she pulled away to get dressed with her husband.

"Thanks for such a great time today," she said before transferring the ten thousand I had earned into my account. "Here's our card if you or your friend would like to make more money in the future."

"Thank you, Domina," I replied.

"You can call me Diane, and this is Rex, my husband." She smiled, letting me know that we were now on a first name basis.

"Thank you, Diane, I look forward to seeing you again."

I crept down the hallway, my heart pounding in anticipation. The sound of a whip crack and a woman's cry echoing through the air sent a chill down my spine. I peered around to make sure no one was watching before I cautiously put my hand on the heavy, wooden door handle.

Another whip crack followed by an agonized cry pierced my ears as I pushed open the door just enough to take a peek inside. My heart stopped at the shocking sight of Brett holding a flogger with a wine slave chained up in a large, wooden frame, her wrists and ankles clamped tightly.

"Again!" commanded another voice, and Brett whipped her breasts with all his might. She screamed out in agony as tears ran down her face.

Holy shit! This was insane. How the hell did they get him to do this?

I opened the door a little farther, slipped inside, and closed the door carefully. As I was about to release the handle and make it in unnoticed, the latch loudly clicked shut. All eyes turned toward me. I froze, embarrassed to have interrupted them.

"Trish," Brett called out.

A woman's voice said, "Yes, Trish, by all means. Come in."

I recognized that voice. That was Grace! I walked closer to see the red marks of the flogger across the wine slave's body. She had red marks on her arms and legs as well.

"Brett, I didn't know you had this in you," I said while slowly approaching them.

"He didn't. I'm helping him with that. Now, please just sit and observe, or you can leave."

I didn't know what to think. I hadn't expected to see her here. How did she find Brett? Did she see our show? *Shit!* I tried to remain calm.

"Grace, Brett isn't even trained with a flogger or any of this. He shouldn't be doing what he isn't trained to do."

"He's fine. I'm coaching him," she smugly replied.

There was no way Brett should be doing this, and I could tell from his grimace that he wasn't comfortable. And what was up with Grace? This wasn't like her at all, but I never really knew the extent of her dark side.

Grace was sitting on a wooden chair, naked, with her legs crossed, wearing a mask and holding a riding crop. She handed Brett a large dildo with wires attached to it. "Brett, place this in my slave's pussy. I want you to push it into her as far as possible."

The woman was barely touching the floor with the iron shackles pulling at her wrists. She was also ball gagged with a decorative scarf through the ball. When he turned to take the dildo from Grace, I realized Brett had red welt marks on his back and arms too. What the hell could have happened in the last hour?

Brett glanced at me, then walked up to the woman and inserted the dildo into her pussy. I was bewildered at the wires coming from it. He stepped back as Grace turned a dial on a small box in her hand. The woman cried out through the gag while her entire body shuddered. Then she turned it off.

"Brett, I want you to fuck her in the ass now. There's anal lube on that table in the red bottle, and you can use that little platform to your left unless you're at a good height."

The expression on Brett's face was more fear than enthusiasm.

He looked to me, then Grace demanded, "Don't look at her, slave, do as I say or be punished!"

He grabbed the lube and made his way over to the platform. He slid a wooden plank with legs behind the wine slave. Before standing on it, he lubed her up generously and massaged her opening. Damn, I had to admit I was impressed with his anal preparation. Much like he had done with me, he pressed his dick against her opening and waited until she relaxed and sucked him in. They both moaned as he pushed in farther, and I could tell they were both enjoying the taboo of ass play. As he started to pick up the pace, they both cried out as Grace turned the dial on the box. Brett became motionless except for subtle shaking and his blank stare that slowly turned toward me.

Shit, he was getting electrocuted.

Grace turned it off. Brett pulled out of the woman and said, "No more of that."

"I'm not done with you yet. You denied me the last time we were together, so I'm going to relieve some pent-up frustration now," Grace exclaimed.

I didn't know what to do. I couldn't believe Grace would go to such sadistic lengths for pleasure.

Before I could really think about what I was doing, I stood up and walked toward him. "I think Brett's done here."

"He's getting five thousand, so I'll decide when he's done," Grace said.

"You can keep your money or give it to the wine slave and fry her cunt some more for all I care," I said. I knew talking to her this way might result in getting fired from Parnum Fectum, but I didn't need the job; frankly, Brett didn't need her that badly either. "Come on, Brett."

He grabbed his toga and followed me out. I helped him get into his toga and fasten the clasp, then we walked down to the cashier's room to collect our money.

We turned in our wristbands while the security guard stood by. The woman behind the counter counted out our cash. We signed for it as she placed it into an envelope for us to take. My eyes welled up, and I discreetly wiped the tears away. I didn't want Brett or anyone else to see me crying. When I saw him getting electrocuted like that, I felt responsible. I should never have left him alone.

As we walked out, the event coordinator walked up. "Hey, you two. I hope you aren't leaving too soon. My guests asked if you could put on another show for them. It would seem you were a bigger hit than we've ever had."

"Thank you so very much," I said. "We would love to come back another time to put on a show, but unfortunately, we need to get going now."

"Aww, too bad. From what I've gathered, we would have been able to pay you another ten thousand."

I didn't think twice. I needed to get Brett out of here, away from what Grace was doing to him. "That sounds like a great offer, and we hope to see you next time. Keep me posted on when you want us again."

We walked out to the car. Brett hadn't spoken a word since I took him away from Grace. I stopped when we got to the car and held his arms to face him. "Are you alright?" I was concerned for him.

"I … I didn't know what to do. She offered me five thousand to do what she directed to the other woman, but the things she asked me to do were horrible. When I refused to piss on her while she was kneeling, she beat me with that crop of hers. It hurt a lot. I didn't want to, but eventually, the woman said it was okay. So, I did. Then she had me slap her in the face a bunch of times, slap her tits, then tie her up and whip her. Each time I wouldn't do something, she beat me with that riding crop. I didn't want to make a scene and ruin this place for you in the future."

Tears ran uncontrollably down my cheeks. I was into some of that, but to push Brett into it the way Grace had was more like an assault than anything else. I thought I knew her better than that. I pulled him in for a hug.

"What you just experienced is not okay. We have strict safe, sane, and consensual protocols, and what happened was wrong on many levels." I looked into his eyes and leaned in to kiss him. "Let's go home."

The ride back was uncomfortably quiet. I tried to lighten things a little, but the response was always short. I decided to let him have some time with his thoughts. It was eight o'clock when we got home.

"How about some wine and a movie? It's still fairly early." I went to the fridge and poured some wine. We had wine glasses on the counter, always ready to be filled.

"Sure. I'm going to go shower up," he said somberly.

"Okay. Here's a glass of wine. I'll take a shower too and rendezvous on the sofa?" I asked enthusiastically.

He looked back at me and smiled. "Sounds good."

I couldn't help but feel he had seen things that were far more than just sexual. Sure, some of the things he and I did were a little aggressive, but I eased him into it, and only if he agreed to it. Grace went wide open sadist on him. She was utterly reckless to have Brett do what he did, which was a side of her I couldn't believe.

I wrapped my hair in a towel and walked back out to the sofa, setting the bottle of chardonnay on the coffee table. Brett came out soon after wearing boxers and carrying his wine. I looked at his red marks and didn't see any cuts or areas to be concerned about, other than his emotions.

He sat down while I paged through some movies on the TV. "What are you in the mood for?"

"That was some sick shit!" he blurted out.

I didn't know whether to laugh or feel sorry. He soon began to laugh and reiterated, "That was some seriously sick shit."

I burst out laughing with him, and with the tension broken, he told me about his experience again. I was glad he was laughing about it now. When he finished his story, I asked, "Did she ever discuss the expectations, limits, or anything like that before you went in the room with you?"

He tilted his head in thought. "When she discussed those things with the wine slave, I was grossed out with the details that were being negotiated and sort of blocked it out. Then the wine slave said ten thousand dollars. I was a little shocked, but Grace accepted. She asked me if five thousand was good, and I accepted that, but I guess I wasn't quite sure what I had agreed to."

"Just so you know, you can leave at any time. Never let yourself be pressured to do what you're not comfortable doing."

He took a sip of his wine, then placed his hand on my leg. "At what point did you get into some of the more extreme things?"

"Well, if you're talking about having large, wired dildos shoved up my cunt to electrocute me, never!"

We laughed.

I thought for a moment and caressed his leg, contemplating really opening up to him. I hadn't realized until tonight just how much I cared for Brett. I guess I knew it at some point in the past, but I kept trying to put my feelings aside. I expected our arrangement to be temporary and wasn't ready to become serious with anyone. It was always just business—until today. When I jumped in to save him, that much became clear. I just wasn't sure how much I was ready to share with him, but I felt it was time to start opening up a little.

"I came out here with who I thought was the love of my life. I wanted to spend the rest of my life with him." I paused, drank the remainder of the wine in my glass, then filled it up again, emptying the bottle.

I shared with Brett the story of my ex, of how I gave up on my aspirations of becoming a CIA forensics analyst to follow him out to California. As I told him this, he placed his hand over mine. Though I was not yet ready to reach out and return the gesture, I let him keep hold of it.

I told him how my ex left me, and then I found Taylor and Megan soon after.

"I realized about a year ago what Grace and Taylor were doing on the side. I wanted to learn what I could from them discreetly, but then they asked me to see if I could get you more confident. It was just business, and I didn't anticipate my feelings to ..."

I pulled my hand away, stood up, and walked into the kitchen. I needed more wine.

"How have your feelings changed?" he asked.

Shit. How did that come out?

"Never mind, I didn't mean anything by it." I opened a new bottle of wine, filled my glass, and brought the bottle back to the sofa. "What movie should we watch?"

Brett held my hand again and smiled. I sighed and leaned into his shoulder as we searched for a movie. I looked down and found my hand grasping his, and surprisingly, I was comfortable with it.

Taylor

It was a relaxing weekend. Not once did I open my laptop. It was a rare occasion that I could lay around the house and read the books I'd shelved for far too long.

I was ready to tackle Monday with a fresh mind. Getting to work early always allowed me to catch up on my email without daily issues distracting me. I had my coffee and a bagel and began tackling my inbox. Ninety-seven new messages. The risk I took for turning work off for a weekend was something worth the pain once in a while.

I heard the department door open. I continued responding to the HR president of another company when Trish walked into my office.

"If that cunt tries anything like she did this weekend again, I'll tie her down, shove a jackhammer up her fuck hole, and leave it on as I walk away!"

I sat back, unsure if I was supposed to laugh or be concerned. I was at least confused. "I have no idea what you're talking about."

"Grace! She fucking tortured Brett with some sadistic shit that would make most people check themselves into an asylum."

I sat forward in my chair. "What the hell are you talking about?"

"Brett and I went to the Roman party Saturday evening. Are you familiar with it?"

"Yeah, I went a few years ago, but it wasn't quite my thing."

"Well, we went to be the main show. I was away from Brett for one hour, and when I found him again, he had welts on his back and was whipping some restrained chick. Grace was there. She found him and forced him to do some sick shit to that woman. Piss on her, beat her, then put some damn electric dildo up her cunt, making him fuck her ass while Grace electrocuted the both of them."

I sat back, wide-eyed and shocked. I had never known Grace to behave that way. Especially knowing what we had at stake with our client next weekend. "I didn't know she was going there, and I'm surprised she … why would she do something like that? Is Brett okay?"

"It's a damn good thing I was there to pull him away and calm him down. He was a wreck for a couple of hours."

"Will he still go through with next weekend?"

"It's questionable. That was some idiotic shit she did."

I sighed, still in disbelief. "I'll talk with Grace." I didn't know how to tactfully change the topic, so I went for it. "On a work-related note, is everything set for the Texas recruiting this week?"

Trish took a deep breath, refocused, and we discussed our strategy for this week's interview schedule. I was finishing up some more emails when I got a text from Grace. *Can you stop by my office?*

I stared at it and shook my head. *This ought to be interesting.*

I walked into Grace's office and closed the door before I walked toward her desk. "Sooo, how was your weekend?" I asked as though I knew nothing.

She raised an eyebrow at me. "What have you heard so far?"

Damn. I should've known she'd see right through me.

"I am curious about why you intended on electrocuting Brett before our prominent client had a chance to have him?"

She put her head in her hands, shaking it. She looked back up to me and said, "I watched the main show they did. It was amazing. But I smoked some hookah with foreign dignitaries I know, which had more than tobacco in it, and I wasn't thinking clearly. Or I was thinking clearly and was in the mood to see how far I could take things. I just let my dark side take over, and it wasn't smart."

Well, which one was it?

She stood up and walked to her window. "I wanted to get them both and see what Trish really knew, but she was gone when I found Brett. I found another woman who was an open-minded sadistic sub. When I asked Brett if he was interested and offered him five grand, he agreed. I thought he heard me negotiating with the sub, but I don't think he comprehended it in hindsight."

"You think? He just graduated college a couple of months ago, and you expected him to go balls deep into all that shit? This isn't like you, Grace. You're smarter than this. What's going on?"

"I know, I know, and I feel bad about it. I got carried away and he resisted a little, but like I do with the others, I gave him a few love taps with a riding crop and he complied. I know I fucked up. Does he want to back out now?"

"You had him piss on that sub?"

"God, yes!" she exclaimed. "I got carried away, I said." She turned away from the window to look at me. "Do you know how he's doing?"

"Trish said he was fucked up for a couple of hours, but he's processing and recovering. She said he will probably follow through with this weekend, but she wasn't sure."

"Shit! We can't afford to fuck that up."

"You should probably talk to Trish. She's the only one who might comprehend what you were doing and is the best one to try to relay it to Brett."

Grace nodded. "I'll do that."

"We leave this afternoon for Texas, so you best get with her today."

I walked out of her office, frustrated at how much I'd put into this company and SD. It had been fun and lucrative so far, but Grace was getting greedy in expanding what we had in both areas. It was beginning to take its toll on me, and it would be difficult to trust anyone else with what we were doing.

I went back to my office and stared at my inbox, showing over a hundred new messages. I stood back up with my coffee cup and walked out by Trish, who was on the phone coordinating the industry day participation for this week. She looked up at me as I poured more coffee. I turned around and leaned back against the wall to wait until she finished.

She hung up and turned to me, not saying a word, waiting for me to say something. Only I didn't know what I wanted to say.

"I talked with Grace, and she feels miserable about what happened. She smoked some bad hookah and wasn't herself. She thought she'd ne-gotiated properly. When she asked Brett, he accepted. She wasn't thinking about whether he was ready for something like that."

Trish sat back and stared at me. I didn't know what else I could have said.

"Brett isn't some tool anymore, and he isn't one of those other engi-neer subs to use. He's …" She looked down to the floor, and I could see from her expression that she was concerned.

"Are you falling for him?" I asked.

"I just don't want to see him shit on and used. I feel guilty for my role in this too. He deserves better."

I stared at her flushed face. She *was* falling for him. It was fucked up enough. I didn't need her judgment clouded about how to handle it. Damn, this is just what we were concerned about in the beginning.

"Has Brett found his own place yet?"

"He's narrowed it down to two places and waiting on approval. Then he has to get some furniture." There was a pause. She was either trying to search for something further to say or waiting for me to say something. She might be fighting her feelings for Brett, but her expressions were telling.

"Are you still wanting to play this weekend at SD?"

She snapped her eyes to mine. I think she was trying to get a read on me. "Why are you asking?"

"Well, you also seem slightly rattled about this incident last weekend."

"Yes, I'm still interested, and I hope you have a good slave lined up for me. But not Todd. I can't do him if he's attending."

I smiled at her. She knew Todd worked with Brett and didn't want a chance for Todd to know who she was or what she meant to Brett. "I'll find someone who isn't part of our company."

"Thanks. I need to get back to planning out the week. Our flight is at four."

I returned to my desk to see a hundred and twenty emails in my inbox. I sighed and challenged my typing skills to address each of them.

Brett

"Move forward." I pushed the thumb lever forward on the remote, and the robot began walking. Todd had an infrared camera aimed at it to detect spots that might be overheating during operations. We had the robot walking around the office for about thirty minutes. The test was successful with no presence of hot spots. Now we were ready to give a demonstration to our client.

I got a call. "Hello?"

"Hi, Brett, this is Mandy from Sunnyvale Rentals. I wanted to congratulate you on your application approval for the apartment with us. When would you like to take care of the lease and move in?"

I had been ready to move, but now I didn't know. "I'm at work and a little distracted. Can I call you back tomorrow to go over the details?"

"Sure, no problem. I have two other applicants for that apartment, so please let us know by tomorrow."

"I will. Thanks."

I thought about this past weekend with Trish finally showing some feelings toward me. Saturday night, she let me hold her hand, and her walls came down a little. Sunday, she spent the day with me looking for furniture for my apartment. She was so funny when no one was looking. She would bend herself over a sofa or a chair, asking me if each pose gave me a good angle to slip inside. I was going stir crazy, but we laughed nearly the entire day. Even during dinner at a local diner, she reached under the table with her foot, massaging my cock while we ate, trying to see if I'd have a reaction. Then when we got an ice cream cone, the way she licked that ice cream drove me crazy. It wasn't just the sex, but how she did so much to please and excite me.

I couldn't help but think she was more than just a colleague helping me until I got an apartment. Unfortunately, I needed to find out before putting a few thousand dollars down on an apartment.

I found Trish on my lunch break to tell her about my apartment. She was sitting at her desk eating a salad she had brought from home. When I knocked at the doorway, she smiled and waved me in. I saw then that she had her earbud in for a phone conversation. She pointed at a chair next to her desk. I sat down and waited for her to finish. She smiled and whispered, "I'm almost done."

I looked around the room, curious to see what an HR office looked like. The last time I was here was my first day when I did all the paperwork, and I never had a chance to look around. There were several filing cabinets, some motivational portraits on the wall, a couple of magazine tables with some vases adorned with Greek or Latin symbols, and a small coffee table with a couple of chairs around it.

"I'll see you this week when we come out there. Enjoy your day. Bye." Trish ended the call and turned to me. "To what do I owe this pleasure? You haven't come to see me since your first day, and then it wasn't really to see me."

I grinned at her and said. "I didn't think you wanted the workforce hanging around the management."

She laughed and gave me a playful shove. "Geez. I guess you see me every evening naked. Why would you want to look at me with clothes on?"

We laughed so hard that I had tears in my eyes. "I had a great time looking for furniture with you yesterday, and the things you can do with ice cream, I'm certain, are illegal in some countries," I said.

She leaned over with a seductive smile. "So, which piece of furniture did you like me bent over on the most?"

"Damn! You're going to get me hard and then send me back to work with a bulge in my pants? And for the record ... I find you hot as hell with clothes on too."

Her look was pure adoration—at least, I hoped it was.

"I received a call that I'm approved for an apartment, and they want to know when I wanted to sign the paperwork."

Her smile didn't break, but she looked down at her desk. "Oh ... that's great. Which one?"

"It's the one about three blocks away from you, with the rooftop pool."

"Oh yeah, that's a great one. And we can always meet for a drink." She glanced up at me, and her smile was slightly different this time. Something was troubling her.

I searched for some sign to let me know she wanted me to stay with her, but she gave me nothing.

"I've enjoyed staying with you."

"Be honest," she said. "You enjoyed fucking me whenever you wanted."

"That was okay." I shrugged.

She laughed in shock and pushed my arm again. "Just okay? You had the best fuck any guy could ever have!"

"You just mean more to me than I expected." There, I said it. My heart instantly raced into hyper-speed, anticipating her reaction.

She reached over and grabbed my hand. "I've enjoyed our time together, and I ..." She sighed and placed her other hand on mine too. "I'm afraid to be involved with anyone right now. I hope you understand."

I was disappointed, and I was sure it showed on my face. "I understand, and I hope when you change your mind, you'll consider me."

She stood and pulled me in to hug me tightly. We stood there for several moments before she said, "I definitely will, Brett." She sat down with tears in her eyes. "I have to leave this afternoon and will be back on Friday. Are you still good to go for Saturday night with Grace's client?"

I tried to paint a smile on my face. I realized I didn't want anyone else but Trish, but I'd go along with it. "I plan on it. Hell, three months of rent for an hour of sex. How can I turn that down?"

"It's not a bad gig if you know how to get the big bucks," she replied.

I remained standing. "I need to get back to work. I hope you have a good trip, and feel free to call if you like." I walked toward the door.

"Brett, wait!" She walked around her desk and kissed me. With her hands on my cheeks, she leaned back and looked into my eyes. "Don't sign a lease just yet. Try to delay them, and we can talk about it this weekend when I get back."

My entire body came alive as I looked into her tear-filled eyes. My vision was becoming blurry as well. "I'll try, and while you're gone, try to remember the show we put on last weekend and let me know how we might change it for next time. I'd like to rehearse until we make it perfect." I grinned at her with a wink.

She laughed. "Get back to work. I'll call you when I get to Texas."

I walked toward the elevator just as Grace walked out of it, reading some papers. She stopped to look at me and lowered her papers. "Oh, Brett. Hi."

I could feel the tension in my jaw, as seeing her brought immediate anger, but I shook it off. I remembered in detail what she had me do last weekend.

"Could you come into my office for a moment? I'd like to talk to you about something."

"Yes, Ms. Skyler."

I followed her into her office.

"Please, have a seat on the sofa." She closed the door and sat down on a chair next to me. "I want to apologize for last weekend. I wasn't myself and was looking for a male slave who would be more accustomed to that type of stimulus. I took advantage of you. I am sorry and should never have done that to you."

I was surprised by her apology, but then again, she wanted me to show up this Saturday for her new client. "I'm fairly new to sex. Kinky sex, that is. And with everything that's happened since meeting you ... I don't know what to think anymore."

"Why didn't you just say no or that you wanted to stop?"

I stared at her, trying to hold back utter rage. "I did, and you beat me, leaving welts all over me."

Her eyes softened, turning her expression into sincerity or re-morse—a look I rarely saw on her. "I'm sorry. I should have taken more time to negotiate the scene and read your limits better. I wanted your first kinky experience with me to be memorable, but not in that way. I guess I had more pent-up frustrations from our last encounter than I realized, but regardless, I should never have pushed you beyond your limits. I normally ensure others respect the code of conduct within our world of kink. I wouldn't blame you if you didn't show up next weekend. But if you do, I hope that you will find it rewarding in ways beyond the financial aspect."

I stood up and looked down at her. "Speaking of financial, I want fifteen thousand for this first one, and then fifty percent on the others, with my having the final say on whether I do it or not."

She looked at me with a slight smile. "I guess Trish taught you quite a bit. Your confidence shows promise, not just in sex, but in everything you do in the future."

Without saying another word, I walked away and went back to work.

The rest of the day, I couldn't help but hear those terms that she discussed with Evelyn, the slave girl, and how she discussed them as though it was an everyday conversation. How could anyone get to that point in their life where they were comfortable talking about light cutting and anal hooks?

The report I had to do from our calibration didn't get done as well as I wanted, but I could review and edit it tomorrow. I couldn't think straight at the moment.

Trish's apartment was empty without her. I opened her bedroom door and took a long look at her room for the first time. I'd come into this room many times but never took the time to see it. The blue and white paisley pattern on her comforter matched the deep blue and white drapery. Her dresser was a beautiful cherry finish while her perfumes, brushes, and jewelry were methodically organized. There was a bronze statue of some strange man with goat legs and horns that caught my attention. One wall had a collage of Marilyn Monroe pictures. In contrast, another wall was more serene, with portraits of forests and waterfalls. Although she opened up to me the other night, there was so much more I wanted to learn about her.

I opened a beer and sat down to watch some random baseball game. I didn't even care who was playing. I just kept replaying the way she ran to me and asked me not to take the apartment, and the tears in her eyes as she said it. What she went through moving here must have been devastating. I was almost certain she had feelings for me, but I could see it was an inner conflict.

And then there was the question of whether I could go through with this side gig on an ongoing basis. As generous as it was, my engineer salary alone wasn't going to pay for my apartment and allow me to help my mom and sister. This was all happening so fast. I'd seen and experienced things in the last several weeks I had never imagined. I needed more time to process it. I *built* robots. I was not *a* robot.

Trish

What a long-ass trip. Delays and running to catch my connection was a pain, but now in my Corpus Christi hotel, I unpacked my suitcase for the week. Fortunately, nothing got too wrinkled. I touched up my hair and makeup and went down to the hotel bar to grab a bite and get a much-needed drink. Taylor was going to join me.

As usual, ten businessmen all looked at me as I walked up to the bar, nearly salivating like I was a lamb walking into a wolf den, and I was wearing a conservative, navy-blue pants suit. I ignored them and ordered a margarita. I didn't mind being gawked at. I'd dealt with it all my life, but I was definitely not in the mood right now. Besides, I didn't think these guys could come close to affording me.

While waiting for my drink, I scanned the room and saw several people having formal presentations in booths in front of a laptop. I turned back to the bar and thought about Brett. Did I really ask him to wait to sign the lease for his apartment? I had always been clear in my mind on what I wanted—well, except for when my ex-boyfriend dumped me. Brett was different, and he had grown on me. I knew he was a quick study from his professional side but hadn't anticipated him taking to his sexual training so well … or enjoying it so much. And then there was the Roman party. He performed that role like a natural. It was *waaay* hotter than any previous time I had attended. It caught me by surprise, and it took a lot to surprise me. Could we continue doing this if we were in a relationship? Or was the relationship helping to take it to a new level?

My drink arrived just as Taylor sat down next to me. "I see you're ahead of me."

"I just sat down a few minutes ago."

"See any prospects?" she asked, looking around the bar.

"Really? I've traveled with you dozens of times, and this is the first I've seen you on the hunt."

She looked back at me with a shrug. "That was before I knew you. Now it doesn't matter anymore, does it?"

I sipped my drink while scanning for potential distractions, but nothing piqued my interest. "I looked when I got here, and nothing caught my eye."

"When you're as gorgeous as you are, I guess you can afford to be selective."

I laughed. "I guess you've experienced that firsthand, especially in your secret business life. Taking care of yourself has its rewards."

"If I only knew at your age what I know now. You'll see in time. Eyes tend to follow the youth. Trust my years of experience on this one."

"Those years didn't keep Brett from ..." I said and immediately wished I hadn't.

Taylor sulked for a moment, and then as the bartender walked up, she asked for the same thing I had.

"Perhaps I got a little complacent and didn't think it through. With our success in the firm and our success in SD, having obedient men who will do anything for us if we fuck them at the end of the night, I've gotten arrogant. I regret how we treated Brett, but fortunately, it may play out well."

"Brett is exceptional," I said. "And he's starting a successful life. I think you'll agree he's come a long way in a short time." I paused a moment, staring into a dark hole behind the bar, and pondered Brett potentially living with me more permanently.

"Yes, and I thank you for helping him get there with such speed. Well beyond what I had considered possible at this point. Definitely protégé material. I can't help but notice your attitude toward him has changed a bit. You're protective of him beyond the limits of HR. You've fallen for him, haven't you?"

I looked up at her, not knowing what to say. Heat rose to my cheeks, and I realized the truth was fully displayed. I couldn't hide it.

"You are, aren't you? Oh, Trish, I had a feeling this might happen."

"It's not like that. I mean, I would never intend on him not being part of SD, or anything else he wants to do." I had a sensation of failure but wasn't sure who I'd failed.

"But if he has you, would you think he would want to do more with other women? Or would you want him to do more with other women?"

I gulped down some of my drink. The guy across the bar winked, but I didn't smile back. I looked to Taylor. "Brett's interests in this are similar to mine … I believe. He's enjoying the challenge of seductions and arousal. He enjoys finding out how to maximize pleasure, and he really enjoys the money that comes with it." Would I get jealous of him with another woman? I enjoyed our time with Megan.

I took another long drink. "If we did form a relationship, I don't think it would hinder that." I took another sip. "In fact, I think it might be even better. We could do things together too, like role-playing. It's still a bit tenuous, but I think I'm the best one to continue developing his trust and encouraging him to explore further. In a way he's comfortable with."

Taylor looked at me and then smiled at the bartender. She took a long sip of her drink, looking through the glass at the man, who had *I'm going to fuck her* painted all over his face.

"What Grace and I built is getting to be more than we initially intended, and I think we're going to lose some of the SD clients we have, and since some of our SD clients provide hefty contracts, I fear it may impact those too."

"Wait, what? First, are you seriously smiling at the cheap suit across the bar? And two, are you considering leaving SD?"

"I never said that, and yes, I did smile at him. I think I might have a pet for the night."

I rolled my eyes. "You also didn't deny it."

She waved a hand but didn't answer.

Two more drinks into felt like the perfect opportunity. "What's Grace really like?" I asked. "Overall, she seems brilliant and has built a great company, but her dark side seems concerning."

"Is this about the Roman party again? She just had a moment and regretted it."

"I'm not concerned, per se, but what she did was very insensitive to someone as inexperienced as he was and still is in many ways. Certainly, in the way she was taking him that night."

She took another sip of her drink and waved her hand again, nearly slipping off her stool. I was beginning to think maybe she'd started drinking before coming down to meet me. "They all need to grow up sometime. So, if you were to run SD, or perhaps start your own type of club, how would you do it?"

I was a little stumped, not sure if she was fishing to see if I had other interests or if I wanted to help guide a new direction for SD. "I don't think combining unique interests is a good idea in one location.

People pay for their unique desires, and if it's diluted, you lose that uniqueness."

She took a sip of her drink and ate an olive. "I like how you think."

All I could do was smile. "What are your thoughts of another place besides SD?"

"Why do you ask that?" she slurred.

"Because you just asked my thoughts about it a minute ago."

"Oh yeah. Are you trying to start something to compete with us and SD?"

That was direct enough. "Of course not. If I were, though, I wouldn't tell you. But I'm not doing any such thing. I have my own clients, and I'm fine with catering to them."

"Would you like to?" she murmured.

"Like to what?"

"Like to start another club, silly, that's what I'm trying to ask you. Pay attention." She ate another one of her olives and winked at the bartender, who smiled at her and then me, obviously aware of how drunk she'd become.

"I don't think I'd be interested in that. It seems like a lot of work. More work than I'm interested in doing."

"What if I told you that I can have a five-year plan for you and Brett to each walk away with over a million dollars?"

I didn't show the enthusiasm I thought she was seeking. I wasn't going to tell her how much I'd already made in a couple of years, but I was intrigued by how she envisioned making this much money.

"I see you're not the least bit surprised at the offer I offered you." She raised her eyebrows to consider her grammar.

"I am intrigued to learn what you have in mind to earn so much money."

Taylor sipped the final drops of her martini and ate her last olive. "I want to create a fantasy suite."

Now that had my attention. "What kind of fantasy suite? What would you be providing?"

"The fantasy kind, of course." She looked around for the bartender, who was purposefully avoiding her on the other side of the bar. I rolled my eyes but realized she wouldn't be discussing this if she were sober.

"We would set up a discreet website and cater on a global scale to the wealthy. We would seek out their greatest sexual fantasies and create it for them, and the fee to do this would be enormous."

I was impressed. "Do you have an example of this by chance, something that you've seen to indicate an interest?"

"On one of my trips a few months ago, I met a sheikh from Qatar. He asked if I knew any place that would set up fantasies."

She tapped her martini glass on the bar to get the bartender's attention.

"So, I asked him. What kind of fantasies? He said he had friends who wanted anything from beautiful women on a small private island to women interested in fulfilling rape fantasies."

"My God, Taylor, that's crazy!" I tried to look alarmed. If she only knew.

"I know, that's what I initially thought too, but I asked him how much he would be willing to pay for that."

The bartender brought a glass of water with some lemon in it. Taylor frowned at him and mumbled, "Thank you."

She leaned back to me and whispered, "He said money is no object if his fantasy is what he wants."

"Taylor, you can't find a woman for him to just rape. These encounters need to be negotiated, rules and limits set to ensure everyone is on the same page."

"Are you kidding? There are masochistic women all over the place who would jump at a chance to make twenty thousand dollars for one night of being used as a sheikh's whore. I'm sure we can put some limits on it."

Although I'd love to have this guy's contact information, I wasn't sure I liked where she was going with this. At this point, it was more than just a fantasy fulfillment; she was looking at its pure monetary aspects regardless of the risk to the people involved.

"I'd have to think about it. I'm okay with some fantasies, and even I like a little rough play, but to place a woman with a man somewhere privately and tell her to collect her money after some stranger rapes her just seems a little beyond my interest, even if it's consensual." I couldn't let on to her that I enjoyed the same type of encounters, but I wanted to learn more.

"Of course, that was just one scenario, but there are millions of dollars out there in people's pockets who want fantasies fulfilled … especially the exotic and taboo ones."

She had a point, and I knew there were island destinations with escorts to fulfill men's fantasies already. And that only scratched the surface on the wealth and power out there in need of an outlet to relieve the stresses of their daily lives. Fortunately, I was in the right business to ensure NDAs and contracts were in place to protect everyone's privacy. Why not cater to the wealthy elitists?

"As I said, I'd have to think about it. It's getting late, I'm going to turn in."

She waved goodbye and turned her attention back to the bartender, which only made me laugh.

I thought about Brett and remembered I said I'd call him. I'd never called him before. Why had I said I would? I was sure he was waiting by the phone for me.

I stepped away from the bar and found an isolated area in the back of the room to dial his number. I was surprisingly nervous waiting for him to answer. The third ring finished, and I was about to hang up. "Hey, Trish! I'm glad you called."

"I said I would call."

"How's everything going?"

"The travel was a pain, but it usually is. I told you I'd call you and didn't want you to be sitting at the phone waiting all night."

He laughed. "I was about to walk out on the ledge. I thought you might have lost my number."

"Now, why would I do that?" I laughed as well. I did enjoy his humor. In that moment of silence, I was comfortable just hearing him breathe on the other end.

"Brett?" It had been a long time since I had allowed my heart to dictate to my brain, but I said, "I thought about it a lot and I'm still nervous about going down this path with anyone, but would you consider living with me for a while longer?"

He failed at his attempt to cover the phone, but I could hear a muffled, "Yes!" I shook my head and couldn't help but grin at his enthusiasm.

"Sure, I could do that," he replied calmly.

I laughed. "Oh really? Did you just yell yes in the background and then come back to me with, 'Sure, I could do that'?"

"You caught me. You know I've developed feelings for you, Trish. I was touched that you're starting to open up to me, and it helps me understand you better. I'll try to be considerate of what you went through in the past, and I can adapt as needed."

"You'll do no such thing. I like you because of who you are. Don't change a thing … unless I tell you to change."

We both laughed, and he replied, "Yes, Domina."

I laughed hysterically, drawing the attention of everyone in the bar, including Taylor.

"We can go down that path if you like. I plan to be at SD this weekend also. Grace and Taylor have a boy toy for me to use while you're playing sex god."

"Oooooh, sex god, I like the sound of that. Maybe I'll get some business cards made."

"Oh my God! You will not." I continued laughing so hard that I had tears in my eyes. I could hear him laughing on the other end too.

"I miss you already, Brett."

"I miss you too, Trish."

Grace

While Taylor was taking care of company business, I looked at the lineup for Saturday. The three Dominae had been members for a long time, and their combined thirty thousand would do nicely to support the cost of the new venue we were looking to expand on.

I looked at the lineup of servi. They were all pretty familiar. On our site, we saw their actual face pictures, but they wore masks at the event. I saw the engineer who was working with Brett last week. He was adorable and well-endowed. He may recognize my voice from work, but he signed an NDA, so I doubted he'd jeopardize his job or attend future events. I'd enjoy him Saturday night.

I looked at the other subs lined up to see which would be a good pick for Trish. I studied each of them for several minutes and decided to let her choose. Taylor would take whoever was left. She enjoyed all of them.

I walked toward my window and looked out at the sunsets over Silicon Valley. SD was built on the premise of strong, high-profile women having a chance to discreetly enjoy submissive men however they wanted for the right price. It was hard for me to let go of the control I'd gotten used to. That showed in my evaluation of Brett, and then again at the Roman party. I just wanted to use him to my pleasure and test his limits, but I got carried away with the other woman who said she would do anything. I wanted to challenge her, but that may have been a mistake. I didn't think of the damage it would do to Brett.

The phone rang. It was Nick from DC. "To what do I owe this surprise?" I asked.

"I'm in San Francisco to meet a client and thought you might be interested in my company since I was in the area."

Nick was the perfect man in my mind. He was different, more confident. My sadistic side didn't come out with him as it did with the other men. I enjoyed how he pleasured me and took me as he wanted, standing up to my alpha and having me bend to his will.

"When are you available?" I asked.

"Tomorrow or Saturday night."

"Saturday night won't work out, but you can come by tomorrow night. Or if you're freshly clean, even tonight might work out." Just hearing his voice made me want to pull him through the phone and have him take me in my office.

"I would love to come down to you tonight, but I'm still with my other client. I'll see you tomorrow."

"Sounds good. I'll text you my address."

I pondered how much Brett was like Nick, just much younger and a little less experienced.

A text message from Taylor popped into my phone. *I quit!*

What the hell? I called her immediately. There was no answer. I called again, and then I called Trish. She picked up.

"What's going on out there? I just got a text from Taylor saying she quits."

"What? I just left her, and she was really drunk."

"Do you know why she would send me a text like that?"

"I have no idea. She was just raving about you being successful and a woman that all other women should be proud of."

"That's strange."

"She was upset about what you did with Brett at the Roman party."

"Yeah, I know she was, but that's over, and we need to press on."

"I'm sorry. You'll have to ask her. I'll find out in the morning and have her call you back," Trish said.

"Thanks, Trish. How was the rest of the trip? Did you get my engineers?"

"We landed a few who confirmed joining the firm. Taylor was pretty happy with the results. We should get some more next week."

"Great work. And Trish?"

"Yeah?"

I wasn't sure what I wanted to say. There was a moment of silence, then I said, "Good work. I'll see you Saturday?"

"I'll be there. Thanks, Ms. Skyler."

We hung up, and I stared at Taylor's text message. Was she really that upset about what I did with Brett? I could see Trish getting pissed, but not Taylor. This didn't make sense.

I packed up my laptop, turned out the lights, and walked down through the building on my way out. I was proud of what I'd built here. I saw a light on in the test area. When I went into the room, I saw Brett's boss, Steve.

"Steve, why are you here so late? You're not eligible for overtime, you know," I joked.

"Oh, Ms. Skyler. Yeah, well, we're a little behind in getting the artificial intelligence working for this robot, and I'm trying to work out some of the bugs. It's personal for me, and I want to see it work one hundred percent for our client."

I did love commitment. And he was here alone. He continued talking, but I wasn't paying attention. He was a man, and I could use a man right now after the brief call with Nick.

"Are you married, Steve?"

"Ma'am?"

"Are you married?"

"Um, yes I am, and I have two great kids."

"I never want you to mention this ever again, and I may never offer this again, but I've had a stressful day. Are you interested in a quick little romp in your office?"

His eyes widened in horror. His chest was heaving with stress.

"It's okay, Steve. I don't want you to get overwhelmed. I'm just in a selfish time of need."

"Ms. Skyler, you are very beautiful, and ..."

He was eyeing me over. I could see his internal struggle. Deep down, he wanted to fuck me, but his scruples were in the way. Perhaps I could help him decide.

I walked up to him, glided my hand along his noticeable arousal, and whispered, "This will be our little secret. You do want to slide yourself inside of me, don't you?"

He nodded but remained speechless.

I hiked my skirt to my waist, took off my panties, and sat on the edge of his desk.

"Come fuck me, Steve."

He walked toward me with a combined look of wide-eyed horror and enthusiasm while unfastening his pants. He looked down at my sex, and although he was a little shaky on his guiding, he eventually slid himself inside. I wrapped my legs around his hips and whispered, "Now, Steve, I want you to fuck me until I have an orgasm, do you understand? I don't care if you come, but don't stop fucking me until I finish."

He nodded and pushed himself in farther. I leaned back on his desk, hoping it would allow him to penetrate deeper as he thrust rapidly. Beads of sweat covered his forehead. He was doing an adequate job, but I was close. I was getting closer and closer, and then I shuddered with delight. I moaned out as he continued. Once I recovered, I realized Steve was still fucking me. "Steve, you can stop. You were quite successful."

He pulled out. "Oh, umm, okay."

I looked down to see he wasn't displaying any signs of his own ejaculation. "Didn't you come, Steve?"

"Um, no, ma'am, I wanted to ensure you came first."

"Well, that's unfortunate. You should have done so when you had a chance. Perhaps your wife can take care of you when you get home."

I picked up my panties, adjusted my skirt, and walked out. I looked back at him standing in his office. He was pulling up his pants while watching me leave. "Good night, Steve, and thanks," I said, waving to him as I walked out the door.

I walked out to my car thinking about whether I should have completed him and then realized he was just another submissive engineer to do my bidding.

Brett

The table was set, the roses were in the vase, candles were burning, and my chicken Caesar was ready. I wanted to give Trish a lovely welcome home. I knew she'd been burned in the past, and I couldn't help that, but I also couldn't help but express my feelings for her. I was excited yet still skeptical about her wavering feelings after saying she was falling for me.

I stood back to check the ambiance. I knew what she said to me, but I had my reservations. She would either like it or walk into her room and close the door. Either way, I guess I'd know where we stood.

She should be here any minute. I grabbed a bottle of her favorite chardonnay, put it on ice, put some light pop music on, and just waited.

Watching the clock is something you should not do while waiting impatiently. A minute seemed to take forever. I searched on my phone for random news to see if something caught my attention when the door opened.

Trish walked in with her suitcase and briefcase and looked around with wide eyes and a smile. "Wow, what's all this?"

"Just a little something to welcome you home." I poured two glasses of wine.

"Hold that thought." She hurried to her room.

Damn ... but maybe she was just dumping off her suitcase. I couldn't help but stare at that clock on the wall again having not learned my lesson from earlier. The wine somehow didn't taste as good as it could with the right enthusiasm. I sighed and bent down to the candles on the table, ready to blow them out.

"What are you doing?"

I turned to see Trish walking out of her bedroom. Her hair seemed a little fuller than when she'd walked in the door, and she was wearing a rose-colored negligee that was just barely sheer enough to see through.

I was shocked at how beautiful she looked and could've kicked myself for doubting. I stared at her as though I was seeing her for the first time.

"Didn't you say you had some wine for me?" she asked seductively, placing her hand on my cheek, then kissing my lips.

"Um, yeah." I handed her a half-filled glass. She took a sip and leaned in to softly kiss me again. It was probably the most endearing kiss she'd ever given me. We sipped our wine as I gazed at her beauty.

"Stop staring so much or you'll spoil your appetite." We both laughed.

I regained my composure. "I hope you like chicken Caesar salad."

"I love it. Thank you for making dinner. I'm always exhausted after flying. This was a great surprise to come home to," she said appreciatively.

"Sit and let's eat."

We ate while she told me about her interviews and the new hires they recruited. She told me how Taylor got drunk and sent an *I quit* text to Grace and then groveled to her about it the next day.

We were near the end of the bottle of wine when Trish asked, "Is it time for dessert?" She winked at me, and then her foot ran up my leg.

I grinned. "It is. Why don't you come with me?"

"Oh, so not here on the table?" She pouted while I laughed.

I led her to her bedroom and removed what little clothing she had.

"I like where this is going so far," she whispered.

I had her lie face-down on her bed. I got undressed, then grabbed the bottle of oil I had set on her nightstand and began massaging her back.

"Oh wow, it's been a long time since I've gotten one of these."

I smiled as I massaged the oil into her skin, savoring every cell to memorize her every curve. "I just want to show you how much you mean to me."

"Brett?" she asked.

"Yeah?"

"I don't want you to move out … unless you want to." She quickly turned her head to see my expression.

I leaned down and kissed her cheek, then gripped the back of her hair and firmly kept her head tilted to face me. She gasped with her mouth slightly open. "I was hoping you would say that," I whispered before kissing her ear.

I released her hair and continued massaging her back.

"But you have to do this for me every night. Oh, and dinner too," she said smugly.

I rolled my eyes. "Hmm, maybe I should reconsider?"

She rolled over under me and looked up into my eyes. "I never thought I would ask this, but … would you make soft, passionate love to me tonight? No kink or aggressiveness. Just soft, passionate love."

My eyes trailed up her amazing body, to her eyes. I could see tears welling up in them and realized my own were becoming blurry too. I leaned down to kiss her softly and slid my hand onto her cheek, caressing it with my thumb. I kissed along her neck and up to her ear. Her skin was soft and warm.

My hands roamed over her entire body, my mouth and tongue following their trail, savoring her all over. When I had her squirming beneath me, I climbed up between her beautifully spread legs and entered her. She arched her back and groaned, bringing my head down to kiss her as I thrust long and deep, slow and fast, unpredictably changing it up. Our kisses were passionate yet tender, our tongues sliding together in a way that mimicked the rhythm of our hips. I sensed she was close as she began grinding up against me.

A moment later, she quietly moaned, and I smothered the sound with my lips against hers. I continued to thrust steadily into her. There were tears in her eyes again.

"What's that matter?" I asked.

"Come for me, Brett. I want to feel you come in me."

She placed her hands on my cheeks and passionately kissed me as I continued thrusting into her faster. Her inner muscles firmly gripped, and she whispered, "Please, come for me, Brett."

I gripped her ass and dug my feet into the mattress, pushing in as deeply as possible. I moaned as I complied with her request. When I regained my composure, I kissed her softly again.

She smiled and whispered, "Thank you for the welcome home reception."

I'd never been in love before, but I couldn't help but think that what I felt for Trish was the very definition. Whether she loved me too—and whether she would admit it—remained to be seen. Her wanting me to stay was enough for now.

I lay down and cuddled behind her with my arm wrapped around her.

"Will you sleep with me tonight?" she asked.

I was shocked and grinned proudly. "Only if I can be the big spoon."

She laughed and held my hand against her chest. "I wouldn't want it any other way."

Trish

I opened my eyes, expecting to see Brett beside me, and I was a little disappointed that he wasn't. I went to his room, but he wasn't there either. I heard the apartment door open and close. He walked in to see me standing naked in the hallway with my hand trying to do something with my bird's nest for hair.

He smiled. "Good morning. I thought I'd get some bagels and coffee for breakfast."

I smiled back at him. "Let me brush these knots out of my hair and I'll be right there." I walked into the bathroom and brushed my hair, staring right through myself. Every thought of Brett made me happy, but I had been crushed too hard in the past and just couldn't make that leap to say I love him. We each had our path, and we had a taboo side gig. How would that play out?

I walked back to the dining table where Brett had my latte and bagel with cream cheese waiting for me. He had a croissant with jam and a coffee.

"I enjoyed last night. Thank you for the welcome home," I said as I leaned in to kiss him.

He blushed and smiled back at me. "As I said, you mean a lot to me, Trish."

"You mean a lot to me too, Brett." I sat down, sipped my latte, and added, "I just don't think I can make it more than that right now."

"Last night was a great start," he said enthusiastically.

I smiled at him for understanding and agreed it was fantastic.

After an awkward silence, I felt the need to shift the conversation. "Are you ready for tonight? Have your first acting career opportunity all planned out?"

"I think so. If Taylor and Grace believe I'm ready, then I think I am."

Ouch. Apparently, my assessment didn't matter.

"Why don't we go to a local vineyard today?" he suggested.

"Sure, that sounds great." I stood up and motioned for him to follow.

"Where are we going?"

"We need to take a shower before we go out." I couldn't keep the grin from my face as he chased me to the bathroom.

* * *

The vineyard was beautiful. We went through their wine tasting and selected a nice bottle of chardonnay, of course. Then we relaxed on the back deck, which overlooked the vines. It was a gorgeous, cool day. I wore a white linen sundress, and Brett wore khaki shorts and a polo with flip flops. Such a stark contrast from the evening ahead of us.

I kept looking at Brett through my sunglasses. There was an internal struggle between my heart and my brain, wanting to tell him my true feelings, but I just couldn't.

"Do you really want to go through with this tonight?" I asked.

Brett sat up in his chair and looked at me, confused. "What? Isn't tonight what you prepared me for? I'm expected to be paid fifteen thousand dollars to have sex with a fairly attractive woman, and you're asking if I want to go through with this now?"

I sighed, realizing the silliness in my question.

"Why are you asking me this? Why now?"

"I don't know, I … just never mind. It was silly."

We were quiet for a little while. I regretted that I'd planted that in his mind. "Maybe we can treat your client together?" I suggested.

"That would be hot. I'd want to be with you all the time. We make a great team."

"We do, don't we? That Roman party, well, the first part, was fantastic. We could do that more often. Just the two of us."

He reached for my hand, and I met his hand halfway with mine. "I'd love that, baby. I committed to tonight. Let's get through that, and then we can do our thing."

I smiled at his following through with commitment, but internally, I was a little bitter. I was afraid Grace would try to push him to do more. She wanted him as a monthly, if not weekly, stud for her clients, and I didn't know if I could trust her anymore. And then Taylor was so out of character in Texas. What was going on around here?

We went back to the apartment to get ready. I was no longer in the mood to play with a sub. I was more concerned with Brett. I didn't want to interfere with what he wanted to do, and it was his first real opportunity, but I couldn't help the worry I felt, or was it jealousy?

I stood in the shower letting the water pound on my back, confused about what I wanted. I knew he loved me, and he wasn't saying so because I'd established our relationship limit. When he made love to me last night, I kissed him with a passion I hadn't known in years, and I realized I wanted that again. I wanted it with Brett. Once we got through tonight, we could break away and I'd be honest with how I really felt about him.

I couldn't stand being in this limbo any longer. I wasn't sure if it was my heart or my mind trying to convince the other to take a chance again. I just knew I was willing, and I didn't want to wait until I talked myself out of it again. And I didn't want another screwup tonight to ruin it.

I wore a thigh-high black dress that showed off my cleavage and calf-high, black, vinyl boots. Brett wore a tight-fitting, black T-shirt that showed off his fantastic definition, black dress slacks, and stylish black boots that looked great with his clothes.

"You don't want to show off any of that delicious chest meat?" I walked up and placed my hands on his chest, caressing the outline of his pecs.

"Chest meat, huh?"

I looked up into his eyes, and he looked back into mine. His gaze found its way down, all the way down—to my soul.

"Should I change?" he asked in a low, seductive voice while he combed my hair behind my ear.

I continued to caress his chest and glided my hands up to his neck. I pulled him down to bring his lips to mine and whispered, "You look great." I patted his chest. "Time to go, sex god."

We arrived at SD with our masks on. The industrial area where the warehouse was located was quite empty with closed companies and not many lights working in the narrow alleyways.

The door opened. Although she had a mask on, we knew it was Taylor. "Greetings. Would you please come in?"

We walked inside, and Taylor guided us to the left. The room we walked into was glamorous and romantic, with a hint of playful sexual devices throughout the room.

"Ah yes, I remember this room," Brett said as he scanned around.

"You'll wait here for your client. Enjoy the champagne, and ensure your client is well taken care of, as we suspect you will."

She turned to me. "Follow me."

This formality was much different from the bar whore I'd seen earlier this week, but I'd play along.

We walked down a hallway, turned left, and walked down another hallway where we came upon several naked men with black hooded masks on their heads. Each had collars on their necks and small chains hooked up to the wall. They knelt on the floor, looking up at me.

"Pick a sub, Domina." Taylor gestured to the men cowering on the floor.

I looked down at the three men sitting there but wasn't feeling in the mood to take any of them.

Each had a card above them showing proof of their STD test results, limits, and desires. That was a smart way to help the Dominae decide their choice of sub.

I figured the man with the smallest dick was probably the most neglected, so I pointed to him. Taylor took the handle of his leash off the wall hook. "Come, servus. This is your new owner for the evening. Obey her in all ways."

"Yes, Domina."

Taylor handed me the loop to the leash. "Pick any open room down this hall." Taylor pointed down a hallway away from where Brett was.

"Come, sub." I tugged on the leash and picked the first open room. We went inside and closed the door.

"How can I serve you, Domina?" he asked while kneeling and staring down at the floor.

The room had a massage table, a large cross on the wall with restraints, a high-backed chair that looked like a throne, and a small, padded mat on the floor.

I sat in the chair. "Massage my feet."

"Yes, Domina." He knelt, unfastened my heels, placed them together beside the chair, and began massaging my feet.

He kissed my calf.

"Did I give you permission to kiss me?"

"No, Domina, I apologize."

I wanted to slap him like most dominants would but sat back instead, letting him continue massaging my feet. It had been a long time since I'd had a foot massage and enjoyed him doing so.

"You may continue massaging my legs but go no farther than my inner thigh." I thought for a minute and realized I should give him a little treat. "You may kiss my legs also, but not my feet."

"Yes, Domina." The enthusiasm in his voice let me know it was exactly what he wanted.

LT Richards

He thoroughly and efficiently massaged my legs as though he was trained in it. Some of these guys learned to please quite well. I was wearing lace panties, so I knew he could see my slit through the fabric, and I enjoyed watching his erection grow as his hands went up my thighs.

I heard a distant knock on a door. I could hear talking but couldn't make out what was said. There was no role-playing in the hallway, so I suspected it was the client Brett would be with tonight.

A feeling started to enter my pores that I was slow to recognize. I could feel it taking over my entire body, raising my body temperature and making my blood flow faster. Was I *jealous?* I jolted upright in my seat, and my unsuspecting sub suddenly stopped and looked at me as if he had done something wrong.

Holy hell, it took me a while to recognize it. I vowed I never would, but I wanted Brett. I wanted him more than I'd ever wanted anyone before, but I didn't want to interrupt him tonight.

"Geez!" I reached down and pushed my panties off. "Eat my pussy, slave, and you better be good at it!"

He grinned. "Yes, Domina!"

I opened my legs, set them on the armrests of the oversized chair, and slid my ass down to the edge of the seat. He began devouring me immediately. I ran my fingers through his hair, hoping it would distract me from what I knew was happening in the other room. I gripped his hair and said, "Suck that clit like you mean it, slave! I want to sense hunger in your technique!"

He mumbled, "Yes, Domina."

His tongue fumbled through my pussy as he continued to please me. At least he made a decent attempt, but my mind wasn't quite into it.

One thing that I'd always prided myself on was not leaving a man hanging. I wasn't enjoying being here, but I didn't want to leave him with blue balls. He obviously had some expectations. I just didn't want him to fuck me.

"Stand for me, slave."

He stood up, and I began stroking his cock. I didn't care if he wanted more or not; I just wanted to get him off and wait for Brett in the car.

I leaned down to suck on his cock while stroking him aggressively. I could feel his legs tense. He was close. "You want to come in Domina's mouth, slave?"

"Yes, Mistress."

He tensed up even more, his hand going to my head, and then he came. His warm cream shot into my mouth, but I let it dribble down to the floor. I continued to stroke him until he finished. I finally looked up at him. "Thank you, Domina," he said graciously.

I smiled, put my panties back on, straightened my dress, and took him by the leash. I walked him out to where I got him and ordered him to sit. I heard Taylor's voice as I placed the loop end on the hook. "Is there a problem, Domina?"

I just wanted to walk out but decided to follow the role-playing dialog with Taylor. "No problem. This slave was very obedient and deserves a special treat. I have a headache and will be leaving now."

As I walked toward the exit, I saw the short hallway to the door where Brett and the other client were located. Taylor was no longer behind me, so I sidestepped toward the door, easing myself closer to find out what I could hear.

I heard his voice say something, and then I heard her voice say *yes*.

I looked at the doorknob and wanted to grab it and walk in so badly. I heard her gasp as a reaction to something he was doing. Brett's whisper was faint, but I heard him say, "I'm going to fuck you so unforgivingly."

"Yes!" she whimpered in return.

My eyes went to the doorknob again, and I told myself to just leave. This job was a lot of money, and I didn't want to be the reason he didn't get paid. I started to turn away, but then I heard the woman moan. Before I knew it, I had opened the door and walked in. I slowly closed it and walked up to both of them seductively. "Good evening. I'm here to see if there was any way I might be of service ... anything at all."

I gazed at Brett, holding her in front of a mirror. She was only in her panties while Brett stood behind her naked. She stroked his cock, and he had one hand on a breast and his other in her panties.

Brett's eyes grew wide as I walked up closer.

"No, no, I only paid for this fine gentleman here."

"I'm offered as a bonus to help with your pleasure." I could only hope now she had some fiber of bi-curiosity.

Brett continued to rub her pussy with his fingers, and she buckled over slightly as she gazed at me and savored the sensation he was providing. Finally, she said, "Would you remove your dress?"

Once I stood there in only panties and heels, she motioned me toward her.

The second I was next to her, she reached out and cupped my breast, rubbing her thumb over my nipple. She looked to be around sixty years old, and she was blond and beautiful. I could swear I remembered her from some magazine like Vogue or one of the others like it. Her body reflected some years, but overall, she was gorgeous.

"I had breasts like this once." She leaned in to replace her thumb with her mouth, sucking on me as Brett continued to explore her mound.

Brett looked at me, raised eyes, and mouthed, "What?"

I mouthed back, "I love you."

His eyes bugged out, and he froze in place. He looked down and then back at me. "I love you too," he mouthed as he continued fondling his client in front of me.

I slowly placed my hand in her hair as she continued to savor my breasts. "I'm Heather. You remind me so much of my college lover, Gayle."

There it was. She did have some bi tendencies. My badass guardian angel had awakened! There was a time I thought she had disowned me. That thing about getting what you put out to the world really was true ...

"Brett and I are here to please your every need, Heather," I whispered and caressed her cheek.

She looked back to Brett. "You said you were going to fuck me?"

I looked to him and then tilted my head to look down toward her ass, using my nonverbals to tell him he better get busy.

He peeled her panties off and then positioned himself behind her. Her grip grew stronger on my breasts as I realized Brett had entered her. She continued sucking on my nipples as I reached under to run my hands over her breasts and her neck. I felt her own hands reach into my panties.

Her fingers gently began to rub my clit as she leaned up to kiss my lips. She was such a beautiful woman. We kissed softly, and she probed inside me with her fingers while Brett continued thrusting into her.

"Fuck her harder, Brett," I whispered, feeling my own pussy getting wetter with everything she was doing to me.

"Yes, fuck me harder, Brett. I may be old, but I don't break easily."

I laughed.

Her hands went back to my breasts, and I noticed tears in her eyes.

"Is everything all right?" I asked.

She nodded. "You're bringing back some fond memories … might I taste you?"

I nodded. Brett pulled out of her, and we walked to the ottoman where I removed my panties and lay back. She knelt between my legs and gazed at my bare mound. Brett stood and watched as Heather leaned into me. She gently ran her fingers through my slit, then looked back. "Brett, I hope you're not done fucking me already."

I tilted my head and motioned him to begin fucking her again, trying to hold back my laughter as I realized he had gotten distracted by the girl-on-girl action.

I kept myself up on my elbows to watch her mouth on my sex as Brett began fucking her again. She slid her tongue up my lips, then swirled around my clit. The sensation was softer than when Brett did it to me, but just as satisfying. I could feel the storm building inside me—and then she thrust her fingers inside. She obviously had experience pleasuring a woman, and I was soon panting and writhing beneath her. She had me soaring near the edge of an orgasm … it didn't take long before I felt that familiar tightening low in my body. That sub may have contributed to it more than I realized.

I quietly cried out as my body tensed and shook under her ministrations. When my climax subsided, I moved back up on my elbows.

"Mmmm, I'm glad I still have the touch," Heather said, smiling with a light sheen on her face.

I leaned up and reached out to pull Heather's lips to mine. "Would you like to suck on Brett's gorgeous, smooth cock with me?" I asked.

I realized I'd interrupted Brett's plan to dominate her, and he was caught off guard, probably confused about how to fit me into this or why I was even there. Since she seemed accepting, I decided to take a semi-lead role in our tryst.

She nodded, and we knelt in front of him. She began sucking on his cock as I smiled up at him, caressing his ass and his balls. I slapped his ass slightly and laughed.

Heather was enthralled with his cock. Her hands glided along the ripples of his stomach while we took turns licking and sucking his cock and his balls, our tongues occasionally overlapping and tangling together as we serviced him. She closed her lips around him and began to suck on him feverishly. She grabbed my hand and put it on the back of her head. I knew exactly what she wanted.

I gripped her hair and began forcing her mouth onto his cock. She gagged multiple times as I continued to push her mouth onto him. I pushed farther as she gagged again, and then I let up.

"Damn, I've missed this," she said while catching her breath. I looked up to Brett and saw the twinkle in his eyes. He was enjoying this just as much as I was.

"I want to watch Brett fuck you now," Heather said.

Eyes never leaving mine, Brett gently laid me down on the ottoman. He pulled my ass closer to the edge and set his cock at my entrance.

The sensation of him opening me was always exhilarating, but now that he kept his eyes laser-focused on mine, it added even more excitement. I wanted so much more than just sex. I wanted him to be part of my life.

As Brett fucked me, I placed a hand on his arm and looked at his face, each thrust causing my back to arch as my heat increased. Heather walked around, running her hands over both of us, reaching down to fondle his balls as they swayed, then shifting her fingers to feel his cock sliding in and out of my pussy. I couldn't help but remember that the last time this happened to Brett, it was from a man.

I motioned her to come to me and reached for her hips to help her straddle my face. Her lips were swollen from Brett's fucking, and I couldn't resist sucking on one side and then the other. While not as sensitive as the clit, I had learned from Megan that it was pleasurable for some women. Judging from Heather's reaction, she was one of those women.

Having opened her like two flower petals, I flicked the tip of my tongue up and down her crevice, pausing to swirl it around her clit before returning to her entrance and slipping my tongue into her as far as I could.

She began to gyrate her hips on my mouth. Brett fucked me good and deep. I loved his cock. I loved everything about him, and I loved him, I wanted to be with him, but I wanted him to have a successful evening.

Heather's hips began to move quicker, and I knew she was close. As soon as I turned my attention to suck on her clit, she gripped my breasts, her body convulsed, and she released. And I do mean *release*. I rushed to hold my breath as she squirted all over my face. I'd squirted before but had never had another woman squirt on me, much less my face.

She stood up. "Oh my God, I'm so sorry. Let me get a towel."

I looked at Brett and watched his surprised gape slowly turn into a grin before bursting into laughter. I gave him a stern look but couldn't hold it and laughed with him. Heather returned with a towel to find us both laughing. After handing me the towel to wipe my face, she helped me wipe my chest and neck. Even in clean-up mode, she had a seductive touch. Brett pulled out of me as I dried my hair.

"I'm truly sorry. I ... I haven't been that aroused in over thirty years. I didn't even know I was capable of doing that anymore." Heather continued to wipe the mess she had made.

Setting the towel down, I pulled her head closer. Our eyes caught, and I was mesmerized for a moment before I leaned in to touch her lips to mine. There was just something about a woman that I enjoyed from time to time, and I was going to remember this one. Not just because Brett and I shared her, but because I found inspiration in seeing a woman her age still enjoy sex so much.

"It's all good. I'm glad we could please you, and I admire you."

"Oh, in what way? You both have given me far more pleasure than I could have hoped for. I didn't realize how much I missed a female touch, and to have them both simultaneously from a couple so clearly over the moon for each other ... it was a treat I could not have imagined."

"I just mean, and please don't take this the wrong way, but I can't imagine not enjoying sex, and sometimes I wonder how it will be as I get older."

"Oh honey, I can tell you it keeps getting better. Yes, as you age, some things will change, but the ways you find pleasure will continue to evolve. It is I who admire you for being so comfortable in your own skin at your young age and so willing to share your man. I am quite sure I wouldn't have been able to do that when I was your age. If I could give you both a piece of advice, it would be to check in with each other often to ensure you stay on the same page as your relationship evolves. Don't be afraid to share your thoughts and feelings with each other. Holding them back will only make things fester. If you haven't already, you will experience jealousy. It's a natural human emotion that even the most poly among us will experience from time to time. Own it. Communicate openly and honestly, and you'll have a long and happy life together."

Brett walked up to her and kissed her. She had just given us a gift far more valuable than her payment, and I would remember her fondly for a long time.

Soon enough, she and Brett were eagerly ravishing each other again. Such a greedy woman too! I liked her even more, if that was possible. Could her advice have melted my jealousy away so quickly? I would have to figure that out later. Right now, there was a little aftercare to be tended to. I walked behind Brett and caressed Heather's back, her neck, and down to her ass with one hand while I did the same to him with my other hand, kissing his back.

Heather reached around Brett to fondle my breast. It seemed another round was in order before aftercare. It was Brett's turn to see if he could get a gusher from her. He guided us to a table against a wall, lifted her onto it, and leaned against her, wiggling his hips until she opened her legs for him. Damn, he had gotten good at nonverbal communication.

"Trish, take my cock and put it inside her." He was getting better at verbal instruction too.

I reached for his cock and brought it to her entrance, letting my fingers slide across his shaft and then up over her clit as he slipped inside. Damn, that was a hot sight.

Brett began fucking her, pushing her shoulders against the wall with every thrust. Heather pulled me closer and started kissing me again. I grazed my fingertips over her supple nipples, randomly squeezing them until she tensed and then released. She took my other hand and moved it back to her clit. It was easier for most women to orgasm with external stimulation. Some used toys while their man fucked them, but I always thought it was hotter when someone else was doing it. It seems I had more and more in common with this woman.

I began rubbing her clit with the palm of my hand, applying pressure as my fingers glided along Brett's shaft. I knew it was a tease, but I wanted to build her orgasm again. I broke away from her kiss and leaned down to her prominent, rock-hard nipples. I could see from the scars that she'd had enhancements, but they were done the way wealth could provide. I took one nipple in my mouth and started to suck on it firmly. She stroked my hair until my eyes met hers.

"I want to feel your mouth sucking my clit. Then I want Brett to pull out so I can watch you suck his cock between strokes."

Damn, who was this woman? We should be paying her. She had turned the scene completely around and was now directing us. Her movements had turned sensual toward us both, and I wasn't sure who was enjoying it more. With her lying on the table, this might be challenging. I looked up to Brett, who seemed to be right on cue. He reached down and pulled the table away from the wall, but Heather's head also fell back. Oh no!

I grabbed her head as Brett pulled her toward him, lifting her ass higher into the air with her shoulders and head now resting on the table.

I trailed my tongue down her stomach. Brett pulled out slightly to allow my access. Fortunately, he was long enough to keep inside of her.

I gave a light, blowing tease on her clit before I placed my mouth over it and sucked her strong and long. I looked up to see her head tilted and her eyes rolled back in her head.

Then I turned to Brett. He had a shit-eating grin on his face. I was tempted to make him wait, but I knew that we were probably over our time limit, so when he pulled out, I obliged and sucked his cock briefly before he thrust back into her with a force that made her grab the back of my head and put my mouth back on her clit. This continued back and forth until it dawned on me that she was edging him and prolonging the encounter. Damn, this woman was brilliant!

Her outstretched arm gripped my shoulder as she lengthened her torso and tried to stretch her legs. Just in time, too, as I didn't think Brett could hold out any longer. I rose and replaced my mouth with my hand, not wanting a repeat of the previous facial. The look on her face was epic, from the hunger in her eyes to the sensual way she ran her tongue across her lips before biting the corner. There was no doubt what was about to happen. She yelled out, "Don't stop. Harder. Harder. Come in me now. Now. Now!"

Brett continued thrusting into her as she squirted all over him. I smiled at Brett proudly and watched the relief in his face as he quickly followed her with his own intense orgasm.

Heather relaxed and tried to catch her breath. Brett stopped but kept himself inside of her. I didn't have to imagine the way his cock throbbed after such a strong release. I could see it written all over Heather's face.

I reached down again to caress her clit, spreading my fingers around his cock and caressing her slick flesh. She reached down and brought my soaked hand to her lips, slowly sucking her sweet nectar off each finger one by one.

"That felt so good. You have no idea how much I have longed for that. This fine man has excellent stamina, and you are one talented lady yourself." Heather complimented us both, and once again, I felt a spot in my heart warm toward her.

I smiled up into his eyes. "Oh, I've realized that." He grinned proudly at me.

Heather slid off the table as Brett held her hand. "It's been a long time since I've tasted a man. Would you mind if I gave you a little recharge and sucked on you one last time?"

I suppressed a laugh, waiting to see how Brett would answer that. I knew he would still be sensitive from his orgasm, and I could hardly wait to see him squirm.

"I'd love for you to clean my cock with that beautiful mouth. Just go easy on me. It's sensitive, especially after a release that intense." We both laughed as Heather knelt in front of him.

"Is everything all right? Trish, what are you doing in here?" It was Grace. She was standing in the doorway wearing her red and black leather dominatrix outfit.

I stood next to Brett, who replied, "Everything is fine."

"I didn't ask you. I asked our client."

Heather turned toward her. "It was fantastic until this interruption."

She backed away. "My apologies," she said and closed the door.

Heather licked under Brett's cock and said, "Now, how about getting another finale out of you?" She grinned.

She began sucking on him slowly, running his length along her cheek as though savoring him. She circled her tongue around his head and then picked up her pace.

She gave him time to recover before aggressively mouth fucking him like a pro. Brett was hard as a rock. Again. Wow. Yes, he was young, but that was still impressive. Heather sucked him and stroked his cock vigorously. I looked up to Brett, and he mouthed, "I can't."

I took his hand and opened my legs, placing his fingers on my mound. He began fingering me and, in a few moments, his concentration was evident. His ass cheeks tensed as he called out, "I'm coming."

He shuddered into her mouth, and when he finished, Heather's mouth played lightly over his tip, and she continued to stroke his shaft. I could see the anguish in Brett's face as his cock was obviously sensitive after coming again.

"Okay!" He gently touched her arm.

She slowed down and continued licking the end of his cock, swirling her tongue around his tip. She swallowed every drop of him. Her eyes were closed as she continued to savor him. "You taste so good. I've missed the taste of a man more than you can know."

She tried to stand. Brett and I quickly helped her up to her feet. She placed a hand on each of our arms and smiled.

"You two make such a great couple," she said. "I am so very thankful you shared yourselves with me. It was one of the best sexual experiences of my life, and you were worth every dime."

I pulled her into us and hugged her. She hugged us in return.

"You're welcome. Everyone deserves to experience pleasure like that," I said.

"Do you two do this often?"

We looked at each other. Brett slowly shook his head. I said, "We don't, but we have considered the possibility of bringing our love to those like you who deserve happiness."

"Well, I hope to book you two again soon."

"The hour is up." Taylor and Grace both walked in this time. "I hope our new protégé lived up to our hype."

I whispered to Heather, "If you want us again, it won't be here."

Heather turned around. "I had a fantastic time. You have some of the best staff I could have ever hoped for. It was just what I needed."

"Fantastic. I knew you would enjoy these two." Grace bumped Taylor with her elbow. "See, I told you sending Trish in here was a good idea."

I tried to maintain my composure. She didn't have to lie.

Grace continued, "Well, I hope you were pleased enough to spread the word. I'm sure we can arrange for these two to perform again, and we may have more getting trained soon. Won't we, Trish?"

Now I was pissed, but I tried to maintain my composure. I held onto Brett's arm. "I'm sure we can work something out."

Heather walked toward her dress, picked it up, and draped it over herself. I glanced at Grace, who was glaring at me, while Taylor was looking at her and assessing the situation.

Heather came over to give Brett and me one last hug. "If you are ever in my neighborhood, perhaps we can have some coffee together. My full name is Heather Cromwell. You'll find me if you look, and if anyone refuses to put you through to me, tell them they're fired … or just tell them your names. They're all good people."

She walked up to Grace and Taylor. "Thank you, Grace and Taylor. I enjoyed myself very much. Goodnight."

Brett

I watched Heather walk out. I hadn't been that enthusiastic about having sex with her when she first arrived, but it was an incredible experience with Trish.

Once she was gone, Grace demanded, "What the fuck was that? You almost jeopardized our operation!"

"Come on, Brett, let's get dressed," Trish said.

"I'm talking to you two. What made you think walking in here was acceptable?" Grace raged.

"I wasn't told I couldn't," Trish replied snidely as she slipped her dress over her head.

She handed me her panties with a wink. "Here, hold these for me."

I looked down at her lacy panties and put them in my pocket.

"Don't get smart with me. I own both of you ... I own all of you!" Grace burst out, looking at Taylor as well. Taylor was staring at Grace's boots, practically cowering.

"How can you say you own us?" I said.

Grace walked up to us. "It's easy. I own your future, and I own your body if you want that future."

I glanced at Trish, who looked like she was about to burst a vein in her neck. Her grip on my hand was like a vise. Trish gave me the best gift I could ever ask for in telling me she loved me, and I couldn't care less if I worked for Grace. I realized I held all the cards, but she crossed a hard line. "You might have been better off trying to make me one of your leash boys. Now pay me my fifteen thousand and we'll be on our way."

"I think your stunt may have lost us a valuable client. Perhaps we'll go back to ten thousand."

"I thought you were smarter than this. Or has your arrogance gotten the best of you? You created a great company. It would be sad if the media learned about your sex cult of male employees forced to fulfill your sick, twisted, and sadistic desires," I said calmly.

Her mouth practically dropped open. "You wouldn't."

"He wouldn't ... alone," Trish added.

Grace backed away. "Perhaps we're parting ways then."

Taylor finally spoke up. "It's been a great experiment, Grace, but I think we should stick to what we agreed to. There is too much at stake to play games or make such demands."

"Who the fuck is playing games? I should have all of you chained and whipped! You're all ungrateful little bitches!"

Trish walked up to her. "We're going to go home now and write our letter to the news outlets detailing everything, including your sex trafficking and torture of submissive employees for your sadistic pleasure. We'll be in at nine o'clock tomorrow morning to receive Brett's fifteen thousand and one year of severance pay for each of us."

"That is NOT going to happen!" Grace exploded.

"Grace, it's better to move on than fight them," Taylor said. "It won't work."

Grace paused as everyone's eyes were on her. Her face was red, and her chest heaved with each breath. I hadn't seen anyone as mad as she was at this moment.

"Fine, you will have your demands, then I want you as far away from here as possible."

Trish and I walked toward the door and stopped. Trish turned around and said, "At what point did you become so arrogant and complacent that you would jeopardize everything you've created? I was considering working with you until I saw what you were truly like at the Roman party. Then this. You're mad with control, and I feel sorry for you."

I took Trish's hand, and we walked out to the car. It was quiet on the way home until Trish broke the silence to ask, "What was your favorite part of the evening?"

I laughed and gripped her hand while glancing at her, trying to keep on my side of the road. "My favorite part was when you said *I love you*."

She unfastened her seatbelt and leaned into my arm. "I'm sorry I didn't tell you before. I wanted to last night and even this morning, but I couldn't for some reason. Then tonight, I couldn't hold it in any longer, and I wanted to tell you louder but didn't want to ruin your fifteen grand."

When we got to the apartment, we took a shower together. We didn't have sex but simply bathed each other and kissed, then toweled off and crawled in bed together.

"I love you so very much, Trish."

"I love you too, Brett. Would you sleep with me again tonight? But this time, I want to wake up with you next to me too."

I snuggled into my position as the big spoon. Moving her gorgeous, wavy hair to the side, I kissed her neck. "I want to sleep with you every night."

Then it hit me. "Wow, we're out of a job tomorrow, aren't we?"

Trish rolled over laughing. "Yes, we are, but no worries. You're very bright. And besides, perhaps we can look into a different career field."

We both giggled and kissed each other good night.

Read other great adventures through the mind of LT Richards:

Our Secret Lives – Our Awakening.

Ryan and Ginger experience the trials and tribulations most new couples experience when beginning their journey in this new frontier. How to find another couple, what to expect on a date, what is a house party, what is that used for, and the all time favorite is, 'wow, I've never done that before'. These and many more questions will be answered in Ryan and Gingers journey which is filled with risk, drama, passion, and of course a lot of steamy encounters. The memorable moments they experience and friendships developed are looked upon as something they never thought possible. Their experience is more than randomly meeting others for sexual pleasures, it's developing friendships which many could never see possible, friendships whereby a simple wink in public is magical, the slightest touch on an arm at dinner is breathtaking, and a smile across the room melts your soul, all while adoration for your own spouse is evident. We hope Our Awakening will wake you as well.

Our Secret Lives – Full Immersion.

In Our Awakening, Ryan and Ginger begin their exploration in the swinging lifestyle. They trip over drama, scary basement encounters, making fantastic friendships, celebrating birthdays, and all the while they notice their adoration and sexual connection between each other grow.

Our Secret Life Full Immersion brings Ryan and Ginger's experiences to new heights with current friends and new friends. They find that their long time vanilla friends are more than curious in their endeavors and in one unplanned evening, they find out how their interests merge. What they didn't expect was their friend's involvement into another lifestyle which drive Ryan and Ginger's explorations to a level they never imagined.

www.ingramcontent.com/pod-product-compliance
Lightning Source LLC
Chambersburg PA
CBHW022027260626
47156CB00017B/424